CW01083662

A LUST
FOR LEAD

A LUST
FOR LEAD

A NOVEL BY ROBERT DAVIS

First published in Great Britain by Swordworks

ISBN 978-1-906512-61-3

Printed and bound in the UK & US

A catalogue record of this book is available

from the British Library

Front cover artwork by Jason Lynton

CHAPTER ONE

After six days of stifling heat, the storm had finally broken. Still air had erupted into a savage fury; harsh winds that stripped the desert raw. The sky had become choked with grit, turning the midday sun into a murky twilight, stained brown, like the colour of dried blood.

At the edge of the storm, the town of Santa Morgana trembled on shallow foundations. It was little more than a shanty, grown up around a weak copper mine in the middle of nowhere. Thin clapboard walls bowed beneath the wind's ferocious energy and tarpaulin roofs strained the tacks that held them down. Some had broken loose already and the tarps flapped in the maelstrom like crows with broken wings. Wood creaked and groaned in a tortured cacophony of stress. The scaffold above the main pit swayed drunkenly, taut cables screaming.

It was during this storm in the spring of 1881 that Death and the Devil faced each other at the edge of town. The two gunfighters stood with ten paces between them, their faces muffled with scarves, hats drawn low to shield their eyes from the driving gusts of sand, their hands poised above their six-shooters, tensed and ready.

The man known as Death was tall and gaunt, with a pale and leathery complexion. His eyes were cold and unfeeling as oblivion, pitiless and devoid of mercy. He stood like a man carved of stone, motionless but for his long white hair whipping in the fury of the gale.

The man they called the Devil had the broad-shoulders of a farm labourer and a handsome, square-jawed face. A look of madness glimmered in his eyes. As wild as the storm, he rolled his shoulders, tapped his feet and drummed his fingers against the stiff leather of his belt, enervated by the thrill of the duel.

A dust cloud blew between them and suddenly the Devil ceased his constant motion. He became as still as his opponent, muscles tensed like stretched wire. Neither man could see. All was darkness and spitting sand, the air hotter than the fires of Hell.

And then the cloud parted.

And each man drew his gun.

The sudden crack of gunfire became the words of a man, spoken harshly and accompanied by a sharp kick in the ribs.

'Wake up, Ennis! It's time to go.'

Shane Ennis surfaced from the dream with a start. He was grateful for the interruption until he remembered where he was. Groaning, he shifted from where he lay and fended off a second kick with his forearms.

It had been a cold night and he had slept on the bare earth, his overcoat wadded for a pillow. Old scars felt stiff and painful and his joints cracked noisily as he rose. The morning air was crisp and contrasted sharply to the hot, sand-choked world of his nightmare. His wrists ached where his tossing and turning had made the ropes that bound them chafe.

The man who had woken him was a bounty hunter, an old grey wolf of a man in faded denims and a brown leather waistcoat. Alijah Noonan was his name, and Shane had learned to curse it in the week that had passed since Noonan and his gang had captured him. Shane was a wanted man in thirteen states and faced the death penalty in just about all of them but Noonan was not taking him to the authorities. Somebody else had put a price on Shane's head that was worth a lot more than the ten-thousand dollars the federal government was willing to pay for him, and it was to this mysterious figure that Shane was being taken. To a place called Saddle Horn Rock, way out in the badlands near the Mexican border.

'Go on, get moving you cuss!' Noonan hauled Shane to his feet and pushed him over to where his horse was waiting. It had been saddled and Noonan's men were ready to set out on the last leg of their journey. One of them spat at Shane as he passed. 'They're gonna hang you today, Ennis.'

'Maybe,' one of the others remarked. 'If he's lucky.'

Shane voiced no comment to their taunts. He had long since lost the will to fight them. He bowed his head and stumbled clumsily to his horse, mounted as he was told and turned to face the southern horizon with a grim sense of resignation.

Today was the last day of his life.

There had been a time, six years ago, when none of this would have happened. Shane had been a different man then, colder and more ruthless. It would have taken much more than a man like Noonan to bring him in.

At forty-one years old, Shane was a gaunt, hard figure of a man dressed in patched and tattered clothes. His hair was long and bleached white by the sun, his face sharp and angular and dominated by cold, pitiless eyes. If the saying was true and his eyes really were the windows to his soul, then Shane's soul was as barren as the desert. He did not look at his captors directly, even when they taunted him and called him a coward. His surroundings passed by unregarded. His mind was elsewhere.

They had travelled far beyond the civilised lands and all around them the desert stretched seemingly into infinity: a sea of rust-coloured dirt that was broken sporadically by islands of coarse dry grass and cacti. Two isolated mesas marked the horizon and Saddle Horn Rock was only a short distance from there.

Shane's thoughts were of his future. Not even Noonan knew who would be waiting for them at Saddle Horn Rock. He had spoken only with middlemen: lawyers who had despatched telegrams to another lawyer based in Santa Fe and who had divulged nothing of his employer's identity. Shane could think of a dozen enemies who might have the resources to go to such trouble. He had killed hundreds of men during the twenty-odd years that he had sold his guns as a professional killer, any number of whom had wealthy friends or family left who might now seek revenge. And likely not a quick revenge at that. Shane expected to be tortured. He expected to die slowly and in great pain.

At least, that was how he hoped it would be.

Shane was not afraid of suffering; it was dying that he feared. He had seen beyond the veil of death and knew what waited for him there. And it scared him so badly that he would gladly endure any pain, any humiliation, if only to prolong his life another second.

It was almost midday when Saddle Horn Rock showed on the horizon. It was a weathered finger of stone that rose abruptly opposite a rounded slope known as Cantle Ridge.

Noonan sent two of his men on ahead to scout things out while the rest of them kept their distance. The desert shimmered in the ferocious heat. One of Noonan's men removed his hat and wiped the sweat from his balding pate. 'You think they'll be there?' he asked.

'They'll be there.' Noonan said solemnly. 'Last chance to turn back, Hooper.'

The man shook his head. Shane had heard them have this discussion several times already. 'You want to?' he asked

'No.'

'Ten-thousand dollars is a lot of money.'

'Twenty-thousand is a whole lot more.' Noonan replied.

But it was risky. There were no guarantees that Noonan's anonymous contacts would be willing to part with such a large sum of money and that was why he had gathered his gang together to make a show of force. They all knew this. They had all come ready for a fight.

The two scouts returned. They were young men, twin boys belonging to one of Noonan's old army buddies. At seventeen, Chris and Cole Dalton were eager to make their mark on the world and to them this ride was an adventure. Cole's eyes were wild with excitement as he described what they had seen: 'They're there all right. Three men. They got themselves a pair of rifles. Third man's packing a six-gun. Looks like he's the leader.'

'A gunslinger.' Hooper mused. 'Makes sense. Old friend, you reckon Ennis?'

More than likely, Shane thought, nerves tightening in his gut.

'What about the money?' Noonan asked.

'They got a horse with two of the biggest wooden boxes you ever saw strapped to its back.' Chris stretched his arms apart to demonstrate the size. 'Like coffins they are!'

'Okay, we're here to do business.' Noonan said. 'Did they get a look at you?'

'They saw us.'

'And?'

'They watched us real good, Al. Especially that gunslinger. He looks like a mean sonofabitch to be sure.'

Noonan nodded his head solemnly. 'We do this like we planned,' he said. 'Hooper, you stick to Ennis like glue. Anything happens. . .'

Hooper pointed two fingers at Shane's head and drew back his thumb like he was cocking a gun. 'Bang!' he promised.

The three waiting men were just as Cole had described them. Two of them carried rifles. Not the lever-action repeating kind that the Dalton brothers were armed with, but the more powerful, more accurate single-shot breach-loaders popular with marksmen. They spread out when they saw the gang approaching, one heading to the shadow of the Rock while the other trekked out wide to the opposite flank.

The gunslinger held the middle. Shane looked but could not see him clearly enough through the shimmering heat haze to tell if he recognised him or not. Behind him, five horses had been roped to a stunted Joshua tree. One carried the two boxes that Cole had boasted were so big. Neither was as big as a coffin, but they were not far off.

Five horses seemed one too many by Shane's reckoning, unless one was intended for him to ride, and that just didn't sit right. He scanned the slopes of Cantle Ridge and found what he was looking for: a momentary flash as the sunlight reflected off a glass lens, betraying the presence of a third sharpshooter, armed with a high-powered rifle and a telescopic sight.

Noonan and his boys were unaware of the marksman's presence and Shane felt disinclined to tell them about him. They rode on as they had planned; the Dalton brothers reining in about a hundred yards from where the exchange would take place, off to either flank. Hooper jabbed his revolver into the side of Shane's head. 'That's far enough, Ennis.'

Shane drew on the reins and held back, leaving Noonan to ride on, accompanied by the fifth man in the gang: Jim Walters, a grizzled old bear with a sawn-off shotgun.

The gunslinger strode out and met them about halfway from the money. Now that he was closer, Shane could see him more clearly. He was in his late thirties with a stocky frame and curly brown hair. A Smith and Wesson Model Three Russian revolver was slung from his belt, rigged for a left-handed draw. He had drawn with his right the last time they had met.

A sudden gust of wind blew grit in Shane's face, bringing sharp memories.

He stood with his hat pulled low and his face wrapped in a scarf as the storm howled all around him. His hand was poised above the handle of his gun and his eyes were narrowed, staring into the blinding wind at the figure that was nothing more than a shadow in the sandstorm's murk. A shadow who had come to kill him.

Shane had hoped this moment would never come. He would have run rather than hold his ground, but the storm had closed in too suddenly and trapped him and now there was no choice but to fight.

His cold, dark eyes showed nothing of the turmoil that raged inside of him, the fear and the joy that competed so savagely for the prize of his soul.

Shane Ennis stood his ground and prepared for what he felt with certainty would be the end of his life.

The wind suddenly dropped. Shane recognised it as a momentary lull that would be followed seconds later by a raging torrent. Then there would be a brief, fleeting calm. The dust would settle and in that moment his opponent would draw, in the instant that the air cleared enough for him to see his target, yet still catch him by surprise.

With that certainty, Shane knew that what remained of his future could be measured in seconds. His heart began to quicken. His senses grew sharp.

The windblast hit, just as he had anticipated. It blotted out everything in a cloud of dust so thick and so hot that it seemed as if the air was on fire. Shane had instinctively closed his eyes to protect them. He felt the sandstorm's heat against his face and when the cooler breeze returned he knew that it was safe to open his eyes again.

He reached for his gun immediately. Through the sandstorm, he saw his opponent likewise draw.

It was all over in a heartbeat.

Thought required too much time; Shane acted on instinct. His hand became a separate entity, no longer a part of him but acting entirely on muscle memory. His arm came up. He held his breath to stop his hand from shaking. Aimed. His finger tightened against the trigger.

He had his opponent dead to rights but in that moment Shane refused to kill him. He dropped his aim by a fraction.

And fired.

The shot caught his opponent on the trigger finger, tore straight through it and shattered his hand. He screamed and pitched away into the storm.

The wind died down abruptly.

'Seven-Fingers Buchanan. I might have guessed it'd be you.'

The gunslinger's smile was fierce and hinted at how much he detested the use of his nickname. Castor Buchanan's career as a gunfighter had effectively ended the day he had fought with Shane. His right hand was a ruin. Only the ring and little fingers remained, attached to a mangled stump at the end of his wrist. He could shoot with his left, but not with anything approaching the skill he had possessed with his right and he was no better these days than any hotshot cowboy.

The loss had shattered his already fragile sanity and Shane saw that the look of madness in his eyes was not nearly as well constrained as it had once been. Men had used to say that he was as evil as the Devil himself. Now he looked the part as well.

He stared straight past Noonan to fix upon Shane and a feral grin spread across his lips.

'Do we have a deal here or what?' Noonan snapped.

'What's your hurry?' Buchanan answered casually. His voice was a low, smooth growl. Many women had been seduced by that voice, only to discover soon after that Buchanan was no gentleman.

'You can see I've brought Ennis.' Noonan said. 'I want to see my money.'

Buchanan shrugged. 'Sure. Follow me. Alone,' he added when Jim Walters made to accompany them.

Noonan dismounted and walked with Buchanan to where the horses were roped. He opened one of the panniers and looked inside. The Dalton brothers watched their marksmen counterparts suspiciously, unaware of the extra man hidden on the ridge.

Hooper kept his revolver pressed tightly to the side of Shane's head.

After a long and tense wait, Noonan closed the box and untied the horse's reins. 'Bring Ennis across!' he shouted.

'You heard him.' Hooper said. He rode close alongside Shane as they started out toward the distant figures. Shane had dreaded this moment. The heat of the sun beat down on him relentlessly and he was conscious that every man had a gun pointed in his direction.

'That's far enough.' Hooper growled.

Shane drew on the reins with his bound hands and they stopped and waited until Noonan was level with them. A few paces behind him, Jim Walters fidgeted nervously with his shotgun.

'I'll be handing you over now, Shane.' Noonan said. 'Thank you. You've made me a very rich man.'

Shane said nothing. He sat patiently while Noonan escorted the horse and its precious cargo safely into his own ranks. Only then did Hooper let up the gun from the side of Shane's head, then turn and ride away.

Leaving Shane alone with his worst enemy.

CHAPTER TWO

'You don't look very pleased to see me, Shane.'

After six years, meeting Shane again had clearly put Buchanan in a good mood. He sauntered over. 'You might at least thank me,' he said.

'For what?' Shane had not spoken in a long while and his voice was dry and cracked.

'For sparing you the agony of a long and boring trial. Not to mention a hanging.' He enjoyed the look of confusion that crossed Shane's face. 'I didn't bring you all the way out here to kill you, Shane. I've something much better in mind.'

The two riflemen had come in from the flanks. They were blank-faced professionals, all in their early-thirties. They kept a good distance from each other and were careful not to stand too close to Buchanan. Necessity had brought them together, but they were not friends.

The marksman descended from the ridge. He was like the others but the way he carried himself radiated a definite malignance. Tall and thin and ramrod straight, he resembled the gun he carried.

The others backed cautiously out of his way. Alone among them, Buchanan was not afraid of him. 'Go after them,' he said, indicating to where Noonan and his men had gone, their passage marked by a diminishing cloud of dust.

'What about Ennis?' the marksman replied.

'He won't give me any trouble.'

The marksman raised an eyebrow sceptically but he voiced no complaint aloud. He mounted his horse and the other two followed him. Buchanan waited until they had gone before turning to face Shane with a leer. 'Alone at last,' he whispered. 'The time hasn't been good to you Shane.'

'I still have all my fingers.'

The jibe was unexpected and cut Buchanan where it hurt. His face twisted into a monstrous grimace of rage and his eyes blazed furiously. Shane tensed, expecting to die there and then, but instead Buchanan twisted away. He bowed his head and Shane heard him breathe deeply for a count of ten. He was calm when he straightened again, although the fury still simmered behind his eyes.

He controls himself better than he used to, but only just, Shane thought.

'Too bad.' Buchanan growled. 'It might be better for you if you didn't.' He drew a Bowie knife from a scabbard under his arm and used it to cut the ropes that bound Shane's wrists. Shane drew away from him, rubbing the circulation back into his hands.

Buchanan sheathed the knife and mounted his horse. 'We've a long way to go Shane. Some old friends are waiting for you.'

'Where are we going?'

'You'll figure it out soon enough.' He kicked his heels and the horse trotted away.

Shane sat, watching as Buchanan rode off. The desert was wide and vast and he thought about making a run for it, but that, he suspected, was exactly what Buchanan wanted him to do. Buchanan was under orders to deliver him somewhere, alive. He was inviting Shane to cause trouble, to give him a reason to kill him.

And Shane was not going to do that, not when it seemed that he had been granted a few more days to live at least.

The dime novels had once called him the most dangerous man in America. Shane Ennis had been a killer so efficient that men had said he was Death itself, given form and sent among the sinners to kill the unworthy.

Those days were long gone. Shane had not so much as touched a gun since Santa Morgana and the stories that were told about him now spoke of a coward who had lost his nerve. That was not the way of it. Shane had his reasons for laying down his guns, but they were reasons that few men would understand.

Buchanan understood them all too clearly and he took every opportunity to show his contempt. He slowed his mount and rode close by Shane's side with his revolver carelessly exposed for Shane to grab it if he chose. Other times, he rode far ahead out of sight, tempting Shane with opportunities to escape from him, but Shane never took them. He had resigned himself to his fate and he had no wish to hasten it by giving Buchanan cause to shoot him. His one satisfaction lay in watching Buchanan grow increasingly irritated the more his games failed to illicit a reaction.

They rode steadily on a north-westerly heading, winding through barren country far from settled lands. Buchanan spoke often but said little. He gave no indication of where they were going or what would happen to Shane when they got there.

They made camp that night and the following morning they rode on, ever northwest. There was no sign of the three riflemen and Buchanan seemed in no mood to wait for them. Likely they were making their own way toward whatever secret rendezvous lay ahead. That Buchanan seemed unconcerned for the safety of the money confirmed something that Shane had begun to suspect: that the money was not his but belonged instead to his employer. Somebody else was holding Buchanan's leash, somebody else who had a vested interest in Shane; though who that somebody was, Shane could not imagine.

They rode for days. One night as they sat around a spitting fire, Shane broke his silence and asked Buchanan where they were going. Buchanan answered him with a sneer: 'You should know that by now.'

'Should I?'

'I'd have thought you would. Where else do you know lies all the way out here?'

It hit Shane then what he was talking about. 'Covenant!'

Buchanan smiled to himself. 'I'm taking you back where you belong,' he said.

Covenant was a ghost town way out in the badlands, so wrapped up in legend now that it was hard to separate the fact from the fiction. Some folk didn't even believe that it ever existed.

In its day, the town had been prosperous and the land surrounding it had not been nearly as bad as it had since become. August Third, 1879 was the day that had marked the end of Covenant's fortunes. On that day, a gunfighter by the name of Jacob Priestley had ridden into town and, seemingly without provocation, had proceeded to shoot everyone that he saw. Afterwards, he had walked out into the desert and shot himself in the head. At least, that was what the story claimed. His footprints had ended abruptly beside a rock, just high enough for him to have sat on, and beside it had been a long splash of blood and a piece of skull with Priestley's coal-black hair hanging from its scalp. The rest of him had never been found.

Things had never been the same in Covenant after that. There were folk who said that the town had become haunted by the ghosts of those whom Priestley had slain, that gunshots and screaming had been heard in the middle of the night. Ghostly figures were seen. Suicide and murder had become a daily occurrence.

The town had been abandoned soon after. People just couldn't stand to live there any more and the place had acquired such a bad reputation that it was struck from the maps.

But that had only been the beginning.

The fire spat, throwing hot embers into the night sky. Shane glared at Buchanan over the top of the flames. In all his worst imaginings he had not thought that he would be taken to Covenant. He did not want to believe it now.

'They'll kill you just as surely as they'll take me,' he said defiantly.

Buchanan shook his head. 'I think they'll make an exception this once. There's another tournament, Shane. Or hadn't you heard? How grateful do you think they'll be if I see to it that you take part this time?'

Shane curled his lip. 'Bullshit!' he said. It was not possible that another tournament was being held at Covenant. He would have heard about it if there was. Even though he had turned his back on the Fastest Guns, he had still kept his ear to the ground. Surely he had not become so out of touch?

The first tournament had been held six years ago. More than a hundred of the best gunfighters in America had been invited to prove their worth in a series of duels to the death, intended to determine which of them was truly the best of the best. Shane and Buchanan had both been invited but neither had gone. The gunfight at Santa Morgana had taken place just weeks before the tournament was scheduled and had seen the end of both their gunfighting careers. The decision not to attend had been the hardest that Shane had ever made and he had regretted it ever since, however much he tried to tell himself otherwise.

He found it hard to speak. 'You're lying,' he croaked.

'You'd like to think I am.' The firelight reflected in Buchanan's eyes, making them blaze. 'You should have known they'd never let you go.'

CHAPTER THREE

Shane did not sleep at all that night. He lay with his back to the hard dirt and stared up at a sky so vast that it made his head spin with vertigo.

Covenant.

A second tournament.

The idea of it was so abhorrent that he didn't want to accept that it was true. *But of course it's true.* Buchanan, with his perverse knack for finding just exactly what it was that would hurt a man had found the perfect way to avenge himself on Shane. The question now was how had Shane not heard about it sooner?

To many, the Fastest Guns were, like Covenant, a myth. Rumour spoke of a secret society of gunfighters who fought with each other in ritualised duels to the death in order to prove their superiority. Their origins dated back to the duellists of the Eighteenth Century but it had only been recently, in the wake of the August Third Massacre at Covenant, that the Fastest Guns had become consolidated into a formal institution. Jacob Priestley was revered as their posthumous messiah and Covenant was their unholy

Jerusalem. In 1881, with the memory of the slaughtered still fresh in the town's deserted streets, the Fastest Guns had held their first tournament and a hundred gunfighters had killed each other until only the six best remained.

Nobody had seen or heard of those men since.

Covenant was not much further away and early the following morning, Shane and Buchanan entered one of the many ghost towns that surrounded it.

The town was a small cluster of buildings, half-buried in the sand. Balls of tumbleweed rolled listlessly across the empty street, blown on a breeze that whispered like far-off voices in the sand. The whole place had the feel of something not quite dead.

Glancing around, Shane noted a strange uniformity in the way the buildings all leaned on their foundations. All of them were pitched at almost precisely the same angle towards the southeast, as if all were straining to uproot themselves and move further away from where Covenant lurked beyond the northwest horizon.

The ghost town was one of about a dozen that surrounded Covenant like desiccated husks in a spider's web. They had all been abandoned within three years of the August Third Massacre, their inhabitants driven out by a mixture of drought and ill-fortune. Covenant's curse had spread since 1879, reaching out like an enormous hand to steal the vitality from everything it touched, poisoning the land and bringing death and destitution.

Shane's horse grew increasingly nervous the further they rode. She flared her nostrils and needed constant correction; a correction that Shane himself was reluctant to enforce. He knew exactly what it was that she could sense around them and shared her unease. Buchanan's horse was unaffected, he noticed. Besides an occasional shaking of its head or worried snort through flared nostrils, it behaved perfectly well.

It's had chance to grow accustomed, Shane realised. *My God, he's not only been here before, he's spent time here.*

It seemed unthinkable. Shane had heard stories of men who had travelled to Covenant. Mostly they were gunfighters, as he had once been, who went there seeking the Fastest Guns. The stories always spoke of the grisly end that befell those intruders. Shane had never once heard of anyone going *and being allowed to leave.*

But things had changed. It was late in the afternoon when Covenant appeared on the horizon and the first thing that Shane noticed about it – the first thing that jarred with his expectations – were the men who guarded its perimeter. They occupied rooftop nests, stood at balconies and upper-storey windows and were armed with heavy-calibre, long-distance rifles.

The Fastest Guns, it seemed, had secretly increased their numbers, though again Shane could not understand how they might have done so without his hearing of it.

The guards issued no challenge as they drew closer; they recognised Buchanan. Shane looked up at them as he rode by. Their eyes were hard, the thoughts behind them clipped and professional. They reminded Shane of the marksman who had lurked on Cantle Ridge. Each had that same killer's edge.

Shane was back among his own kind.

They rode into town along the wide thoroughfare known as West Street. Covenant was a corpse of a town. Its buildings slumped on their foundations, their dirt-encrusted walls sagging, sloughing strips of old paint like rotting skin. Its windows had been mostly boarded-up or smashed. Those that remained intact were coated in a layer of hard, scabrous dirt. In places, the rooftops had caved in. In others, whole buildings had collapsed on themselves.

The air was hot and fetid. Shane smelled gunsmoke, as if a full-on battle had only recently been fought. Eight years on and still the memory of August Third remained, leaking out of the town's every pore.

Further in, some of the buildings began to show signs of being lived in. Wooden boards had been torn from the windows and the dirt scrubbed from the glass, admitting light into the rooms beyond. Men watched him suspiciously as he passed. By the hungry look in their eyes, he judged that they were contestants, sizing him up in preparation for the tournament. A few of them were men that he recognised, at least by their reputations.

Shane felt as though he was watched by other eyes as well, though he saw nothing more. The sensation made his flesh creep.

West Street met with the South Street thoroughfare at the exact centre of town in a crossroads. The old town hall stood on one corner, its clock tower looming over the junction like a sentinel. The hands on its clock face had long ago rusted solid and become stuck at the strike of noon.

Buchanan hitched his horse outside a building that had once been the finest hotel in town, the Grande. It was a majestic building that still clung to a faded dignity even as it slumped into decay. The steps of its wooden porch flexed under Shane's weight as he followed Buchanan inside, into a lobby that had been built with the hotel's name in mind. Sunlight slanted through tall windows, lighting on the tarnished frame of a chandelier and an ornate stair that climbed the wall to a gallery overhead.

A brass bell sat on the front desk and Buchanan slapped his hand against it repeatedly, breaking the austere silence. After a short while, a door opened upstairs and a tall black man appeared at the gallery. He stared down at Buchanan with a look of cold disdain.

24

Grinning, Buchanan sauntered to the foot of the stairs. 'Is your master at home?' he asked.

The man did not answer him but flicked a curious glance towards Shane. The faintest suggestion of a grin twitched at the corners of his lips. Shane did not like that grin; it had a distinctly predatory look about it and he instantly decided that he did not like this man. This man was dangerous.

He descended the stairs with smooth, graceful steps, seeming to glide, the hem of a long, grey overcoat dragging on the steps behind him. A delicate, long-fingered hand brushed against the handrail, stirring up flakes of dust. Buchanan stepped out of his way as he reached the ground floor, affording him space the way a lone wolf avoids a bear. It was only when they stood side-by-side that Shane realised just how tall the man was: he towered a full head above Buchanan, who was himself over six feet tall.

The giant glided past Buchanan and Shane caught himself instinctively backing away as he drew closer. 'You must be Shane Ennis,' he said. His voice was soft and had a strange accent that Shane could not identify. Shane forced himself to meet the stranger's gaze, and found himself staring into eyes that were as fathomless as his own.

'I got him.' Buchanan said proudly.

'So I see.' The man turned and beckoned for them to follow him into a dimly lit hall.

'Have the other contestants arrived?' Buchanan asked.

'Ennis is the last,' the giant replied.

'How many have tried to kill each other already?'

'None.'

Buchanan snorted derisively. 'Well that's no good. They're supposed to be killers, aren't they?'

The giant stopped beside a door and gestured for Shane to pass through. The room beyond was murky with dust. Tall windows dominated the far walls but their surfaces were so encrusted with years of accumulated grime that the light that shone through was stained a dirty shade of brown. In the centre of the room was a semi-circle of armchairs, each covered with a muslin cloth. Other furniture – broken and mouldering – had been stacked against the walls.

A man stood at the window, facing out through a small circle that he had wiped clean of dirt. He turned as Shane entered the room. He was grey-haired with tanned skin and a trimmed moustache and beard. His boots were made of soft leather and were worn with brown woollen pants, a white shirt and a brown waistcoat and jacket, all expensively-tailored by the look of them. At his side was a bone-handled Colt 1873 Single Action Army revolver, rigged for a right-handed cross-draw. The look of the man said that he was no stranger to the weapon, although his bearing did not indicate that he was a gunfighter by trade. He lacked the constant wariness that men in Shane's former profession learned to possess. Judging by his confidence and the authority in his stance, Shane guessed that he was a military man, or had been once.

This was Buchanan's employer, the man who had fronted the money to buy Shane's capture. Shane was slightly disappointed that he was nobody he recognised.

'You got him. Excellent,' the man congratulated Buchanan. 'Noonan gave you no trouble?'

'None at all.' Buchanan answered with a smile. 'Penn and the boys will be along with your money shortly.'

'Good. If there's one thing that I appreciate, Mister Buchanan, it's not having to pay for the things I want. Mister Ennis!' He extended his hand warmly. 'I've been very much looking forward to meeting you, sir. My name is Colonel Hartshorne.'

Shane had never met him but he had heard of him by reputation. Nathaniel Hartshorne had fought for the Union under General George McClellan and had earned himself an unsavoury reputation for being a butcher. During the Battle of James Point in 1861, rumour had it that he had pressed an attack upon Confederate forces despite their surrender, and had slaughtered an entire company of unarmed men.

After the war he had gone on to amass a considerable fortune on the stock market. Asked once how he picked his investments, he had confessed that he regularly consulted with a medium and that he cast his own horoscopes before embarking on any new venture.

Word in occult circles was that Nathaniel was secretly a practitioner of the black arts and that it was no medium he consulted, but a demon instead. It was rumoured that he had found something during the war – or that something had found him – wandering the battlefield among the dead and the wounded. It was to secure a deal with that something that he had led his brutal assault at James Point, and because of that deal that he had since become the thirteenth richest man in America.

But money wasn't enough for Nathaniel. For the past eight years he had invested thousands of dollars into archaeological expeditions around the world. He had plundered tombs and ancient cities in Egypt, Africa, Tibet and India, supposedly searching for some form of supernatural power.

So far as Shane was aware, he had no connection to the Fastest Guns. What he was doing in Covenant was a mystery.

Shane ignored the occultist's proffered hand. After a moment's embarrassed hesitance, Nathaniel withdrew it.

'You'll have to excuse the means by which I brought you here,' he said. 'As I'm sure you can appreciate, I very much doubted that you would have come had I simply asked you. Won't you take a seat?'

Buchanan threw Shane into a chair. Dust erupted from the muslin sheet. Shane had no sooner recovered his breath when Nathaniel extended a glass of cognac to him. 'Drink?'

Again, Shane refused. Nathaniel was indifferent. He sat opposite Shane and sipped from the glass himself, savouring it before swallowing. 'Really, you should try to enjoy my hospitality Mister Ennis. I'm given to understand it that comfort is something that you cannot expect to look forward to where you're going. You should make the most of it now.'

'Fuck you.'

Buchanan stepped threateningly close, his fist raised, but Nathaniel stayed him. 'I think that Mister Buchanan would gladly hit you all day,' he told Shane. 'But then how could you be expected to compete in the tournament?'

'Who says I'm going to anyway?' Shane growled.

Nathaniel held his cognac up to the light and contemplated it. He swirled the liquid with a deft rotation of his wrist. 'Let me answer you with another question if you will, Mister Ennis. If I put you on that crossroads tomorrow with a gun in your hand and set another man opposite you, likewise armed; and if I then tell you that man will shoot you unless you shoot him first, would you choose to die? No, I think not. I know you, Mister Ennis. Buchanan has told me a lot about you; the rest I can fill in for myself. I've seen the things you've seen. I embrace them.'

He lowered the cognac to his lips and drained the glass. 'You *will* compete in this tournament, Mister Ennis. You really don't have any other choice.'

* * *

Shane's eyes had grown accustomed to the Grande's dark interior and the sunlight blinded him as he stepped outside. He shielded his face with one hand. Faded lettering on the wall of a building across the street identified the place as O'Malley's Saloon, home, the sign boasted, to the best Irish whisky in the county. A man stood in the open doorway, staring at Shane.

'Know him?' Buchanan asked.

'No.' Shane lied.

They unhitched their horses and Buchanan took Shane to a stable off West Street. It was a barn-like building whose rafters were thick with cobwebs. Some fifteen horses were already stabled there. Some had clearly been in town longer than the others and had grown accustomed to its atmosphere, just as Buchanan's had. Shane again marvelled that Covenant had tolerated a human presence for so long. It went completely against everything that he thought he knew about the place.

The stables were tended by an ostler with a surly disposition. Shane got the impression that he was there to guard the horses more than take care of them. He found his mare an empty stall by himself and rubbed her down and brushed her. She was nervous about being left on her own and she nuzzled him urgently.

'Easy, girl,' he whispered. She had been his only companion for years and he wondered what would happen to her after he was gone. He patted her lovingly on the flank and found her some grain to eat. There was a hoof pick lying on a wooden block close to the feed bags. Buchanan saw him look at it and smiled knowingly, aware of what Shane was thinking. He also knew that Shane didn't have the nerve.

'Come on,' he said. 'Nathaniel wants you to get cleaned up.'

Shane left the hoof pick where it was and followed him outside. They walked back onto West Street, where a pair of riflemen passed them by. 'They're not contestants.' Shane observed.

'No.' Buchanan replied. 'Nathaniel calls them his invigilators. They're here to make sure everyone plays nicely.'

'Does that include you?'

'Hell, I *always* play nicely. It just depends on what kind of a game you happen to be playing.'

He led Shane down a narrow alleyway into a yard, enclosed by leaning walls and a ramshackle fence. At one end was a shed in which were three tin baths and a hearth for heating water. Buchanan showed him where there was a pump across the yard, then left him to it.

Alone, Shane filled his bath. He could not shake the suspicion that, even though he could not see anyone, he was being watched. His bath water was steaming when a soft tread alerted him that he had company. He expected it to be Buchanan, returning to taunt and threaten him some more, but instead it was the man from O'Malley's Saloon. He leaned himself in the shed's open doorway and glared at Shane through slitted eyes. 'I heard you'd be competing this time,' he said. 'I had to kill three men before I got an invite, just so I can finally be the man to put you in your grave.'

Shane unbuttoned his shirt. 'What's the matter, Sullivan? You like me so much you've come to watch me undress?"

'No, I just come to look you in the eyes, tell you I'll be seeing you in Hell real soon.'

Shane turned slowly away and finished undressing. 'You'll have to save me a seat,' he said. The man swore at him and left him to his bath. It had been a good long while since Shane had bathed and the hot water felt good against his skin. He scrubbed himself clean. After a while, Buchanan returned with a razor and clean clothes.

'I heard you had a visitor.'

'Nobody special.'

Buchanan leaned his back against the wall and grinned. 'David Sullivan. I heard he was looking for you a while back. You the man that killed his brother?'

Shane didn't answer. He had killed lots of people.

After he had washed and dressed, Shane was taken back to the crossroads where a cell had been prepared for him in Covenant's jailhouse. The building was a squalid brick extension added onto the side of the town hall and courthouse. In it, eight years ago, Jacob Priestley had shot three prisoners through the bars of their cells and the bullet holes remained, the mortar surrounding them coloured brown where the dead men's blood had splattered. Only one of the cells had been empty on August Third, and that was the one that Shane was now put in. Some work had been done to strengthen it: the bars were set in fresh stone and the lock on the door was new. Buchanan produced the key from a chain around his neck and locked him in.

A guard was stationed in the next room and Buchanan spoke to him as he left. 'No visitors. Anyone wants to speak with him, you send them to me.'

Shane walked over to the bars and tested them for strength. He was not surprised to find that they were properly secure. If he had any notion of escaping then he had left it far too late to put into action now. Feeling wretched, he sat on the edge of his bunk and put his head in his hands. He had always known that he would end up in a situation like this. For six long years he had known it was inevitable, but had run from it nevertheless. Now, the weight of his fear, all his certainty, bore down on him and crushed him with despair.

What made it worse, what really made him hate himself, was the joy he felt deep inside: that this was where he wanted to be. That finally he was where he belonged.

A noise outside made him cross to the window. His cell looked out into an alleyway, down which it was possible to see out to the front porch of the Grande on the opposite side of the street. Three riflemen had drawn up outside the hotel. Shane recognised them as the men from Saddle Horn Rock. Tethered in a line behind them were five horses that had once belonged to Noonan and his men, and a sixth that carried the money boxes containing the twenty-thousand dollars that Nathaniel had paid for Shane's capture.

Nathaniel's servant met with them and Shane overheard one of them refer to him by his name: Whisperer. He had them carry the boxes inside, then the horses were taken away to be stabled. Shane returned to his bunk and sat down to brood.

CHAPTER FOUR

It had all started when a Chicago newspaper printed a story exposing a list of senators who had been receiving bribes from members of the Prosperity Union Investment Company. Congress had formed a special committee charged with investigating the allegations and bringing those involved to justice. It was to blossom into the biggest political scandal since Credit Mobilier.

The year was 1881.

Shane lay atop a low rise in the southern plains, spying on a ranch about a mile away. It belonged to a man called George Babson, who had recently gone to town and hired six gunfighters to protect his home. The reason was that he had a new houseguest: his brother-in-law, a man by the name of Benedict Hunte.

It was Hunte that Shane had come to kill. He was the lynchpin of the Prosperity Union scandal, an accountant who knew the names of everybody involved. A lot of powerful men stood to suffer if what he knew was ever made public, and one of those – a US congressman – had hired Shane to ensure his silence, permanently.

Hunte was no fool; he had guessed what his co-conspirators

would do to him if they thought he was going to spill the beans, and when Congress had sent for him to give evidence at a special hearing he had chosen to skip town instead. It was too bad that he had run to his sister's family for safety. Tracking him had been just too damned easy.

Getting to him was going to be trickier, however. The ranch was located way out in open country, making it difficult for anybody to get close without being seen, and it was well-protected with men and firepower.

Shane slithered back out of sight and retreated to the small copse of trees where he had tethered his horse. As he drew close to it, he saw a rider approaching from the west. It was getting time for the spring round-up and Babson had a number of cowboys working for him, some of which had been patrolling the land since Hunte's arrival. Shane quickly ducked out of sight among the trees.

The rider was a younger man than Shane by maybe five or six years and looked handsome and strong. He wore a Smith and Wesson Model Three Russian revolver and, judging by the way he carried himself in relation to it, Shane figured that he was not one of Babson's men. This man was a professional killer of the kind that Babson could not afford and had likely come to kill Hunte.

Shane was not overly surprised to find that he had competition. Given the number of powerful men who were liable to suffer if Hunte testified, it was not unthinkable that several of them might have despatched assassins to ensure he didn't make it to the committee. Shane held back among the trees and watched as the man rode closer. He was headed straight for him, no doubt figuring, as Shane had, that it was a good place to leave his horse while he climbed up onto the ridge to get a feel for what he was up against. When he had drawn within fifty paces – close enough that he was in pistol range but far enough away that only a well-aimed shot could kill – Shane stepped out into the open. He kept his guns holstered but his hands ready.

The man reined in before him and mentally assessed him before deciding not to go for his gun either. 'Looks like I chose me a popular place to take a rest,' he said.

'There's not a lot of shade in these parts.' Shane replied. The exchange was amicably done.

The man nodded past him at the ridge. 'I hear the Babson ranch is over there.'

'It is.' Shane confirmed.

'I heard he bought himself some gunfighters.'

'Nobody special, but add them to what he's got and there's more than twenty guns there now, and no cover for close to a quarter mile in any direction.'

'Sounds like it'd be best to go in at night.'

'That's what I figured.'

Shane walked over to his horse and unhitched the reins without ever once letting the man slip out of his peripheral vision. He was ready to reach for his gun at the slightest provocation.

'You're Shane Ennis, aren't you?'

Shane did not reply. He mounted his horse and turned her around in the direction of town. The stranger fell in beside him. 'You are, aren't you? Shit and buggery!' He whistled through his teeth. 'I never thought there'd come the day when I'd meet you. I'm Castor Buchanan.'

'The man who shot Rick Valentine?'

'Hey, you've heard of me! Ain't that a breeze.'

Castor Buchanan was a killer with the sort of reputation that a certain breed loved to foster. To him, killing was less a vice and more a pleasure. He was a brutal and sadistic man whose fondness of torture and rape bordered on the demonic. He was also a very talented gunfighter, almost as good as Shane in fact. 'I wouldn't have reckoned on you having heard of me, a big shot like you,' he said.

'I keep my ear to the ground.'

'Like a fucking Apache.' Buchanan laughed. 'Hey white man, heap many men want you dead.'

'Very funny.'

They rode on in silence for a time. Presently, Shane began wondering if they had rode far enough that a gunshot would not be heard at the Babson Ranch and contemplated killing his rival before Buchanan got the drop on him instead. He was just about to reach for his gun when Buchanan spoke: 'It could get messy.'

Shane stayed his hand. He could not be sure if Buchanan had read his intention or not, but if the man wanted to talk, Shane was of a mood to let him.

'The two of us being hired for the same job like this; we can't both get paid, now can we?' Buchanan grinned like he had said something funny. 'So we kill each other now and get it over with, but what does that solve, right? We still got all those men back at the ranch to contend with and that's not likely to be easy, not for just one of us on his own. So whaddya say we team up? We can settle our differences afterward. Partner?'

Shane would later regret not killing him when he had the chance, but at the time he had weighed his options and foolishly answered: 'Sure.'

It was getting late in Covenant and the daylight was beginning to fade when Buchanan came to collect Shane from his cell. He was taken across the road to O'Malley's Saloon.

Shane saw other men go in ahead of them. 'Nathaniel's drawing lots tonight to decide who fights who in the first round.' Buchanan explained. 'No prizes for guessing who's already asked to fight against you.'

'What did Nathaniel tell him?'

'Refused him of course. The matches are picked at random, those are the rules.'

'The Fastest Guns never used to care much for rules.'

'No.' Buchanan agreed. 'But you'll find there've been a few changes made since you knew them last.' He stepped up to the saloon's butterfly-wing doors and pushed them open.

The atmosphere in the saloon was tense and fragile as glass. Shane counted about a dozen men spread throughout the room, each with at least the space of a table separating him from his closest neighbour. A flight of stairs climbed to a gallery on the first floor, where whores had used to ply their trade in small private rooms. Three of Nathaniel's invigilators occupied the gallery now, armed with Winchester repeating rifles and standing vigilantly over the men below.

Everybody had turned to face the new arrivals and Shane felt the weight of their scrutiny bear down upon him. Buchanan shrugged it off and strode across the room to the untended bar, where he poured himself a drink. Shane joined him.

'Did you ever see such a mean bunch of desperadoes all crammed into one place?' Buchanan said loudly. He slid a shot glass full of whisky into Shane's waiting hand. Shane did not drink it but slowly turned to sweep his gaze across the room.

He recognised most of the contestants gathered there, by reputation if not by face. Among them was John Devlin, the insane mass-murderer; Daniel Blaine from Canada; and Escoban Cadero, an outlaw king from the desert wastes of northern Mexico. They had come from all over the continent to compete, not for money, but to be recognised as the best of the best.

Seated with his back to an old piano was Nanache, also known as Nathan Sanders, a renegade Apache spiritwalker. He wore a faded blue US Army jacket and a grisly necklace made of finger bones, each of them supposedly cut from the hand of a gunslinger he had killed.

Across the room was a man with a star-shaped scar on his face that identified him as Evan Drager. He had been shot in the head five years ago but had miraculously managed to survive. The wound had left him in a coma for twenty-seven days, after which he had woken and proclaimed himself to be the Fastest Guns' new holy messiah, spared from death by the bullet's own mercy. Since then he had amassed a small cult following.

Not all of the contestants were men. A hard-faced brunette sat with her back to the wall. She wore a man's clothes and had a .44 calibre Forehand and Wadsworth revolver strapped to her thigh. Shane had never seen her before but he knew by her reputation that she could only be the woman they called Vendetta. No other woman alive was more deadly with a gun.

She was not the only woman in the room, although the other was certainly not a contestant. She was a pretty young thing, maybe eighteen years old, with a trim figure and long blonde hair that was black at the roots. She sat on a young man's lap, himself not more than a year or two her senior and Shane was appalled to find that a man had brought his girlfriend to watch him compete.

The girl was looking at Shane. 'You never told me Shane Ennis was competing,' she whispered excitedly.

The boy stopped nuzzling her and looked up. 'Oh yeah, hey!

38

Whatever.' He reached his hand around her and gave her arse a squeeze.

At that moment, the butterfly-wing doors swung open and David Sullivan strode in. Everybody looked up at him and there was a moment of reckoning, then it passed and Sullivan stalked to the bar. He paused beside Shane, glared at him hatefully, then snatched up a bottle of beer and found himself a table far from anybody else.

Shane went to find a seat of his own but Buchanan laid a restraining hand on his shoulder. 'Here's just fine,' he said.

The butterfly-wing doors swung open again and this time it was Nathaniel who came in. He was followed by Whisperer and two more of his invigilators who, once inside, took up flanking positions guarding the door.

Nathaniel walked over to the bar and poured himself a drink. He nodded to Buchanan and Shane. 'Nice to see you here, Mister Ennis. In fact,' he said, turning to include the rest of the room with a sweep of his arm. 'It's good to see *all* of you here.'

He stepped away from the bar, moving out into the centre of the room where everyone could see him. 'In this room I see fifteen of this country's finest gunfighters. I salute you all,' he said, raising his glass. 'Welcome to the second tournament of the Fastest Guns.'

Buchanan whooped and began to applaud but he was alone in openly displaying his enthusiasm. The other contestants remained tight-lipped and insular. Nathaniel took his drink with him to the stairs and climbed halfway to the gallery. From up there he towered over everyone in the saloon, imposing his authority on men who normally followed no rule save their own.

'It has been six years since the last tournament was held,' he said, his voice rich and flowing. 'Since then, a new generation of gunfighters has emerged and it is time for the greatest among them –

39

you! – to settle who is truly the best. This time there can be only one winner. For the rest of you there is only death and the anonymity of failure. But for the victor–' Nathaniel paused, savouring the moment – 'Lies the greatest of all treasures: immortality! The immortality that will come from being recognised as one of the legendary Fastest Guns.'

Shane glanced around the room and saw that all of the faces staring up at Nathaniel burned with ambition.

'There are rules.' Nathaniel said. 'These men with the rifles whom you are all no doubt familiar with by now are here to see to it that you abide by them. If you do not–'

Every invigilator in the room cranked the lever-action of his rifle in unison, jacking a cartridge into the breach. Nathaniel let that formidable sound echo around the room before he continued: 'I trust that I make myself clear.'

There was a deadly silence.

Nathaniel went on: 'You are all in this to the end. In coming here you have made a commitment that you cannot go back on. You will have seen the men stationed around the perimeter of town. They will shoot anybody who tries to leave. They will also shoot anybody who tries to enter.'

He counted the second rule off on his fingers. 'There is to be no fighting outside of the tournament. You will each of you shortly be paired with an opponent drawn at random and given a time when you will fight. You will fight *only* with that opponent and *only* at the allotted time. Any act of fist-fighting, wrestling or any attempt to draw down on another contestant will be met with lethal force, without hesitation, by my invigilators.

'Lastly, no fight will be deemed to have finished until one of the combatants is dead. You will all fight to the death and if you do not kill your opponent with the first shot you will carry on shooting, reloading if necessary, until he is dead. The last man left standing at the end of the tournament will be deemed to be the winner by virtue of being the only survivor.'

Several of the contestants began glancing around at each other, trying to gauge who would win and who would die. Shane had made his own predictions already and they did not bode well. There was not a single fighter in the room that he was not confident he could beat, assuming of course that he chose to fight at all. He was not being cocky. It was not without good cause that men had once claimed he was the best gunfighter who had ever lived. Six years on and he was undoubtedly out of practice, but even so he knew that it would not take long for him to get back into his stride.

He just didn't know if that was something he wanted to do. The risk was too great that if he started killing he might never stop.

Whisperer passed Nathaniel a bag, which he held up for everyone to see. 'In this bag are the names of each contestant. Sadly, there is one contestant who is absent this evening. Her name will be drawn for her and she will be advised of her time and pairing in due course.'

'Who is she?' It was David Sullivan who spoke. 'And why ain't she here?'

'Her name is Chastity, and she is currently resting. Chastity is . . . different.' Nathaniel replied.

Shane had never heard of any gunfighter who went by the name of Chastity, and there were few enough women gunfighters that, if she had any reputation at all, he should have heard of her. The fact that he had not struck him as unusual. Lately, too much information that he would have expected to have heard had managed to slip him by, and he did not think it a coincidence.

41

Nathaniel began drawing names from the bag. 'The first match of the first round,' he said. 'Will be held at half-past ten tomorrow morning, and will be fought between. . . Matt Nesbitt and David Sullivan.'

The two men each turned to look the other over. David Sullivan, the unrelenting bounty hunter and Matt Nesbitt, the die-hard lawman. Whisperer chalked their names up on a chalkboard at the foot of the stairs. Shane was relieved that his name had not been one the first to be drawn. He tensed when Nathaniel drew the second pairing:

'Escoban Cadero and the absent Chastity. To fight at half-past-eleven.'

Cadero, the scarred Mexican outlaw, wrinkled his face in disappointment. He knew nothing of his opponent, whether she was a challenge or if he could beat her easily. He poured himself a drink and knocked it back.

Nathaniel drew again. 'The third match will be held at half-past-twelve and will be fought between Vendetta and Luke Ferris.'

The woman gunfighter barely acknowledged the call. She stared at her table, where she had been drawing abstract images in a pool of spilt beer.

Nanache and Daniel Blaine were drawn next, followed by Tom Freeman and Kip Kutcher. Freeman was a serious-faced black man from North Carolina with more than eighty kills to his name and Kutcher was the young man who had brought his girlfriend with him. Shane was able to place him now that he knew his name. Kip Kutcher was one of a dozen or more wild young men who had made a name for themselves tearing up the Comstock Lode. He was a renowned fast draw. Supposedly, not once in over fifteen gunfights had he been the first man to draw. He was handsome and clean-shaven and dressed fine with a shiny Colt Peacemaker slung from his belt.

'The sixth match will be fought between Evan Drager and John MacMurray and will take place at half-past three.' Nathaniel announced

Drager nodded his approval. MacMurray, an engineer in the US Army, went back to cutting into the tips of his bullets with a pocket knife. He was renowned for his signature-kill ammunition. He cut a cross into the tip of each bullet he fired. This caused them to deform on impact, inflicting massive tissue damage. One shot was nearly always enough to kill, the massive weight of impact literally dragging the victim's blood from his heart. The cross incisions had led most people to call him 'The Christian'.

Shane tensed as Nathaniel reached into the bag for the fourteenth time, knowing that his own name was sure to be drawn soon.

'The seventh match.' Nathaniel announced. 'Will be between Valentino Rodrigues and the Gentleman, and will be held at half-past four.'

Whisperer chalked their names up on the board. Rodrigues was a Mexican assassin and the Gentleman was one of a new breed of city gunfighters from the streets of New York. A shy and neatly-dressed man with tortoiseshell-rimmed spectacles, he looked more like a banking clerk than a gunfighter.

Nathaniel drew the last pair of names. At half-past-five the next day, Shane would fight John Devlin.

After six years abstinence, he would either kill or be killed.

The meeting ended as soon as the last pairing had been called. Vendetta kicked back her chair and was the first to leave. One by one, the saloon began to empty. John Devlin made a point to make eye-contact with Shane before he left. He was a young man, not much in his twenties but he had eyes as deep and cold as gun barrels.

'He shot fifteen kids in a schoolhouse.' Buchanan told Shane. 'Killed their teacher and half the posse they sent to find him. That man sure likes to kill.'

Shane had already heard Devlin's story and likened him to a lesser Jacob Priestley. He did not think that he would lose against him, although the thought of winning made him feel cold with dread. He began to think of what would happen to him but was distracted when Kip Kutcher walked up and stuck out his hand in greeting. Shane ignored him but Kutcher had the sort of ego that glossed over small details like rebuffal.

'Wow, it sure is an honour to meet you Mister Ennis. I'd like to introduce myself, my name is Kip Kutcher. That's Kip with a K, Kutcher with a K. And this here's my girl, Madison.'

The girl ducked her gaze, feigning bashfulness. 'Pleased to meet you, Mister Ennis.'

Shane fixed her with a withering stare. He knew her kind: gunfighter groupies. They clung to a man like lice, drinking up his fame to compensate for their own lack of character. Shane had tolerated a few in his time but never one as striking as Madison. Towards the end he had grown to scorn them for they had distracted him from what he had believed was the purity of the kill.

The girl had no place being in Covenant and Kutcher should have known better than to bring her along.

'It's not often that a man gets to meet a *bona fide* legend.' Kutcher told Shane. 'So I'll understand if you're feeling a little shy.'

He laughed at his own joke. 'Seriously, I thought you'd retired. Don't you know that gunfighting's a young man's game now?'

Shane did not rise to him, only turned and reached for his whisky glass. He was wondering if getting drunk would go any way to solving some of his problems. He decided not.

Madison dragged her boyfriend away and they left the saloon, laughing. Nathaniel came over. 'So what do you think of the new generation of gunfighters, Mister Ennis?'

'I think the Fastest Guns' standards must be slipping.'

Nathaniel laughed politely. He turned to Buchanan: 'You and I have matters to discuss. Why don't you show Mister Ennis back to his accommodation? We'll speak again, Shane.'

Buchanan put his hand on Shane's arm and steered him to the door. It was dark outside. The embers of a rust-coloured sunset burned on the edge of the horizon leaving Covenant to skulk in blackness. The air was still, quiet and foreboding.

'Less than twenty-four hours, Shane.' Buchanan said as they crossed the street. There was excitement in his voice. 'Don't tell me you don't feel it too: that fear, that anticipation. Knowing that tomorrow you're going to take a man's life, Shane. Doesn't that feel good to you?'

Shane was in no mood to talk about how he felt. He was excited but he was also afraid and the worst part of his fear stemmed from the fact that he was excited. He did not want to feel good about the prospect of shooting a man tomorrow but it was so hard for him. He had lived by the gun for the greater part of his adult life and, however much his conscious will despised it, his heart would always crave the power he had once wielded with a gun in each hand.

Back then he would have never fallen so low as this.

They entered the jailhouse and Buchanan took a lantern from the guard in the sheriff's office and used it to light the way to Shane's cell. Its flickering light set Buchanan's eyes ablaze. 'I know you feel it,' he said knowingly.

He locked the door and took the lantern with him back to the sheriff's office, closing the door behind him so that Shane was left in darkness. Despondent, Shane sat on his bunk and counted Buchanan's footsteps as they receded into the distance. When he heard the front door slam, he rose and crossed to the window. There, he could see Buchanan as he crossed the street to the Grande. He saw Buchanan pause at the foot of the porch and turn to face the sunset.

Waiting for something, Shane thought.

And then it began. As the last of the sunlight faded from the horizon, the town began to creak and groan.

It was as if the town's foundations were contracting in the cooling night air, except that the temperature did not seem to have dropped at all. Wood groaned and screamed and in places there were violent banging noises. The sounds built in number as every building in town joined the cacophony. Shane jumped back from the window as the wall of his cell began to groan. The floor shook beneath his feet.

The noise built to a tortured howl and then, slowly, a sense of order began to emerge. It was subtle at first, but then grew more noticeable and Shane realised that every building was gradually settling into rhythm with its neighbours.

The sound became a lullaby. It started at the centre of town and rolled outwards, then crept back again.

Out and in again.

Out and in again.

Shane could almost imagine the buildings bending and flexing like stalks of corn in the wind.

Out and in again.

It sounded as if the town was breathing.

Buchanan stood at the foot of the porch for a while, letting the town's song caress him. He had not felt anything like it since the Fastest Guns had turned their backs on him after Shane had ruined his right hand. It would have been better if Shane had killed him that day – at least then there would have been a proper end to things – but Shane was weak. He was frightened by what the Fastest Guns would make of him, and so he had spared Buchanan's life and severed him from the truest love he had ever known.

Buchanan had spent years training to shoot with his left hand. By many standards, he was still a force to be reckoned with, but even on a good day he was nowhere near as good as he had used to be, shooting with his right. The Fastest Guns only accepted gunfighters of the highest standard and no matter how hard he tried, however violently he raged, he knew that he would never be good enough for them again.

His life had been meaningless since he had lost his right hand, up until now.

The door swung open and Whisperer appeared from the shadows. 'Shall I leave you a moment alone?' he asked sardonically.

Buchanan snarled a terse reply.

'We have work to do,' the occultist reminded him sternly. 'Colonel Hartshorne wishes to speak with you.'

'Of course he does.'

Nathaniel was in his study, the same room in which he had received Shane earlier in the day. He reclined in a cloth-covered armchair, sipping fine cognac which, as always, he refused to share with Buchanan.

'How is he?' he enquired.

'How is who?'

'You know who.' Nathaniel said firmly.

'Shane is fine. Miserable, but then he always was a gloomy cuss.'

'Do you think he'll fight tomorrow?'

'Of course he will.' Buchanan had no doubt. 'His soul belongs to them. If he dies, they'll take him. He knows that; it's why he hasn't put up a fight yet. Besides, he *wants* to be here. He just won't admit it.'

'It's been six years. I doubt he's even practiced at all. You're certain he's still got what it takes?'

'Six years or sixty, it makes no difference.' Buchanan replied with certainty. 'Shane was the best. He always will be. He'll be a bit rusty, that's for sure, but even at his worst he's still more than a match for anyone here.'

'Including Chastity?'

Buchanan paused. Even he had respect for the girl's talent. 'Your girl's good, Nathaniel, I'll grant you that, but what she's got doesn't compare to the kind of skill that develops over time and with practice. My money's still on Shane.'

Nathaniel grinned. 'I find the loyalty you have for him very touching.'

'Fuck you! The fact that Shane beat me is all the proof you need that he's as good as I say he is. You wanted bait; they want him! Just be sure you're ready when the time comes.'

'We'll be ready.' Nathaniel assured him. 'Our trap is set.'

CHAPTER FIVE

The Babson ranch was a fair spread with a two-storey house, half a dozen sheds and two bunkhouses. George Babson had worked fifteen years to build it into what it was, and he would lose it all in just a single night of violence.

Shane and Buchanan had left their horses among the trees on the far side of the rise and proceeded the rest of the way on foot. It was a dark and moonless night and they moved silently across the low ground, communicating solely through a system of coded whistles which, when heard from a distance, sounded like nothing more ominous than the wind.

Babson had posted guards. Two men walked solitary patrols and a third sat on a rocking chair on the front porch, a shotgun cradled in his lap. Babson's money had bought him loyalty, but not quality. The man on the porch was asleep and the other two had fallen into routine, as bored men were prone to do.

Shane and Buchanan dropped to a crouch in the tall grasses and Buchanan signalled that he would cut around back. Shane whistled agreement and remained where he was while Buchanan scrambled off into the darkness. The next time they met, Benedict Hunte would be dead and they would be enemies again. Shane looked forward to it. He had come to recognise Buchanan as a man whose skills were equal to his own, and he was eager to test himself against him in combat.

A period of time passed in which the guards walked two circuits of their patrol, each time treading exactly the same path. By the time Buchanan gave the signal that he was in position, Shane had planned his attack. He crept quietly to a shack near the edge of the ranch and waited in the darkness. Soon enough, one of the guards walked past him. He was a young man, not yet old enough to grow a proper beard. He did not see Shane but searched in his pockets and drew out a cheroot. Shane struck him from behind while he was trying to light it, clubbing him across the back of the head with the butt of his revolver and knocking him unconscious.

The man had a belt revolver holstered by his side and Shane took it from him. He left him where he lay and stepped out boldly from behind the shack. He was of a different height and build to the unconscious guard but, from a distance and concealed in the dark, he doubted that anyone watching from the house would know any better. He crossed to the first of the two bunkhouses, drew a gun in each hand and then kicked down the door.

He was inside and shooting before anyone had time to respond. Two men died instantly in their beds, while three more had time to scramble for their weapons. Shane fired like a machine, thumbing back the hammers of both guns and pulling the trigger in a murderous rhythm of death. The flash of exploding cartridges illuminated the room in fractured bursts.

One man drew a gun and fired in return. Shane flattened himself against a wall, discarded a spent revolver and drew another, with which he shot the man in the head.

Outside, men had begun shouting in alarm. A series of shots rang out from somewhere on the opposite side of the ranch as Buchanan began his half of the attack. Women began to scream.

Shane looted the dead of their guns. His own guns were Colts and though they were fine and accurate weapons they were slow to reload and he did not have the time. He stepped outside with his purloined weapons, aimed one and fired at the man on the porch. He was awake, and ducked as the shot blew splinters from the doorframe beside him. Shane fired with his second gun and this time he did not miss. The man fell dead.

The door of the second bunkhouse suddenly burst open and a gang of men emerged, their guns blazing. Shane dropped to the ground and rolled sideways, shooting on the move. The men were gunned down. Others jumped over their bodies and scattered among the other buildings for cover. Shane was quickly caught in a crossfire and forced into shelter behind a log pile.

He discarded his empty guns and drew fresh ones. Thinking that he was empty, a pair of men rushed him and he gunned them down. He pirouetted, coat tails billowing, and fired two shots in opposite directions, killing two more.

Kicking down a door, he skirted through one building and came out the other side, catching a gunman by surprise. He shot another through the bunkhouse window and the slaughter was complete.

He tossed aside a pair of smoking guns and advanced toward the ranch house.

A man shot at him from an upstairs window and the bullet whipped past Shane's ear. He retaliated with a lethal hail of bullets and a moment later the window exploded, the gunman toppling out to land on the hard earth below. Shane stepped up to the front porch and relieved the dead sentry of his shotgun.

There was mayhem inside. Shane kicked through the door, then stepped back immediately. A shot from within ripped the doorframe into splinters. Shane thrust the barrel of the shotgun around the door and fired. As he stepped inside, an elderly man and a boy of fifteen were both picking themselves up from behind cover. Shane emptied the shotgun into the old man's chest then tossed it aside, drew a revolver and shot the boy. He stole a fresh gun from the dead, stepped over the bodies and followed the sound of fighting deeper into the house.

Buchanan had taken the fight to the upper floor. Shots rang out above and a man's voice was shouting for the women to take the children and run. As Shane reached the stairs, the pretty young wife of Babson's eldest son came rushing down. She was dressed in her nightclothes and dragged a four-year old child by the hand.

Shane did not even think about what he was doing. He levelled his gun and shot them both. He did it so quickly, so instinctively, that it was not until afterwards that he realised what he had done. He stopped in mid-stride, looked down at the woman, saw the look of shock upon her face. The boy looked peaceful, as if he was only sleeping.

'You bastard! They did nothing to you.' George Babson himself stood at the top of the stairs. Shane shot him, then shot him twice more as he fell. He stepped aside as the body tumbled down the stairs.

The sounds of gunfire elsewhere in the house had come to an end and the battle was over. Shane reloaded his guns and went to find Buchanan.

* * *

The smell of gunsmoke lingering in the cell made Shane think that he had not woken from his dream and that he was still back in the ranch house. He sat bolt upright on his bunk, suddenly alert and it was only then that his sense of reality came back to him. Damn, but the dream had been vivid! It lingered so fresh inside his mind that his ears still rang with the sound of gunfire and his guilt burned in the depths of his heart.

Guilt. It was a stranger to him. He had felt it for the first time that night at the ranch and it had left an indelible mark on him, one that had set in motion a chain of events that had brought him. . .

Here.

The sunlight slanted in through the barred windows, casting diagonal lines of shadow across the far wall. The air was hot and stuffy and laden with dust. Slowly, Shane stretched, easing the pain in his joints and back. A few old scars troubled him with aches. He crossed to the window for some fresh air and looked out upon the alley.

Today, he thought. He wondered if it would happen today, if killing Devlin would be all it would take to plunge him back into the nightmare that he had barely escaped from before. He looked up at the sky and tried to calculate what time it was. His fight was scheduled for five-thirty that afternoon and he estimated that it was currently sometime around seven. That gave him ten hours. After that he was not really sure what would become of him.

He sat and brooded. Some time later, the door to the sheriff's office opened and Buchanan arrived with his breakfast. He was in a rare good mood and called out in a sing-song voice as he entered: 'Wakey wakey, rise and shine!'

He slid the tray of hash browns, sausage and egg through a grate in the bottom of the cell door. 'Tournament begins in two hours, Shane. Are you raring to go?'

Shane said nothing but stared glumly at his meal. He had no appetite that morning and could not bring himself to drink, even though he was thirsty.

'Somebody's got their grumpy head on this morning.' Buchanan chided. 'I've got something that'll cheer you up.' He reached behind his back and produced a newspaper that he had tucked into the waistband of his woollen pants. 'One of Nathaniel's men rode in with it last night,' he explained and tossed it through the bars. 'Read it,' he said. The jokiness had suddenly gone from his voice.

The newspaper was a copy of the Carson Daily Gazette, dated a week ago. The main headline immediately caught Shane's eye. 'Shane Ennis Killed,' it proclaimed. Beneath it was a photograph of a dead man propped up in his coffin, flanked on either side by the men who had shot him. One of them had his arm in a sling.

The article claimed that Shane Ennis had been killed in a shoot out with three local men, who had recognised him while drinking in a saloon. Attempting to perform their civic duty and arrest the known criminal, they had approached him, whereupon he had drawn a gun and commenced firing. He had shot one man in the arm but, vastly out-gunned, he had been shot dead in retaliation.

Shane put the newspaper down and looked across at Buchanan, who was grinning like a loon. 'How does it feel to be a dead man, Shane?' He was clearly enjoying himself. 'I think it's a good likeness, don't you?'

The dead man did indeed bear a striking resemblance to Shane. He was the right height and build and had similar white hair. The grainy quality of the photograph made it even harder to tell that he was not the real Shane Ennis.

Shane had prayed for years that something like this would happen. Every bounty hunter that had ever sought for him now thought that he was dead. He was a free man again. It was a kick in the teeth that such good fortune had happened now, when it was too late for him to make good of it.

Buchanan smiled to see the anguish written on his face. 'You should have killed me when you had the chance.' Buchanan told him.

Shane did not answer. He sat and stared at the article. *I should have killed you a long time ago*, he thought to himself.

He had found Buchanan at the end of the hall, standing over the bodies of two of Babson's men and grinning like a madman. His face was splashed with blood, none of it his own. 'Shit, was that fun or what?'

Shane said nothing. Killing the woman and her child had dampened his enthusiasm for the night's proceedings and he wanted to be done and gone from the place as soon as possible so that he could put it out of his mind. He had never killed a child before and could not understand why he had done it this time.

He became aware that Buchanan had asked him a question.

'Did you get him?' Buchanan repeated.

'Who?'

'Hunte. Who do you fucking think?'

Shane shook his head. 'No.' He didn't think so.

Buchanan was jaunty. 'Well, let's go find him then, shall we?'

They searched the upper floor room by room. In one, they found Babson's youngest daughter. She had tried to hide herself under her bed but Buchanan heard her whimpering and dragged her out. He slapped her across the face. 'Where is he?' he shouted. 'Where's Hunte?'

The girl was too hysterical to answer. Buchanan subdued her with a punch that knocked her senseless, then tied her up. They did not find Hunte, but in one room further down the hall they discovered an open window and a rope of knotted sheets that hung to the ground below. Clothes were scattered from an open case and it was clear that Benedict Hunte had made a hurried escape.

'Well that's just fucking great!' Buchanan swore violently.

Shane shared his sentiment but did not voice it. He thought of the dead woman and her child again. It was doubly unprofessional of him to have killed them but let his intended target get away. 'We'll find him,' he promised resolutely.

They picked up Hunte's trail outside. He had run to the corral, where he had opened the gate and panicked the horses so that most of them had fled. Hunte had presumably taken one of them but the confusion of tracks was so great that they would have to wait until daylight to make sense of them.

Shane turned to face Buchanan, his hand straying towards his gun. The need for an alliance between them was ended now that Babson's men were gone.

'Fuck it!' Buchanan said. 'I ain't in the mood.'

Shane could have shot him anyway but it would have been an empty victory. Some day in the future he knew that their paths would cross again, and when that time came they would fight each other on equal footing. How else could they learn for certain which of them was the better man?

Until then, they went their separate ways. Buchanan stalked back into the ranch house and soon the Babson girl began to scream. Shane blanked the sounds from his mind and walked away. As he left the ranch, he passed the sentry that he had knocked unconscious. The boy was awake and rising to his feet. Shane coldly shot him through the head without breaking his stride.

Sunlight streamed through the boarded-up windows of the house that Kip Kutcher had claimed as his own. It pierced the gloom in beams that were heavy with dust and lighted on him as he struggled into his pants.

'Do you think there'll be any action on the side?' he asked.

His girlfriend lay half-wrapped in the tangle of their bedroll, her tanned skin glistening with sweat. Her hair was bedraggled and lay half across her face and shoulders in sleepy disarray. 'There must be,' she mumbled. 'Why wouldn't there be?'

'I don't know. Most of the people here seem kinda stiff.' Kip answered. He had tried to get a game of cards going the other day but no one had been interested. The invigilators were strictly business and the other contestants hadn't wanted anything to do with him. Only the Canadian, Daniel Blaine, had been willing to speak with him and he had expressed no desire to play against a card shark.

'They just don't know how to have a good time is their problem.' Madison said. She wriggled one arm free of the bedroll and lifted it above her head, stretching languorously and arching her back with a moan. She ended the stretch by rolling onto her side, facing Kip and studying him with heavy-lidded eyes.

Kip was just nineteen years old, a stringy, handsome youth with a mop of yellow-brown hair that flopped down over his brow. His ribs showed through the skin of his chest and his arms were skinny, but he was impressive in so many other ways. He picked up a shirt from the debris that constituted his unpacking, shook it to rid it of any insects that had crawled in during the night, and put it on.

'Just remember what I told you,' the girl warned him. 'Freeman is good. He's killed more than eighty men.'

57

'But I bet he isn't as fast as me.'

She smiled. 'No, he isn't. No one is.'

'Then we're cool. Hey, do you want to hear something really wild?'

'What?'

'I overheard some of the invigilators talking yesterday. You know Colonel Hartshorne put up a reward for whoever could bring Shane Ennis to him? Well, Buchanan killed the men who found him and brought it all back here.'

The girl raised herself up onto her elbows, suddenly wide-awake. 'What, all of it?'

'That's right, and I bet you can't guess how much it was. Twenty-*thousand* dollars, can you imagine that? Just for one man.'

Madison was amazed.

'I'm wondering if maybe they'll add it to the prize money.' Kip said. 'I wonder how much that'll make it.'

'They still haven't said?' Madison asked.

Kip shook his head. 'Not yet. But there's got to be something. Being ranked as one of the Fastest Guns is all nice and fancy and everything, but you can't have a tournament and not have prize money. What'd be the point?'

The girl smiled. 'What would you do with the money if you won?' she asked.

Kip walked over and crouched beside her. 'Baby, I'd spend it all on you.'

'Mmm, good answer,' she said, and pulled him to her.

CHAPTER SIX

Shane was released from his cell at ten o'clock and taken out onto the street where the other contestants had begun to gather in anticipation of the tournament's opening bout. It was a bright and clear morning, the sky a bleached shade of pale blue in which the sun burned like an open sore. Scarcely a breeze disturbed the turgid air.

Nathaniel's invigilators were out in force. Four stood on the rooftops overlooking the crossroads while six more guarded the streets. Two more flanked the Grande's porch, where Nathaniel reclined, eating an orange in the shade, Whisperer towering behind him.

There was a bench against the courthouse wall and Buchanan seated himself at one end. Shane was disinclined to sit with him and chose to stand instead. He leaned against the remaining upright of the half-broken porch and let his gaze roam across the assembled gunfighters.

Kip Kutcher and his girlfriend sat on the boardwalk opposite, the girl reclining in the sun while Kutcher chattered inanely. She was dressed in a pair of tight buckskin pants and a man's white shirt that she had tied short, exposing the smooth, flat skin of her midriff. Her appearance attracted looks from several of the men, David Sullivan being one of them.

He sat on the edge of the boardwalk outside of O'Malley's, absent-mindedly playing with a handful of dirt. He would let it slide between his fingers into his open palm, then switch hands and repeat the process again and again, nervously occupying himself until the time came for him to face Matt Nesbitt on the crossroads.

Shane hoped that Nesbitt would win. He despised David Sullivan. Out of all the bounty hunters that had pursued him during the last six years, Sullivan had been the most determined. Had it not been for him, Shane might have vanished into obscurity years ago but Sullivan had always been there wherever he had fled, following him like a shadow and never giving him chance to rest. Twice, Sullivan had almost succeeded in catching him, and on one of those occasions he had put a bullet in Shane's leg that still caused him to limp sometimes when the weather was humid.

Matt Nesbitt was a grim and solemn-looking man in his late-thirties with a square-jaw and fierce, unforgiving eyes. He was every bit as imposing as his reputation made him out to be. In 1878, Nesbitt had brought order to the town of Averil by killing every man who broke the law. Three years later, he had done the same at Valour, and then again two years after that at the notorious cattle town of Packard's Well. There were some who said that he was a man in love with violence and that the only law he enforced was a law of his own choosing. He was famously precise in all things, from the symmetrical cut of his moustache to the polished buckle on his belt. He reached into his pocket for a watch that had been a gift to him from the grateful people at Valour, checked the time, then snapped the watch shut. He straightened his waistcoat, adjusted the cuffs of his shirtsleeves and strode out into the crossroads to take his place.

Realising that it was time, Sullivan let his last handful of dirt fall to the roadside and brushed his hands off on his pants before following his opponent.

They took up position on either side of the crossroads: Nesbitt to the north and Sullivan to the south. An expectant hush settled over the town and even Kutcher fell silent as they all waited for Nathaniel to give the signal for the tournament to begin.

Shane held his breath.

'Gentlemen.' Nathaniel rose to his feet and laid his hands on the wooden porch rail. 'The tournament will begin when you are ready to fire.'

His voice travelled clearly over the crossroads.

The two contestants stared at each other but neither of them moved.

And then Matt Nesbitt suddenly wrenched his gun from its holster. He shot from the hip, the flat of his palm striking three times against the hammer in rapid succession, fanning off a blaze of shots. They hit Sullivan and tore straight through him as if his body was made of wax, the first striking him in the belly, the second in his chest and the third ripping through his shoulder and picking him up, spinning him around and flinging him to the ground.

As he landed, his head rolled over and his dull, lifeless eyes – fixed wide in a look of frozen astonishment – flung a last accusing stare towards Shane.

The tournament had claimed its first victim.

Invigilators came in from the sides of the street and dragged the carcass away while Nathaniel offered his congratulations to the winner.

'Next match in one hour!' he called, and the contestants dispersed until then.

Buchanan was laughing, slapping his knee as he rocked backwards on the bench. 'And that man actually thought he could beat *you*?' he said. 'The Shane I used to know would have killed him years ago.'

Shane very nearly had. It was in 1879 that he had shot David's brother. Chris Sullivan had been the sheriff of a Wyoming cattle town known as Ladd's Corner. He was a good and honest man, which had been his downfall. A local beef baron had taken offence to him locking up his boys when they got rowdy and so had taken steps to remove him. Chris had stood firm, backed up by his deputy and by his younger brother. David was a drifter in those days and had come to town looking to bum a few dollars off his brother to cover a gambling debt. Together, the three of them had fought off every attempt to put pressure on them and finally Shane had been called in to put an end to it all.

News travelled quickly in Ladd's Corner, as it was prone to do in any small town, and Chris had gotten wind that Shane was coming. He had known that he hadn't stood a chance of survival but he had stayed anyway and faced Shane like a man. David had not been so courageous. He had skipped town and had not heard of his brother's death until three days after it had happened.

'I bet you wish it had been you.' Buchanan whispered in his ear. 'Wouldn't you have rather been the one who killed him?'

Shane did not want to think about it. Of course he wished it had been him. To Shane's way of thinking, David's mission of vengeance had been an affront to his brother's memory. Chris Sullivan had been a man of principle and Shane had respected him. David, meanwhile, was a coward who had waited five years – until long after Shane had laid down his guns and sworn never to shoot again – before finding the courage to avenge his brother's death. Shane would have loved to have been the one to kill him, and he would not have shown him the mercy that he had shown his brother by making it quick.

But that was not the sole reason that Shane would have liked to have taken Matt Nesbitt's place. A part of him longed just to fire a gun again, to handle the power that had once been his to command. He yearned for it, but at the same time he was afraid of it. For Shane knew the secret of the Fastest Guns and he had barely escaped from them the last time.

The second match drew the contestants back to the crossroads. It was Chastity's turn to fight and so far the enigmatic gunfighter had yet to be seen by any of the contestants. Shane was eager to catch a glimpse of her and learn her measure, as was her opponent, Escoban Cadero.

The Mexican bandit leader swaggered from O'Malley's and drained the last of a bottle of beer before tossing it aside and letting it break against the saloon wall. Hands on his hips, he searched about for his opponent, then strode boldly out into the crossroads to wait for her.

He was a singularly foul-looking man. In the deserts where he lived, the springtime winds blew up sandstorms so violent that they were known to strip the flesh from a man's bones. Cadero had weathered countless such storms, often using them as cover when he raided the villages and ranches of that land, and his face and arms were covered with scars where the sands had bitten deep. His beard and moustache were thick and matted with grease, his hair long and wild. His eyes were as black as the night and narrow from squinting into the ravenous winds.

He took advantage of Chastity's absence to choose to stand on the northern side of the crossroads, superstitiously avoiding the spot where David Sullivan had died. Having taken his place, he heaved at his shirts with meaty hands and tore them apart, exposing a muscled chest that was coarse with thick, black hair. The sunlight glimmered on half a dozen gold chains that hung around his neck.

He roared, flecking spittle from his rotten gums. 'Where is she then? Where is this little *puta* who would fight me?'

There was no answer and Cadero laughed contemptuously. 'Perhaps she has dresses to mend, or is too busy cooking dinner, no?'

He raised his voice in a sing-song: 'Come out, *senora*. Don't be shy. Escoban has something for you.' He gestured obscenely.

His challenges echoed desolately through Covenant's abandoned streets and a long moment passed in which nobody moved. Then, the door of the Grande hotel creaked slowly open.

Nathaniel emerged, followed by Whisperer, and they were not alone. They were accompanied by a thin, pale woman. She was in her mid-thirties with long brown hair that hung straight and without style. She moved timidly, her eyes pointed down at the ground and by her manner Shane judged that she was used to being beaten.

She led a child by the hand: a young girl who could not have been more than seven or eight years old; who wore a pink dress and had ribbons in her hair. Incongruously, she also wore a gun belt fastened around her waist, the holster empty and about the right size for a small pocket gun.

Shane turned and shot Buchanan a withering glare. It was unconscionable that someone so young was competing. Buchanan only grinned. 'She's not what you expected, is she? Don't be fooled by how she looks. That little bitch might even give you a run for your money.'

Shane felt the deepest revulsion. He turned back to see that the girl had been passed over to Nathaniel, who was now leading her down the wooden steps from the porch. There was something odd about the way she moved, her steps wooden and unbalanced, as if walking was unfamiliar to her.

'Nathaniel found her in an asylum in New England.' Buchanan explained. 'One of the doctors there sold her to him for twenty bucks.'

She had reached the foot of the steps and Nathaniel steered her toward the crossroads. Her feet scuffed in the dirt and Shane noticed that her attention was elsewhere. Her eyes, unblinking, seemed fixed on something that only she could see.

Escoban Cadero thought she was a joke. 'What is this?' he demanded. 'You expect me to shoot a child?'

'If you can,' Nathaniel replied. 'But I assure you it won't be as easy as you think.'

'You play games with me.'

'No. No games. Chastity has the same right to be here as any of you.'

Cadero shrugged. 'It makes no difference to me,' he said. 'It will not be the first time that I have killed a child.'

Nathaniel had to steer the girl by the shoulders to get her to face Cadero. Even then, she seemed unaware of his presence. Her gaze wandered, eyes distant. Her arms hung uselessly by her sides.

'She's got no mind.' Buchanan explained. 'No will. Nothing. That girl's a clean slate.'

His meaning was perfectly clear to Shane and it provoked an anger in him that was fiercer than anything he had known in years.

A clean slate.

The idea of it was so terrible that he did not want to believe it was true, and yet the proof was right there in front of him.

He watched as Nathaniel reached into his jacket and withdrew a small, double-action .41 calibre pocket revolver. With only a three inch barrel it was just the right size for Chastity's small hands. Nathaniel set it in her holster and, before he left, he whispered in her ear. 'Make daddy proud,' he said, and then hurried from the crossroads as if he had just lit the fuse on a stick of dynamite.

Escoban Cadero snorted irritably, still convinced that he was being fooled with. Chastity was not even looking at him. She stared blindly at the roadside, her head cocked to one side, arms limp.

Then she blinked. The change that came over her was so abrupt that Shane's breath caught in his throat. Her eyes suddenly became focussed and her head straightened on her shoulders and turned about mechanically to face towards Cadero, who gasped with surprise. *'Que pasa?'*

'Now he's for it.' Buchanan said, his voice an excited whisper.

'Contestants!' Nathaniel shouted. 'You may fire when ready.'

Escoban Cadero reached instantly for his gun.

And the side of his head exploded in a violent shower of blood.

His body stood there, gently swaying back and forth while the contents of his head pattered down around him like a heavy shower of rain. Then his knees gave way and he crumpled on the spot.

He had not even had time to draw his gun from its holster.

Shane was awestruck. He had never seen anybody draw so fast. All around him, the town was gripped in silence as people stared, dumbstruck by Chastity's skill.

The girl stood motionless, her arm extended and still pointing her diminutive revolver at the spot where Escoban Cadero had stood. She had not moved at all since she had killed him, remaining frozen on the spot as if held in a state of shock. There was a look of confusion in her eyes, as if she was unable to make a connection between the body on the ground and the man who had stood before her. It looked to Shane as if she was disappointed that she had killed him already. It had all been over too quickly for her. She wanted to kill him again.

The invigilators who were supposed to take away Cadero's body were understandably reluctant to go forward while she was still so dangerously poised. Nathaniel derided them for their timidity.

No will of her own, Shane thought, and cursed bitterly to himself. The girl's plight cut through his own self-pity and he grieved for the loss of her innocence.

Cautiously, Nathaniel walked up behind her and gently reached out his hand to encircle her wrist. 'It's over now, cherub,' he said, speaking softly. 'All done for today.'

The girl cocked her head sideways and looked up at him, uncomprehending. The look of cold hatred in her eyes was something that Shane had never thought to see in a child so young. Nathaniel prised the gun from her hand.

Chastity suddenly threw back her head and screamed. It was a noise of pure, animal loss, as if Nathaniel had reached into her body and torn out her soul. The force of it was incredible. Even at a distance, it sent a stab of pain ripping through Shane's ears that made him flinch. Those contestants closest to her blocked their ears with their hands.

Nathaniel had clearly expected her reaction and had beaten a hasty retreat to the side of the road. 'Bethan! Take her inside.'

The girl's nanny came scurrying over and gathered Chastity

67

into her arms. The girl fought violently, striking with balled fists and kicking while the woman tried to subdue her. In the end, Nathaniel had to shout for one of his invigilators to grab her, and the girl was unceremoniously tucked under one arm and carried back into the hotel while Bethan fluttered at her side, making ineffectual shushing noises to try and calm her down.

Her screaming became muffled as the door was closed behind her and the resultant silence was uncomfortable, with nobody knowing what to make of what they had just witnessed. Nathaniel smiled reassuringly, dismissing Chastity's outburst as just an ordinary child's tantrum. He turned and nodded across the street to Buchanan, who nodded back in reply, some comment going unspoken between them. Nathaniel then joined Whisperer and the two men disappeared into the Grande.

'She's quite something, isn't she?' Buchanan said.

Shane was not interested in making small talk. He wanted the facts. 'How long?' he asked.

'Nathaniel's had her shooting for a couple of months now. She took to it right away, didn't even need to be shown or nothing. Girl's a complete natural.'

'How many has she killed?'

'Not many.' Buchanan replied. 'Ten, maybe twelve.'

Not many? Shane wanted to laugh except that it wasn't funny. Nathaniel had taken a child with no will of her own and turned her into the perfect killer, accomplishing in her what it had taken Shane more than twenty years of practice to achieve.

Chastity was damned, just as surely as he was.

And she had had no say in the matter.

CHAPTER SEVEN

Shane had returned to the Babson ranch at first light the following morning, his arrival scaring crows into flight as he led his horse through the stink of the battleground. His mind cold to the events of the night before, he knelt outside the open gate of the corral and examined the hoof marks that were left there.

Benedict Hunte had fled westwards. He was no great horseman and in his panic he had exhausted his mount in the first hour of riding. Thereafter he had been forced to travel slowly and by midday Shane had caught up with him enough that the chase looked certain to be over before nightfall.

Shane was glad. He was eager to get the job done and put the events of the previous night behind him. The murder of the Babson woman and her child still haunted him, sitting badly on a conscience he had not known he had until he had woken that morning.

It was the senselessness of the incident that bothered him the most. Shane had never killed a child before. He had shot over a hundred men and more than his fair share of women, but he had never found reason to shoot a child. He was not altogether convinced that he'd had a reason this time either. Quick hands were something that every gunfighter was fast to develop if he wanted to survive, but however quick the hands the eye was always faster and Shane had known who his targets were before he had pulled the trigger.

He had known and he had still done it and he did not know why. It was almost as if, for a brief moment, somebody else had been in control of his body and that bothered him because it made him wonder if he was going mad.

He pondered heavily on these thoughts while he rode and by midday he arrived at the town of Wainsford.

His appearance earned him suspicious looks as he rode into town. A mother hastily dragged her children indoors out of his way and a shop sign in the window of the general store was hastily flipped over to read 'closed'. Shane drew up outside a fine-looking hotel and he hitched his horse beside it and went inside. A bell, situated above the door, rang to announce his arrival and a man called out from one of the other rooms, asking him to be patient. 'I'll be with you in a minute.'

Shane was not feeling patient and tracked the voice to its source: a middle-aged man dressed in a floral-print apron, who was spring-cleaning. He looked embarrassed to have been discovered and hastily shed the apron, casting it aside. 'Belongs to the wife,' he muttered. 'We're dining with the vicar tonight; I didn't want to get my clothes dirty. You must want a room real bad, mister.'

'A man came into town recently. Did you see him?'

'You a friend of his?' The hotelier clearly did not believe he was.

'I want to know where he is.'

The look in Shane's eyes and the tone of his voice convinced him to answer. 'He's across the street in the marshal's office. Marshal

Fletcher come by and arrested him just a half-hour ago. If you're looking for a bounty, mister, I guess you're too late.' He gave a nervous laugh which Shane silenced with a glare. Hunte getting himself arrested was a complication he could have well done without.

'This Marshal Fletcher, he got a deputy?'

'He's got two. Alan Grant and young Ben. They're more than capable of taking care of things, mister.'

Shane cursed silently to himself. Killing lawmen always meant trouble and if there were three of them then that made matters even worse. He left the hotelier to his spring cleaning and stepped outside.

Word of him had spread across town and the marshal was waiting for him as he walked out the door. With him was a young man who held a 12-guage shotgun, which he pointed right at Shane's chest.

'Howdy,' the marshal said amicably. He was an elderly man with wiry grey hair and a moustache like a steel brush. He was thin but had the sort of lean physique that suggested he was still a force to be reckoned with. 'You know, I didn't believe it at first when I heard that Shane Ennis was in town but now I see it with my own eyes. What you doing here son?'

Shane declined to answer. 'Am I under arrest?' he asked.

'No, you're not. Ben here is just my insurance. You've got a nasty reputation Mister Ennis and my old bones ain't what they used to be. Now I believe I asked you a question.'

'I'm looking for someone.'

'And who might that be?'

'Just someone.'

The old lawman sighed wearily. He knew that Shane had come into town looking for Hunte. Shane was a professional gun for hire and Hunte was a man with a high price on his head; it didn't take a suspicious mind to put two and two together. Fletcher was outmatched but he managed to look cool. 'So what's this someone look like?' he asked. 'It could be that maybe I've seen him around.'

'I'd like to tell you, marshal, but to tell you the truth I haven't seen him.'

'That might make it hard for you to find him.'

'Hard.' Shane agreed. 'But not impossible. I got a pretty good idea I know where he is.'

'You fixing to cause trouble in my town?' Fletcher asked.

Shane looked him levelly in the eyes. 'Not if I can help it,' he said.

The marshal nodded, understanding him perfectly. 'Well then,' he said. 'In that case I'll leave you to go about your business. Oh there is one thing: Benedict Hunte rode into town a little while ago and I understand there's quite a price on his head. I've got him locked up in the jailhouse and there's some federal marshals coming to pick him up in a couple of days. Until they get here though, me and the boys are likely to be a little nervous so I'd stay out of our way if I were you. I'm not threatening you, you understand; I'm just saying. A man like you has a reputation and we don't want any misunderstandings around here now do we?'

Shane smiled slightly, admiring the old man's nerve. 'No, we wouldn't want that at all.'

'So everything's clear?'

'Perfectly.'

'Well, good day to you then.'

Shane tipped his hat to them and watched as they retreated back toward the jailhouse. He had hoped to have been able to intimidate them into giving him Hunte without any trouble, but it seemed as though things were going to be a little more complicated than that.

He swore quietly to himself. Hunte was becoming more trouble than he was worth.

The stroke of noon was the Gunfighter's Hour. It was sacred to the Fastest Guns and Shane thought it curious that no match was fought to honour it. Instead, the contest between Luke Ferris and the woman, Vendetta, took place, like every other match, at half-past the hour.

Vendetta was the woman that evil men feared. Ten years ago, her husband had been murdered by a gang of outlaws led a famous gunfighter named Michael Brett. The local sheriff had been powerless to do anything about it, being too scared and too underpaid to risk his neck over something as trivial as justice, and so Mary Elizabeth Becker had learned to handle a gun, changed her name to Vendetta, and sought her own retribution.

It had been bloody and dangerous. Vendetta had pursued her enemies relentlessly and only Michael Brett had managed to elude her. In 1881 he had competed in the first tournament at Covenant, from which he had never returned. Since then she had wandered the continent, fighting for others that the law was powerless to protect and championing the causes of those too weak to fight for themselves.

Shane had it on good authority that Michael Brett had been one of the six men who had won the first tournament and was willing to bet that Vendetta had come to Covenant to complete her revenge. To do that, however, she would need to win.

She squared-off against her opponent with a look of tough determination smouldering in her eyes. Luke Ferris was a handsome man in his late twenties whose deceptively laconic nature concealed a vicious talent for murder. He wore no gunbelt but simply had his gun tucked into the waistline of his pants. It was a .44-40 calibre Remington with an inch-long brass spur protruding from the handle for use in close-combat. With it, Ferris had killed close to three-dozen men. He was a notorious train and coach robber, wanted dead or alive in Nevada, Utah, Texas and Oklahoma. He stood with his left shoulder slouched, hands idle, the stub of a cigar hanging from the corner of his lips.

When Nathaniel called it, both fighters burst into an explosion of speed. Their hands reached instantly for their guns, flicked back the hammers and drew.

Two gunshots rang out almost simultaneously, thundering through the silent streets of town. Vendetta's hat was blown from her head and fell, spinning, into the dust behind her. As it landed, a sudden hush closed upon the crossroads as if a smothering fist had tightened, choking all further sounds.

Then there was a heavy *thump* as a body hit the ground.

Luke Ferris had been the quicker of the two by a mere fraction of a second but his haste had proven costly. He had fired high and his shot had missed the top of Vendetta's skull by just an inch and a half. Vendetta had been more accurate. Her shot had found its mark and split Luke's heart in two, separating the left and right ventricles before cleaving through his shoulder blade in an explosion of blood and shattered bone.

She stooped now, retrieved her hat and dusted it down before putting it back on and tilting it to shield her eyes from the sun. She then walked calmly from the street.

The other contestants dispersed and did not return to the crossroads until the fourth match was due to begin. The renegade

Apache, Nanache, took his place on the crossroads opposite the Canadian, Daniel Blaine, and stared at his opponent with hate-filled eyes.

Nanache had served in the US Army as a scout during the Geronimo Campaign. He had been promised ten ponies and his freedom in exchange for his services, but when Geronimo surrendered the US Government had broken its word and sentenced 'friendly' Apaches like Nanache to share Geronimo's exile in Florida. Nanache had escaped from the prison train and become an outlaw rather than suffer that fate. His bitterness at being betrayed after years spent fighting his own kinsmen had turned into a deadly hatred for the US Government and its people, and over the following years he had built a name for himself as a ruthless killer of men, women and children. He was known to torture his victims slowly to death, to cover them in pitch and set them on fire or stake them out in the sun for the buzzards to eat alive. The Federal Government had issued a thousand dollar reward for his capture, dead or alive, but so far he had killed every bounty hunter who had ever searched for him.

He wore his old US Army jacket as a mark of spite, decorating it with *kachinas* made from beads and feathers and horse's hair. At his side, he wore a seven-inch bone-handled knife and a Colt 1873 Single Action revolver.

Blaine was an enormous man with a thick chest and hairy arms. He stood ramrod-straight, his feet planted a shoulder's width apart and his knees slightly bent. He was a competition marksman by profession and a murderer by habit. His gun was custom-made to his own specifications and was based on a Remington 1875 revolver, rechambered to take a .50 calibre cartridge and fitted with an Alvan Clarke telescopic sight above the barrel. With its monstrously powerful cartridge and five times magnification, he boasted that it was lethal at ranges of up to a hundred yards.

Nanache fingered the grisly necklace of finger bones that hung around his throat.

'That's a pretty rosary you have there.' Blaine told him. 'But praying to your heathen gods won't save you.'

Nanache regarded him coldly. 'Every one of these bones is the trigger finger of a gunfighter I have killed. This one,' he said, stroking one of the small, yellowed bones. 'Was fast on the draw. Whereas this one,' he said, stroking another. 'Came from a man who shot well. Now *I* shoot well and *I* am fast on the draw. Not only have I taken their bones, I have taken their skills as well. When this is over I will take *your* finger and *your* famous marksmanship and I will go into the second round better than I am today.'

Blaine did not know whether to take his boasts seriously or not. He curled his lip. 'First you'll have to beat me, chief.'

The two contestants glanced sideways as Nathaniel came to the edge of the porch and called for their attention. They tensed. Blaine shook his fingers to loosen them and heighten his responsiveness. Nanache checked his footing.

Nathaniel raised his voice. 'You may fire when ready.'

It was over in seconds. Nanache's shot hit Blaine hit in the neck. The bullet clipped off the underside of his jawbone and ricocheted into his spine. His head jerked sideways, blood spurting from his mouth as fragments of his shattered jaw ripped through his tongue and into his pallet.

He rotated slowly on the spot, hand still rising to bring his heavy revolver to bear.

Nanache fired again and this time Blaine hit the ground. He twitched once, then lay still. The invigilators moved forward to collect his body but Nanache waved them back. He holstered his gun and walked over to Blaine's body, where he knelt and drew his knife. Prising the gun from Blaine's tightly clenched hand, he straightened the man's trigger finger and carefully cut it off at the root.

'You may take him now,' he told the invigilators, and stepped aside to let them carry him away.

CHAPTER EIGHT

The sound of hoof beats on the road outside his window startled Shane from his thoughts. He rose and parted the curtains a crack so that he could see outside.

The horseman was a wild-looking man, dusty from the trail, with a revolver worn prominently in a shoulder holster and a pair of knives strapped across his back.

He was the fifth bounty hunter to have arrived in Wainsford in the last couple of days, and Shane did not think that he would be the last. Word had gotten out that Hunte was in town and now bounty hunters from all across America were flocking in, each one vying to be the man who killed Hunte.

Marshal Fletcher had stopped greeting them as he had greeted Shane and now just watched from the jailhouse porch. He was outnumbered and outgunned and praying that the federal marshals would arrive soon.

Shane withdrew from the window and let the curtains fall back into place, dimming the light. It was hot and stuffy in his hotel room and Shane's naked body was greased with sweat. He crossed to where he had laid his guns out on the floor and sat down, cross-legged in front of them.

Both were Colt 1873 Single Action .45 calibre revolvers. A lot of people criticised the Colts but Shane had always preferred them over competing manufacturers because they were finely balanced and leant themselves easily to the kind of fast handling that he preferred.

Some gunfighters chose to personalise their weapons with ivory or solid silver handles, or with stylised engravings on the frame and barrel, but Shane disliked such affectations. A gun was a tool, not an ornament. The only modification that he had made to his guns was to have the barrel of one of them shortened from seven and a half inches to just five inches long. This made it faster and easier to draw and it was this gun that he fired with his right hand, for while Shane could shoot accurately with both hands he was marginally better with his right.

He had arranged both guns on the floor before him pointing outwards. Both had been cleaned and oiled reverently and the blackened metal gleamed in the dusky light. Their scent, acrid and sharp, reminded him of the smell that lingered after sex. It was perversely erotic.

Both guns were fully loaded and the hammers cocked. Danger radiated from them. A slight knock was all that it would take to set them off. A door could be slammed in another part of the hotel and the vibration might cause the hammer to fall, discharging one of the powerful .45 Long cartridges. Capable of penetrating through as much as four inches of solid timber, the result of being on the receiving end of one of those bullets was likely to be fatal and as Shane sat there, meditating on his weapons, he fancied that they *wanted* to be fired, that they *wanted* to kill and that, while he was a necessary medium by which they could achieve that desire, they would gladly kill him if there was no one else around.

The idea that his guns could think and that they had desires of their own was nothing new to Shane. He had often thought as much. During the long times that he spent alone, travelling across the country he had formulated quite a complex mythology for them.

A gun existed solely to kill. Unlike a knife that could be used for a variety of purposes, a gun was singular in its design. It was good for nothing else. Shane had admired that simplicity ever since he was a boy. He had been envious of it. Human life was so full of questions and uncertainties, so bewildering in comparison that the world of the gun had seemed seductively well-ordered to him, and he had sought to emulate it in his own way of life. He had many times sought to find solace in them as he did now, meditating on them and seeking to perfect his state of mind and be more like them, to eliminate doubt and focus purely on the task at hand.

This time, however, the clarity that he sought kept eluding him. He kept thinking back to that night at the Babson ranch. Each time, he vividly recalled the look of surprise on the woman's face, the splash of wet blood.

What was more, he kept thinking about how he had not felt in control of himself at that time but rather as if some other mind was working him while he had been just a spectator. He stared at his guns, his body sheathed in perspiration, and wondered if he was going crazy.

Outside, the bounty hunters were gathering and Shane knew that he was wasting time. The more bounty hunters that arrived in town, the more competition he would have to contend with, and yet he felt unmotivated to do anything about it. He sat in his room, plagued with strange doubts and staring at his guns.

And trying to deny something that he knew in his heart was

true.

He blinked and came out of his reverie as if waking from a dream. The contestants were gathering again. It was time for the next match.

'Half-past one, Shane. Not long for you now.' Buchanan told him. 'Isn't it exciting?'

Shane said nothing. He had tried not to think about the passage of time and how it was steadily running out on him. Only two more bouts remained after this one and then it would be his turn. Four hours in total before he stood on the crossroads and held a gun for the first time in six years. The prospect filled him with a confusing mixture of emotions: part dread, part excitement.

Right now, the present match belonged to Kip Kutcher and Tom Freeman. On the opposite side of the street from Shane, Kutcher was counting out six bullets into his palm. He held them out to his girlfriend. 'Blow on them,' he said.

The girl was puzzled. 'What?'

'For luck,' he explained. 'Like when gamblers shoot dice.'

She smiled to herself and indulged him, blowing gently. Kutcher slotted the bullets one by one into the chambers of his Colt 1873 Peacemaker. He was trembling with nervous energy, not frightened but invigorated. His eyes were wild.

He got up and sprang down off the boardwalk with a lightness in his step. Tom Freeman stood lounging against the hitching post outside of O'Malley's, waiting for him. He was a handsome black man with closely-cropped hair and a muscular physique. He wore his shirt with the sleeves rolled up and was smoking a cigar.

Kutcher grinned at him. 'I promise I'll make this quick.'

'You'd better hope you can shoot your guns as fast as you shoot your mouth.' Freeman replied.

'My friend, I can talk so fast that I can be running six conversations all at the same time, but my hands, well they move even faster than that.' Kutcher boasted. To demonstrate, he waved his hands rapidly in the air as if drawing imaginary guns, moving them at such a whirling speed that they became a blur. Freeman was unimpressed. He stubbed out his cigar on the hitching post, checked his heavy Schofield revolver, and followed Kutcher out onto the crossroads.

Kutcher took the north and Freeman took the south, facing off to each other. Kutcher waggled his fingers to get the blood flowing while Freeman stretched out the tension in his neck, turning it first to one side and then the other, his bones popping audibly.

Nathaniel rose to his feet on the porch of the Grande and called for them to make ready.

The two fighters tensed and the street became deathly silent.

The moment stretched.

And then Nathaniel called it.

In an instant, both fighters drew. Kutcher's hands once again became a blur as he slapped the hammer back with one and then drew with the other.

In the very next instant, the .44 calibre bullet fired from Tom Freeman's Schofield revolver smashed through Kutcher's ribs like they were made of glass.

It was followed by another and another, and Kutcher fell to his knees. His eyes were wide with shock and he did not appear to be able to make sense of what had happened to him. He looked down at himself in bewilderment, saw the blood that stained his shirt and reached out with a shaking hand to touch it. Finally realising what had happened to him, he gave a small cry of alarm. Blood dribbled from the corners of his mouth and ran down his chin.

Freeman calmly walked the distance that separated them and shot Kutcher through the elbow, causing him to drop his gun. Kutcher opened his mouth to scream but was silenced as Freeman suddenly thrust the barrel of his revolver into his mouth. He used it to turn Kutcher's head until they were looking eye-to-eye. 'Looks like your hands aren't as fast as your mouth, son.'

He glanced sideways to where Kutcher's girlfriend stood. She watched helplessly, her hands tightly clenched, not making a sound. A girl like her had seen plenty of men die.

Kutcher tried to call out to her but gagged on the revolver in his mouth. He choked, spitting up blood that landed on Freeman's boots.

Tom Freeman stared at him in disgust. 'She's a pretty girl,' he said quietly. 'What was it, you think, that attracted her to a nobody like you? Was it your pretty-boy face or your smart mouth?'

Tears began to roll down Kutcher's cheeks. Freeman exaggeratedly cupped a hand to his ear as if waiting for his answer. Seconds passed. Kutcher slipped in and out of consciousness.

Hearing no answer, Freeman gave a shrug. 'Guess it couldn't have been your smart mouth then,' he said. He tilted his gun sharply, so that it was aimed straight up through the roof of Kutcher's mouth, and pulled the trigger.

The shot rang out loud and was followed afterwards by a long silence, broken by the heavy *thump* as Kutcher's faceless body toppled over into the dirt. Tom Freeman wiped the blood from his hands and from the barrel of his gun and strode casually away. He tipped his hat to Kutcher's girlfriend as he passed her.

The girl barely seemed to notice him. Her face was blank, drained equally of both colour and expression. She looked as if she was having difficulty coming to terms with what had just happened. Her eyes began to shine with tears as the shock subsided, but she admirably held on to her composure. When the invigilators came to drag Kutcher's body away, she stepped down off the boardwalk and quietly followed them.

Shane did not expect that she would survive much longer. Covenant had a way of dealing with its unwelcome guests and now that Kutcher was dead the girl had no further excuse for being there. The town would swallow her up and nobody would miss her.

A part of him wondered if maybe he should feel sorry for her, but he had problems enough of his own and none of his pity to spare.

Only two more bouts remained and then it would be his turn on the crossroads.

The next hour passed quickly and it was not long before another pair of gunfighters stepped out to face each other. This time, the fight was between Evan Drager and John MacMurray.

Evan Drager was a freak of a man. Shot in the head five years ago, his injury had left him with a large star-shaped scar that covered the left-hand side of his forehead, leaving him partially bald. All of the muscles along the left-hand side of his face had been paralysed by the injury and it was only the right-hand side that showed any expression; the left remained slack.

'This could be interesting.' Buchanan commented. Like Shane, he had never actually seen Drager fight, although he had heard the rumours. In the days before his injury, Drager had been a man of little repute, a brawler, a cattle rustler and a small-time crook. He had picked a fight with the wrong man coming out of a saloon in Dodge City and the rest was history. It was a .45 calibre bullet that had split his skull and it was nothing short of a miracle that he had survived.

The bullet had penetrated his skull and lodged itself deep within his brain, where it still remained, completely beyond the reach of any doctor.

A kindly Samaritan had taken him in and nursed him during the long month that he had lain in a coma. He had been a changed man when he had woken. Drager claimed that the bullet had spoken to him while he had been unconscious. It had shown him visions of a future in which terrible wars inflamed the whole world, spawning guns of such awesome power that they could annihilate whole cities. The bullet had told him that he must prepare for this coming age and, to help him in his mission, it had promised him that no shot he fired would ever miss.

He had since developed into a formidable gunfighter and his reputation, coupled with his feverish charisma, had attracted a small cult following who had sprung him out of jail some nine months ago.

Old-hand gunfighters like Shane and Buchanan were sceptical of his claims and the Fastest Guns themselves had yet to formally accept him but, nevertheless, there were few who could say that there was not something special about him.

His opponent was the 'The Christian', John MacMurray. He was a stocky man with a wrinkled, pig-like face and a humourless attitude. As Shane watched him, he pinched his nose with one hand and blew out one nostril and then the other, clearing them messily before wiping his hands off on his dusty pants.

Drager faced him with his hands gently clasped before his waist, radiating an air of ministerial calm. He looked like a preacher about to deliver a sermon.

'No way is he the new Jacob Priestley.' Buchanan said dismissively. 'I don't care what anybody says. I wouldn't follow him.'

Shane said nothing. He was keeping his own opinions to himself. He looked across to where Nathaniel stood, Whisperer present by his side as usual. Nathaniel called for the two men to make ready and they both tensed.

At Nathaniel's signal they both drew. Their hands moved so quickly that it was hard to see who fired first. MacMurray went down, hissing through clenched teeth as Drager's shot punched a hole in his chest. At the same time, his own shot ripped into Drager's left thigh. The specially-cut bullet deformed instantly, mushrooming in size to almost twice its original width. Blood splashed across the hot sand.

MacMurray was mortally injured but still alive. Tottering on his remaining good leg, Drager fired a blaze of shots that hammered deep into MacMurray's torso, denying him the chance to fire a second shot in return, firing again and again until MacMurray pitched over backwards and fell dead. Only then did Drager lower his smoking gun and limp painfully to the side of the road.

Shane turned and looked meaningfully at Buchanan, who merely shrugged. 'I still ain't following him if he is,' he muttered.

CHAPTER NINE

Shane had waited until sunset before leaving his hotel room. The streets of Wainsford were bathed in the cool blue shadows of twilight while the sky overhead burned like fire, shades of orange, red and gold melting against the horizon. A coyote howled in the distance and was shortly answered by its mate.

Shane paused momentarily and checked his holster before setting out along the street. On his right, the jailhouse loomed darkly on the other side of the road. Shane had watched the marshal and his boys turn the place into a fortress over the past couple of days. They had barricaded the windows and hacked loopholes into the walls, giving them a clean line-of-fire in every direction. Twelve gunfighters had arrived in town and the marshal was hopelessly out-numbered.

About half a dozen of the men lurked just out of sight, concealed in alleys and doorways on both sides of the street. One of them glared at Shane as he walked by. Shane met his gaze and held it until the man backed away, muttering an apology.

Shane continued on along the street. He had not gone far when he saw a surreptitious movement out of the corner of his eye.

Another man stood in an alleyway across the street and, thinking that Shane had not noticed him, he drew his gun.

Shane moved in an instant, spinning and dropping to one knee. His whipped his gun clear of the holster and fanned off a pair of shots before his opponent had time to register the danger. Both shots hit their target and the man staggered from the alley, clutching at his bleeding chest, and fell down in the road.

Hearing footsteps behind him, Shane whirled about and saw that it was the man he had just passed. He had his gun drawn but Shane didn't give him time to use it. He fired off another pair of shots, drew his second revolver and fired again as the man fell.

Further down the road, somebody began to applaud. Shane turned and brought his guns to bear but checked himself when he saw that it was Marshal Fletcher. The old man still walked his evening rounds, defying the men who would kill him in order to show that there was still a law in town. He openly carried a Winchester rifle and Ben walked on the opposite side of the road, shotgun in hand. That shotgun was presently trained on Shane.

Shane holstered his guns. 'You going to arrest me, Marshal?'

'No.' Fletcher replied. 'It looked like self-defence to me.'

Even if it hadn't been, Shane doubted that Fletcher would have put him in jail, not while Hunte was in there. It would just be asking for trouble.

'I reckon it was you they were waiting for.' Shane said.

'In that case I suppose I should thank you. You may have just saved my life.' Fletcher signalled over to Ben, who lowered his weapon. The boy's eyes scanned the darkness for anybody else who might cause trouble.

'I'd be mighty obliged if you feel like shooting any more of them while you're at it,' Fletcher said.

'Are you deputising me, Marshal?'

'No, just an old man making fun. We've not seen much of you these last few days. You found the man you were after?'

'I found where he is,' Shane replied casually. 'But he's out of reach for the moment.' His meaning was not lost on Fletcher but the old man made no comment. 'Your federal marshals haven't shown up yet.'

'They'll come.'

'You reckon?' Shane had his doubts. Federal marshals were paid even less than a town sheriff and were seldom known to stick their necks out for anyone, especially if someone bribed them not to. 'A man would have to be a fool to come here.'

'We've got plenty of fools in town already; a few more ain't gonna hurt.' Fletcher replied.

Shane laughed. 'No offence, Marshal, but the men you've got flocking into town: they're getting paid a hell of a lot more than your Federal Marshals will be.'

'Not all men fight for money, Mister Ennis.'

'All of the good ones do.' Shane replied cruelly.

'And what of you? Do you only fight for money?'

Shane hesitated. Lately he had been asking himself the same question. It wasn't money, it wasn't even pleasure, and fame wasn't as important to him now as it had used to be. 'I'm just doing what I'm good at,' he replied lamely.

There were hoof beats from the edge of town and both men turned to see a new bounty hunter come riding in.

'Well, I'd better see about getting this mess cleared up.' Fletcher said, motioning to the bodies that were strewn around.

Shane left him to it. He glanced down the road at where the newcomer had hitched his horse outside the hotel. There was something familiar about him but in the dark it was hard to make him out. Shane turned and walked on to the town saloon, where he pushed his way through the butterfly-wing doors and strode up to the bar.

It was mostly deserted. The locals were too scared to drink there with all the bounty hunters hanging about. Most of the men who weren't watching the jailhouse were in the saloon, drinking. They eyed Shane suspiciously. He was a lion among the wolves and they knew it.

Shane ordered a whisky and mentally assessed them while he drank. He discreetly observed who was friendly with who; who looked dangerous and who he guessed would be the first to run when the bullets began to fly; which of them would be his allies and who was better off dead.

He was thinking on this when the butterfly-wing doors swung open and the newcomer strode in. He paused in the doorway. 'Well, aren't we just balls-to-the-wall with gunfighters in here!' The newcomer was Castor Buchanan.

He had always been excitable. Now, as the hour of Shane's match grew near, Buchanan grew wild. Springing from his seat, he stalked over to join Shane at the edge of the boardwalk. He grabbed the wooden upright with his good hand and swung off it, leaning over so that his face was close beside Shane's.

'You can't deny it, Shane. It's *in* you,' he enthused. 'And don't lie to me and tell me that you don't want it; you and I both know you do. We're alike, you and I, two of a kind. I want it, you want it. You just don't have the guts to accept it the way I do.'

Shane was not really listening. He was aware of the content of what Buchanan was saying but the actual words he just tuned into the background.

Across the street the other contestants were gathering once again, this time for the seventh match of the day, the battle between Valentino Rodrigues and the man they called the Gentleman.

Rodrigues was a handsome man: tall, dark and suave, with slicked-back hair and a fluid, cat-like grace. He was dressed in fancy black pants and a ruffled shirt, with a jacket that was heavily embroidered in silver and white thread. He wore a pair of Remington revolvers, one chambered for a .38 cartridge and the other chambered for a .44-40.

He strutted and he preened as he strode out in front of the crowd and offered his opponent a theatrical bow. The Gentleman returned the gesture with a shy nod of his head.

Rodrigues may have been playing to the crowd but it was the Gentleman they were interested in. The East Coast city gunslingers – called 'Button Men' by the mobsters of the Italian, Jewish and Irish gangs who hired them – were an enigma to the rugged gunfighters of the West. Their fancy clothes and diminutive revolvers led most to call them sissies but, in New York and Detroit and Chicago, the term 'Button Man' was a mark of respect. A mobster who called on one to erase his enemies knew he would get the job done, as easily as if he just reached out and pressed a button.

The Gentleman had earned his name because of his impeccable good manners. He spoke rarely but when he did it was with a stiff British accent.

Before stepping onto the crossroads, he removed his pinstripe jacket and rolled up his sleeves. His gun – a Webley British Bulldog .44 calibre double-action revolver – was worn in a shoulder holster under his left arm. He straightened his glasses and took his mark opposite Rodrigues.

The two men waited for Nathaniel to give them the signal.

They waited.

And waited.

And then Nathaniel called it.

The fight was over in seconds. As Rodrigues drew, he dropped to one knee. Sweeping out his other leg to the side and flinging one arm for balance, he dodged the Gentleman's rapid fire and shot back with deadly accuracy. His bullet passed between the Gentleman's eyes, neatly clipping his spectacles in two, and blew out the back of his skull. He fell as if he had been pole-axed.

Rodrigues rose smoothly back onto his feet and bowed to Nathaniel like a matador, then again to everybody else who was watching. The other contestants regarded him icily. There was nothing in the rules to say that a man could not dodge if he wanted to and now that Rodrigues had set the precedent others were sure to follow. In the second round, nothing could be taken for granted.

Shane was not thinking that far ahead, however. The match was over and it was his turn next. His stomach twisted itself into a knot.

Buchanan, still in a maniacal mood, clapped him excitedly on the back. 'Better get you a gun,' he said.

Shane closed his eyes. He had never wanted this moment to come.

The sun rose on the town of Wainsford, beginning the fourth day since Benedict Hunte had rode into town. The streets were empty save for the bounty hunters, who kept constant vigil on the jailhouse. The wind was lonely as it blew, stirring up the dust so that it drifted above the ground like a mist.

Shane stepped out of the hotel.

There was a new feeling in the air that morning, a sense that violence was soon to erupt. Fletcher had stopped walking his rounds. The streets were too dangerous for that now.

It was all about ready to kick-off.

Castor Buchanan stood a short distance away by the side of the road. He had his back to Shane but knew that he was there. He did not move as Shane walked over to stand next to him. Both men were silent for a long time.

'Seems like every fucking bounty hunter in the country's in town.' Buchanan growled. 'The marshal must be shitting his breeches.'

Shane did not reply. The silence stretched between them, becoming taut.

'I heard you rode in a couple of days ago.' Buchanan said, almost accusingly. 'What you been doing?'

Shane turned to stare at him. His bleak, expressionless gaze challenged Buchanan to come out and say whatever it was he was skirting around. Never one to back away from a fight, Buchanan obliged him.

'They say you've been shut up in your room, jerking off.'

Shane didn't particularly care what people thought he had been doing. By the end of the day, most of them would be dead.

Buchanan turned his attention back towards the jailhouse. 'They've been talking to you, haven't they?' He said it so mildly that Shane thought he had misheard.

'What did you say?'

Buchanan didn't answer. He smiled secretively and nodded to himself. 'I thought so.'

A chill crept through Shane's body as the realisation sank in that Buchanan hadn't been talking about a group of people; he had been talking about Shane's guns. It sounded ludicrous. Shane wanted to believe that he was being paranoid but the smugness in Buchanan's attitude told him otherwise.

Warily, Shane dared to ask: 'Yours too?'

Buchanan nodded.

'For how long?'

'A while now, but I think they've been in my head since the beginning.'

Shane knew exactly what he meant. He felt the same way. 'It's like I didn't want to believe it at first,' he said. 'I thought I was going crazy.'

Buchanan nodded. 'It was the same for me. They tell you about the tournament?'

'The one in Covenant?'

'That's the one.'

Shane's mouth felt dry. He hadn't told anyone about the tournament. It was an idea that had come into his head one day. He couldn't remember when. If Buchanan knew about it too then that meant it was real, and that meant everything else that Shane had begun to fear was real too.

'I figure this thing with Hunte is some kind of a test.' Buchanan told him. 'Sort of like a qualifying round. Only one of us can go through to fight at Covenant.'

Shane thought about how he had recognised Buchanan as an equal the moment they had first met, how he had seen it in the way he carried himself and in the look in his eyes. He thought about how badly he wanted to go up against him in a fair fight to prove himself. 'I think you're right,' he said at last.

Buchanan nodded. 'We work together to kill the rest of these losers,' he said, looking pointedly at the bounty hunters who were watching the jailhouse. 'And we kill Hunte. Then we'll settle things properly, you and I.'

The two men looked at each other, and Shane nodded. 'Agreed.'

CHAPTER TEN

Nathaniel sat on the front porch of the Grande, flanked by his two bodyguards and smoking a cigar. As ever, Whisperer lurked behind him, keeping to the shade and regarding everything with a look of supercilious calm.

As Buchanan crossed the street to join them, he mentally suppressed his hatred of them both. For the time being, he needed them.

'Well, Buchanan?' Nathaniel called out to him. 'How have you been enjoying the show so far?'

'It's okay. Have you noticed how it's only the fighters I picked who've gone through to the next round?'

Nathaniel's smile was replaced with a frown. 'That's not entirely true. The woman, Vendetta, made it through. And Chastity of course.'

'Vendetta don't count; Ferris was one of yours as well. And I never said Chastity couldn't beat Cadero. I only said she won't beat Shane.'

'And your predictions for Shane?'

Buchanan smiled. 'The same as before. He's going to win this tournament.'

One of Nathaniel's bodyguards laughed at him. Buchanan shot him a withering stare and the man instantly fell silent.

'You're confident that Mister Ennis will shoot then? Yesterday when we spoke, he seemed quite adamant that he would rather die,' Nathaniel said.

'You underestimate him. He wants this almost as much as I do.'

'He hides it well.' Nathaniel observed, glancing over to where Shane sat, staring gloomily into the distance.

'He always did.' Buchanan replied. He climbed the steps and joined Nathaniel on the porch. 'How are we doing?' he asked quietly.

Nathaniel twisted about and gave Whisperer a querying look. Obediently, the tall man closed his eyes. There was a moment in which his expression became distant. 'We have their attention,' he said at last.

'They're watching? Now?' Buchanan eagerly glanced around him, looking at the empty windows and doorways that lined the street, hoping to see something. Whisperer laughed at him.

'They are close, but not *that* close.'

The mocking tone of his voice raised Buchanan's temper. He started forward, his good hand tightening into a fist. The two bodyguards moved to bar his path.

'Calm yourself, Buchanan.' Nathaniel snapped. 'Whisperer is correct. It is too early for you to see them. Be patient. They will come to us in time.'

'They had better.' Buchanan snarled. He was tired of waiting. He had waited six years already and now that his goal was at hand it was frustrating to find it still just outside of his reach. He breathed deeply, fighting against the rage that swelled up inside of him. Slowly, he brought it under his control.

'You cannot rush the occult.' Nathaniel told him. 'Why don't you take Mister Ennis' gun back to him? Let that amuse you for a while.'

Buchanan grinned, his anger forgotten. Taunting Shane would be fun. He was looking forward to seeing the expression on his face when he showed him his surprise.

Shane discreetly watched them talking from across the street. The conversation ended and Buchanan went into the Grande. Nathaniel said something to Whisperer and the tall man nodded in agreement.

Shane would have liked to have known what they had talked about. There were certain things about the tournament that didn't add up, and either he didn't know as much as he thought he did or else there was something strange going on.

It wasn't that he particularly cared. He did not expect to survive his fight with Devlin and looked no further into his future than the twenty minutes he believed he had left. If Nathaniel was up to something then it could hardly affect him but, still, he was curious. If Nathaniel really was fucking with the Fastest Guns then he was playing with fire and likely to get burned.

All along the street, contestants who had wandered away to pass the hour alone were returning. It wouldn't be long now, Shane told himself.

He thought back to that night at the Babson ranch and recalled how it had felt when he had shot the woman and her child. It hadn't been the first time that he had shot someone without really wanting to but it was the first time that he had actually been aware of it. There were men – women, even – that he had callously shot out of hand and never stopped to ask himself why. He had done that for years and had just always assumed he'd had a reason.

Shooting the child had been different. He had been unable to justify it, not by any standard, and it had opened his eyes.

It was said among the Fastest Guns that beyond skill there is mastery.

But Shane had wondered, if that is the case, then who is the master and who is the tool?

He had not liked the answer.

Buchanan returned bearing a mahogany box and a gunbelt, which he gave Shane to put on. Shane did not argue. He fastened the gunbelt and adjusted it until he was satisfied. The feel of it was natural, as if a piece of his body had been missing for a long time and he had only now discovered what it was.

Buchanan held out the box. It was fancier than it needed to be. Its surface had been lacquered and buffed to a shine and it was inlaid with brass catches. 'Open it,' he said.

Shane was afraid to touch it.

'Open it.' Buchanan repeated, and this time the command was reinforced by Shane's jailer, who drew a revolver and cocked it in his direction.

Nervously, Shane reached out and released the brass catches. His fingertips were electric as he opened the lid and exposed the gun inside.

It was a Colt 1873 Single Action .45 calibre revolver. Not a new weapon as Shane had expected; its frame was scratched from years of use. It had been customised: the barrel was a couple of inches shorter than the factory model. Shane remembered paying a gunsmith to have it done.

It was his gun, the self-same weapon with which he had destroyed Buchanan's right hand. The gun he had thrown away at Santa Morgana.

'You wouldn't believe how many people I had to kill to get hold of that gun.' Buchanan told him. 'It was about a year after you shot me that I decided I wanted it. I rode back to Santa Morgana but by then it had moved on. One of the miners had taken it with him to Nevada, lost it in a game of poker there. Word had gotten out that it used to belong to you and it was sold to a collector. A powerful man, with protection. Not very good protection it turned out, or at least, not as good as me.'

Shane stared at the gun. He was sure it was not just his imagination that made him think it was staring back at him.

'I'd got it into my head that I wanted to kill you with your own gun.' Buchanan continued. 'I liked the idea of it. I was going to start with your hands and feet and work inwards, one shot at a time. Then I met up with Nathaniel and, well, everything just seemed to fall into place.'

'Destiny.' Shane said.

'What can I say; the two of you were meant to be together.'

The gun had been lovingly cleaned and oiled. Shane could tell that it had seen some neglect since he had abandoned it, but Buchanan had restored it. The gun lay nestled on a velvet cushion, the metal gleaming in the afternoon light. It was beautiful and Shane hated it.

Nervously, he reached out to touch it, running his fingers along its barrel and tracing the contours of its cylinder, the loop of the trigger guard. As soon as he touched it, he felt it in his mind. He recoiled as if stung.

Buchanan laughed. 'You're going to have to get better

acquainted than that, Shane. Go on,' he said. 'Take it. You know you want to.'

He was right; Shane did want to. It called to him and he touched it again, stroking his fingers along it before taking it into his palm. It felt so perfect in his hand that his fear was momentarily forgotten. Then he remembered himself and cursed himself for a whore. After six years of abstinence it had taken only a few seconds for the gun to become a part of him again.

Now he wanted to shoot with it.

He held it up for inspection, checking that the barrel was clear and the mechanism smooth and professional. Buchanan had taken good care of it.

It was not loaded however.

'Patience, Shane.' Buchanan chided. He dug around in his pocket and produced a single .45 Long cartridge. Holding it out, he teased Shane by refusing to give it to him, only dropping it into his palm when the game grew tiresome.

'You'll understand if I only give you one.' Buchanan said. 'But I wouldn't want you to get carried away. Can't have you doing a Priestley, now can I?'

Shane wasn't listening. He took the cartridge and inserted it into the Colt's side loading gate, then spun the barrel until the loaded chamber was under the firing pin. It was all exactly as he remembered it, as familiar as the day he had thrown the gun away.

'Knock him dead,' Buchanan whispered excitedly.

Shane stepped onto the crossroads on legs that felt stiff and wooden and not his own. It was like being in a daze. The gun was not yet in control of him. In fact, he barely felt its presence at all. He was simply numb.

He could not believe that it was all really happening. Everything had acquired a dreamlike quality and he felt as if he would awaken at any moment to find that everything that had happened to him in the last few years was only a nightmare. He imagined he would wake up and find himself at Santa Morgana and he fervently wished it was true. But in his heart he knew better. This nightmare was his reality.

And his time had just run out.

John Devlin was waiting for him. He was like a younger, paler, more fanatical mirror-image of Shane. They could have been father and son they were so alike. Devlin was only twenty-two years old. He was tall and willow-thin, with a pale complexion made whiter in contrast by the black clothes that he wore. His straight black hair fell halfway down to the small of his back and was held in place by a small black ribbon, tied in a bow. He could not quite master the same expressionless gaze as Shane, but his stare was bleak and if his eyes were the window to his soul then his soul was a maelstrom of screaming torment and pain.

Devlin was a maniac. He had once shot up a schoolroom in Ohio in an attempt to emulate Jacob Priestley's rampage in Covenant, killed more than a dozen young children and their teacher, then gunned down half the posse they had sent to catch him. He had twice been sentenced to hang and twice had escaped from the gallows, once so closely that he still had a rope scar on his neck. All of this he bore with pride, believing that it made him special somehow, better than the rest of the world which had so wisely chosen to shun him.

Shane found his mark opposite him and looked down at the blood that stained the dirt. He wondered if his own would shortly mix with it. The crossroads seemed vast and open, the sky above him almost impossibly broad. Shane felt open and exposed, conscious of the people that were watching him. Nathaniel reclined lazily on the edge of the porch, a half-smile on his lips. Whisperer, behind him, his expression oddly knowing but otherwise unreadable. Buchanan, his eyes throwing off sparks he was so excited.

The invigilators were curious, the contestants wary. Shane noticed that Kip Kutcher's girlfriend had come back to the street and was watching him. She, like all the others, was wondering if the stories about him were true. Had he really lost his edge? Was he a coward like everybody said he was? And if so, would John Devlin kill him now?

Shane really didn't care what they thought. To be honest, he didn't much care about anything any more. He felt drained of all emotion, used up and desiccated by the burning heat.

Devlin stared at him and Shane stared back.

He heard the floorboards of the porch creak as Nathaniel rose from his chair, that telltale signal that preceded the call and, in that moment, Shane's entire future condensed into a handful of seconds. In those brief moments of time, his mind raced.

He had not yet decided for certain what he would do, whether he would shoot Devlin or simply let himself die. Whatever he chose, the end result would be the same. The Fastest Guns had taken hold of his soul and they would claim him one way or another, dead or alive. His only real option was whether to give himself up to them willingly or fight them every step of the way.

Nathaniel's voice broke his train of thought. 'Gentlemen,' he called. 'The time has come. You may fire when ready.'

Devlin drew and Shane's decision was made for him.

It was over before he knew what was happening. Seconds later, staring down the barrel of his gun as Devlin fell, he realised he had drawn and fired.

A numbness filled his soul. He could sense the gun's exaltation raging through him and felt its triumph. But, mercifully, that triumph did not last long. The gun had been loaded with only a single bullet and it was impotent now that it was empty. Its silent scream of rage went ignored as Shane slowly lowered it and took a deep breath. He felt his chest expand, filling with air, the sensation real and grounding.

Out of the corner of his eye he was aware that Buchanan was approaching him, but he did not care. He had survived. His mind was still his own. For six years he had feared shooting a gun, dreading that it would consume him in one gulp. He had let that fear grow inside of him like a cancer until it had seemed that there was nothing else.

He felt empty now, burned out and hollowed. But like a forest that had been razed by fire, new shoots were beginning to sprout.

Buchanan came up beside him. 'Good to see you haven't lost your touch.'

Shane turned and hit him. The punch caught him across the jaw and Buchanan was knocked to the ground. Immediately, half a dozen rifles were aimed at Shane. The ratchet of their lever-actions echoed across the street as the invigilators readied themselves to fire. Shane slowly backed away and held up his hands to show that he wanted no more trouble. He tossed his revolver aside.

Buchanan stared up at him from the ground, his eyes wide. Shane said nothing. He had no need to; his eyes said it all. They were cold and desolate as the void and, staring into them, Buchanan was rendered speechless. He waved his hand slowly and indicated for the invigilators to stand down. They complied and Shane turned abruptly on the spot and walked away. He stalked back to the courthouse and went inside, where he went straight to his cell and slammed the door behind him.

Still lying in the dirt, Buchanan rubbed his aching jaw. 'Welcome back, Shane,' he said. 'It's been a long time.'

There was a gathering at O'Malley's that night. Buchanan came to collect Shane a little before sundown and they crossed the street in silence.

Shane felt as if something had changed inside of him. Killing Devlin had been like a splash of cold water and it was as if he had woken from a deep sleep. The last six years felt like a bad dream. There was a sureness in his step and he walked with his head held high.

When they came to the saloon doors, Buchanan paused to let Shane go first. He strode in, ignoring the faces that turned to stare at him, and crossed straight to the bar; where he grabbed himself a bottle and a glass and moved on to find himself a table. This time, Buchanan let him go and did not move to join him.

Shane pulled up a seat alone with his back to the wall and pushed another chair out in front of him on which he propped his feet. He poured himself a drink and leaned back and studied the contestants who had made it into the next round.

They were all present, all except Chastity, and each sat with several tables between them and their nearest neighbour, filling the saloon even though there were only a handful of them. They were watched over by Nathaniel's invigilators and the atmosphere was tense. Nobody spoke.

Several of the windows had been opened but inside it was still hot as Hell. Tobacco smoke drifted, mixing with the smell of liquor and sweat and the underlying scent of gunsmoke, mould and dry wood.

The woman, Vendetta, sat where she had sat the night before, one foot resting on the seat of her chair. Her hat had a noticeable hole in its crown. Evan Drager stretched his injured leg out in front of him. The Apache, Nanache, had a fresh finger bone hanging from his necklace.

Shane noticed that Kip Kutcher's girlfriend, Madison, had come along. She sat way back in the shadows and looked to be keeping out of Tom Freeman's way. Freeman, for his part, seemed uninterested in her. He sat with his back to the wall and was watching the other contestants discreetly, sizing them up.

The chalkboard on which Whisperer had scratched up everybody's name stood propped against the wall as it had been last night. The names of the dead had been scratched off and from the empty spaces chalked up to the right of every match it was easy to deduce the pairings for the second round. The winner of the first match would face the winner of the second; the winner of the third would face the winner of the fourth, and so on. Matt Nesbitt was drinking heavily because of this, for his next opponent would be Chastity and he knew that he did not stand a chance.

Shane's next fight would be against Valentino Rodrigues, the man who had killed the Gentleman. He would be a more difficult opponent than John Devlin had been but Shane was confident he would win. Shane drained his glass and poured himself another.

The doors opened and Nathaniel's bodyguards entered, followed by the man himself, with Whisperer close behind. He was full of praise for the contestants. 'I salute you all,' he said. 'Today's round separated the wheat from the chaff. You have each of you shown the speed and the skill worthy of a true gunfighter. But that is not enough. Tomorrow we will divide you still.'

Whisperer walked past him and began chalking up the names on the board, confirming what everybody had already deduced about the second round's pairings.

'The first two matches tomorrow morning will take place at ten and eleven on the hour. Matt Nesbitt and Chastity to begin, followed by Vendetta and Nanache. The second two matches will be fought in the afternoon at one and two respectively. The pairings are . . .'

Shane had stopped listening. He had noticed that once again Nathaniel had avoided the Gunfighter's Hour of twelve noon. He wondered why.

'Those of you who succeed tomorrow,' Nathaniel continued. 'Will earn the chance to further distinguish yourselves in the semifinal. Those of you who do not will die as unremarkably as those who failed today. May the best of you prevail.'

He walked over and joined Buchanan at the bar. With the business of the meeting concluded, many of the contestants began to leave. Matt Nesbitt stayed where he was. Sullenly, he filled his glass back up to the brim and sat there staring at it.

Somebody walked over to Shane's table. It was Nanache. 'You shot well today,' he said.

Shane smiled wryly to himself. 'You want to add my fingers to your collection?'

'If I could do that, I would not need my collection,' the Apache said. He sat down opposite Shane. 'You could have competed here before. I would like to know why you refused.'

'And I'd like to know why you're talking to me. I thought you hated white men.'

'That is true, but you are no man.' Nanache replied. 'You are like he is,' he said, and he nodded toward Whisperer.

Despite the heat, Shane suddenly felt cold. 'And what's he?' he asked.

'*Devil-kind*,' Nanache replied. The word was familiar to Shane. 'No longer of this world, not yet of the next.'

After all of the others had gone the only two people left in O'Malley's were Matt Nesbitt and the girl, Madison. Both sat alone and in silence. Shane had been taken back to his cell, Nathaniel had returned to the Grande and the invigilators had gone back to their patrols.

The saloon lay mostly in darkness. A few lanterns burned, offering a dim source of light in places, but in others the shadows were deep. The place felt empty.

Nesbitt stared at his glassful of whisky. He had not touched it in more than half-an-hour, but simply sat and stared and thought about what would happen to him tomorrow. He thought about the death of Escoban Cadero and how the little girl, Chastity, had killed him before he had even had chance to draw his gun.

Matt Nesbitt did not want to die.

He did not look up when the girl came over and sat opposite him. For a long time they both sat in silence. Then the girl spoke. 'Are you going to drink that?' she asked.

Nesbitt thought hard on it for a while then leaned back in his chair and pushed the glass away. 'No,' he said. 'I'll need a clear head in the morning.'

The girl shrugged. She too had seen Chastity fight that morning and understood what Nesbitt was up against. 'You'll need more than that,' she said doubtfully. She reached over and took his glass.

'Finish it.' Nesbitt told her, leaving her the bottle. He kicked back his chair and left the saloon.

Madison watched him go, wishing that he had stayed to keep her company. She stared at the glass for a moment, then downed it in one. The harsh liquor burned her throat but it felt good and she poured herself another and downed that one too. She had spent a good deal of her adult life in saloons and gambling dens and cheap hotels and Madison could handle her drink better than some men she knew. Kip had never been a very good drinker. After two shots the alcohol would go straight to his head and he'd start singing. She smiled. Kip had always got frisky when he was drunk and she remembered him fondly.

She had never meant for him to die, not like this.

Her eyes began to water with fresh tears and she rubbed them viciously. She did not want to cry any more. She had always thought herself tougher than that. Angrily, she poured herself another glass of whisky. She was clumsy and slopped a little bit onto the table. Behind her, she thought she heard someone laugh.

She called out: 'Is somebody there?'

The darkness swallowed up her voice, muffling it. Madison could not see anybody else in the saloon with her but still she had a creeping sensation that she was being watched. She began to get uneasy and, snatching up the unfinished bottle, she hurried to the doorway.

She reached it just as the town began its nightly chorus. The wood beneath her feet groaned and the walls shuddered noisily. Madison started and ran outside, jumping off the boardwalk onto firm ground. All around her in every direction, every building was making the same noise, wood popping and cracking as if the whole town was about to fall down. She had heard it many times already but still it made her nervous and she headed out into the middle of the crossroads, where she thought she would be safe if anything did collapse.

From where she stood, the sound was even more creepy. She

listened as it settled into rhythm, each individual building gradually falling into time with its neighbours until the sound rolled in towards her like a wave advancing up the shore, then turned and rolled back out again towards the desert.

In and out.

In and out.

The timing was as consistent as the ticking of a metronome and it moved through all four quarters of the town at the same pace. It was far too regular to be natural. Madison did not understand what caused it, but then there was a lot about Covenant she did not understand and more besides that she wished she had never found out about in the first place. Kip was dead and she wished that she had never insisted that he come here. Again fighting the urge to cry, she hurried down the street until she reached the house that she and Kip had claimed as their own.

The house had once belonged to a family with a little girl. Madison had found an old rag doll on the day they arrived and, though it was a little dusty, she had adopted it for her own. It was perched close to the bedroll that she and Kip had shared and she gathered it into her arms as she sat and swigged straight from the bottle of whisky.

Finally, she could hold off her sadness no longer and she broke down and cried.

When the messenger had brought Kip his invitation to compete, Kip had initially not wanted to attend. 'It'll just be a bunch of psychos, Maddy. No fun at all.' Madison had known that really he was afraid that he would die, but that hadn't bothered her at the time. She had only known Kip a few weeks and while he was fun to be with he was not as good a gunfighter as he liked to think he was, and Madison liked gunfighters. Proper ones.

She had figured that if Kip took her to Covenant then she would be able to replace him with somebody better, maybe even one of the Fastest Guns. He was only supposed to have been a temporary thing, a stepping stone. She had never expected to fall in love with him.

She slugged miserably from the bottle and wiped her eyes with the back of her sleeve. She had never felt so wretched before in all her life and now she did not know what else to do with herself.

As she drank, she failed to notice the figure who stepped silently out of the darkness on the opposite side of the room. He was tall and wore a long, leather coat and a hat whose brim was pulled down low to cover his face in shadow. Pale, grey smoke rose from his body, smelling strongly of fulminate.

Madison did not notice. She had her back to him and was too wrapped up in her grief to hear him as he drew a long-barrelled revolver and thumbed back the hammer.

'Wait.'

A second figure emerged from the shadows next to the first and closed a slender hand around his wrist, forcing him to lower his aim.

The first turned to the newcomer, questioningly.

'We have made an accord.' The second whispered, his voice like distant gunfire. 'No one is to die. Yet,' he added.

Unobserved, both figures melted back into the darkness.

CHAPTER ELEVEN

They were the six most powerful men in Wainsford: a banker, traders, a rancher and two lawyers; the men who ruled the town, who influenced, shaped it, milked and bled it dry. They were the six members of the town council and Shane had not been entirely surprised when they had asked to speak with him. He only wondered that it had taken them so long.

'It would only be a temporary arrangement, you understand?'

Shane said nothing. The six men were all used to getting what they wanted and it showed. All wore power suits, gold watches and polished shoes. All, that was, except for the lawyer, Boyd, who did not care what other people thought of him and wore an ill-fitting suit, stained and mildewed, his hair unstyled, greasy and unkempt. He smelled of stale sweat and tobacco and cheap gin.

The six men were confident, domineering, and Shane took great pleasure in unnerving them with his dead-eyed stare until the point that even Reynolds, the fat rancher, shifted uncomfortably on the edge of his chair.

It was Boyd who was doing most of the talking. 'You'll be

paid five-hundred dollars,' he said. 'How you do it is up to you but we want Fletcher out before the end of the week. This situation has gone on quite long enough.'

Earlier that morning, as Shane and Buchanan had talked on the boardwalk, the town council had gone to the jailhouse and formally terminated Fletcher's employment as town marshal. 'You've been neglecting your duties,' Boyd had told him, speaking to the locked jailhouse door. 'This town is overrun and instead of protecting us you're holed up like a coward. This is unacceptable.'

Since only the town marshal was supposed to use the jailhouse, they had demanded that Fletcher and his men vacate it immediately, to which Fletcher had replied in no uncertain terms. After a lengthy argument he had eventually flung his marshal's badge out the window and it now rested in the palm of Shane's hand, where Boyd had put it.

Shane did not know if the councilmen were just trying to preserve their interests in the town or if somebody more powerful had wired them before the telegraph lines had been cut, but they had not hired him to get rid of the bounty hunters in town; they had asked him to get rid of Fletcher, Ben and Alan Grant, and in so doing had effectively given him a free hand to do what he liked with Hunte.

Hunte's name had not been mentioned once in all of the discussion and it was clear that the councilmen wanted no complicity in whatever became of him. If there were any repercussions for what happened in town then Shane had no doubt that they would hang him out to dry. He expected no less, but that didn't mean he had to play by their rules. 'I want to be sworn in,' he said. 'In front of witnesses. The hotel manager and his wife will do. And I want my contract in writing.'

The banker, Patterson, was not keen. 'I don't think that's necessary,' he said evasively.

'Hunte's wanted in front of a Congressional Committee. If he dies because of this, I'm not having my head put on the block.'

Boyd was slick. 'We'll swear you in,' he agreed. 'And have everything done up in writing. Effective immediately, you will be marshal.'

'And I want a deputy.' Shane said.

Boyd's face twitched in irritation. 'I'm not sure we can find–'

'I already have someone in mind.'

'Fine.' Patterson said. 'Employ him. But you'll have to pay him out of your own pocket.'

'Yes. About the money,' Shane said, turning to face him with his dead-eyed stare. 'It's not enough.'

In truth, the money was fine; Shane just enjoyed fucking with them.

The tray scraped as it was pushed into his cell, bringing with it the smell of greasy fried bacon and lukewarm coffee. It was not Buchanan who delivered it but one of the invigilators instead, a solemn-looking man in his early-thirties who left without saying a word.

Shane rose from his bunk and rubbed his head with his palms. He felt different this morning. Perhaps it was just that he had slept well for the first time in six years, but he felt clear-headed and composed. What was more, he had an appetite and wolfed down his breakfast, mopping up the last drips of fat with a crust of bread. He paced over to the window when he was finished and looked out, angling himself so that he could see to the end of the alley and look onto West Street and the crooked walls of the Grande hotel. The sun beat down on another hot and dry morning with scarcely a cloud in the sky to offer any shade. A pair of invigilators walked by.

It was all exactly as it had been the day before, only this time Shane saw it with different eyes. It was as if he had been seeing in black and white and now the colours were back again. Details that he had only half-noticed the day before now caught his eye: the way one of the two invigilators favoured his right leg over his left; the tilt of the third step that led up to the Grande's porch, which was more precarious than the rest. Little details that were insignificant on their own but which added up to make a larger picture.

A picture that became a map or a diagram that went some way towards forming a plan of escape.

Shane stepped back into the shade. He had been thinking a lot about the newspaper that Buchanan had brought him yesterday, about how the world outside of Covenant thought he was dead. Before yesterday, Shane had been convinced that he had nothing worth living for. Now he knew better. Outside of Covenant he was a free man, free to stop running and free to start over again. If anybody ever said that he looked like Shane Ennis he could laugh and remind them that Shane Ennis was dead, he just had the misfortune to be a man who looked like him. His name . . . his name could be whatever he wanted it to be.

Shane Ennis was dead.

All he had to do was escape from Covenant.

He turned as the door to the sheriff's office creaked open and Castor Buchanan strode in. 'Well, something's got you looking sparky!'

Shane did not answer him but waited sullenly while he unlocked the door to his cell.

'Come on, out you come. Round two, Shane. Time to show us what you're really capable of.'

As Shane stepped out of his cell he deliberately dropped his shoulder into Buchanan's chest, driving the wind from his lungs. Buchanan was pushed sideways. A second later, his temper exploded and he hit Shane like a cannonball. His arm came up across Shane's throat and drove him hard against the bars of his cell, pinning him there and choking him. Buchanan pressed his face close, eye-to-eye, the light of his madness glittering like sparks from a tinder box.

'I let you get that shot in yesterday,' he snarled. 'But don't think you're so fucking important to what we're doing here that I won't lay you out if you fuck with me again.'

He pulled his arm away and Shane dropped to his knees, gagging for breath.

'There's plenty of ways I can hurt you and still leave you well enough to compete.' Buchanan said. 'Just remember that.' He hauled Shane up and propelled him towards the door. Shane staggered where he was flung, colliding bodily against the wall. He was shaken and his throat felt raw, but inwardly he felt victorious. He had wanted to test Buchanan's reaction and what he had learned was very encouraging. Buchanan's temper was still volatile for all that he had learned to control himself, and it was still the easiest means by which he could be manipulated.

Shane would remember that for when the time was right.

The streets were already lined with contestants and invigilators, all of whom had gathered for the morning's first match: the fight between Matt Nesbitt and Chastity.

Shane walked to the edge of the boardwalk and sat down on his own. Buchanan settled on the wooden bench behind him while Shane's jailer stood nearby, watching Shane with narrowed eyes. Buchanan's temper was still unsettled and Shane could feel his anger radiating from him, the emotion evident in the way he breathed loudly and shifted restlessly on the bench. Shane noted that it took him a while to calm himself completely.

A sullen breeze that did nothing to ease the morning heat blew dust across the road. Shane let his attention wander slowly, first to the invigilators – whose body language he discreetly studied, ascertaining who was good and who merely wanted to be – and then the contestants.

To his surprise, Kip Kutcher's girlfriend was still around. Shane had not expected to see her again, figuring that the town would have disposed of her during the night, and yet still she was here, looking in fine health but for what looked like a bad night's sleep and a hangover. She had tricked her eyes out with liner and powdered her face but she had not been able to hide all of the signs that she had spent most of the night crying.

The fact that Kip's death had upset her so badly, or rather, the fact that she had tried to conceal it surprised Shane almost as much as the fact that she was still alive. It implied a level of self-respect and pride that women of her kind seldom possessed in any great quantity, and he wondered if maybe there was more to her than he had first assumed. He made a mental note for future consideration and turned his attention to Matt Nesbitt, who was pacing back and forth by the side of the road.

He wore his nerves like an overcoat: plain for all to see. Like the girl, he showed signs of having passed a sleepless night but that was to be expected. Having seen Chastity fight, there was not a man in Covenant who would have put money on Matt Nesbitt surviving this round and it was a measure of his courage that he had come to the crossroads at all.

He periodically stopped his pacing to check the time on his

pocket watch, or draw his Merwin revolver and check it over before returning it to the holster; acts of nervous repetition that nonetheless passed the time for him until the door of the Grande was opened and Nathaniel emerged with his bodyguards, Whisperer, Chastity and her nanny.

Pointlessly, Nesbitt checked his watch for the final time, snapped it shut, and went out to take his mark. He walked with his head held deliberately high as if he could fool anyone that he was not afraid. The only prayer he had was that he would meet his fate with dignity and not die like a coward.

Nathaniel took Chastity from her nanny and led her to the crossroads. As with the day before, the girl's face was expressionless, like something sculpted in fine bone china with wide blue eyes painted on above a straight, flat mouth. Her steps were clumsy, feet scuffing in the dirt, so that Nathaniel almost seemed to be dragging her half the time. The hand that he held might have belonged to someone else for all the awareness she had of it.

The mood along the street became apprehensive. Everybody watched as Nathaniel positioned her opposite Matt Nesbitt and drew out the tiny pocket revolver. The girl stared vacantly straight through it and into the middle distance beyond.

Nathaniel tucked the weapon into her holster, then straightened her shoulders so that she was facing Nesbitt more squarely. He then hurried to the side of the road.

Nesbitt stared at her, his brow furrowed with concentration. Everybody knew what was going to happen next.

The girl seemed unaffected for the space of three heartbeats and then her posture straightened. She drew herself up from her slouching stance and raised her head, eyes swimming into stark focus, piercing Nesbitt with her gaze.

Nathaniel called it, seeing that she was ready, and both fighters reached for their guns.

Two shots rang out in rapid succession.

The first struck Nesbitt in the hip, shattering his pelvis into splinters of bone that lacerated his kidney and spleen. The second shot hit him in the chest going faster than the speed of sound. It ripped straight through his lung and burst the left ventricle of his heart, filling his chest cavity with blood. He staggered sideways, clutching at his side, blood frothing on his lips. His gun slipped from numb fingers and hit the dirt. Seconds later he sank down on his knees next to it and cursed Chastity with his final breath.

The third shot caught everybody by surprise.

It was unexpected and broke the post-match silence like a hammer breaking glass. It was followed moments later by a dull thump as one of the invigilators fell from his perch on the clock tower and hit the ground, dead.

Startled, everyone looked to see who had fired.

The culprit was in plain sight for all to see. Chastity stood with her tiny revolver pointed at the spot where the dead invigilator had stood, thin wisps of grey-white smoke curling from the barrel.

The surviving invigilators reacted at once, bringing their guns to bear on her. Nathaniel shouted at them. 'No! Stop!'

A fourth shot rang out.

It was not the piercing crack of a rifle but the angry cough of Chastity's revolver and a second invigilator fell in a burst of crimson. The girl had moved with phenomenal speed, going instantly for the man who had moved the fastest.

Shane and the other contestants instantly went for cover. Chastity moved, turning on the spot with balletic grace, scanning the multitude of moving targets for the one who next represented the greatest threat to her and settling on a third invigilator. The man had her in his sights but held his fire on Nathaniel's order. For some reason, Chastity held her fire as well and a tense stand-off was achieved. The little girl stood in the middle of the crossroads, surrounded by five invigilators. Others came running and Nathaniel shouted at them to stand down. 'She is not to be harmed,' he ordered.

The invigilators obeyed him insofar as they did not shoot, but they kept their rifles trained on her diminutive figure. Peering out from behind the water trough where he had dived for cover, Shane studied her technique. She was completely at ease with the situation. She kept turning in a slow circle, gun moving in a controlled sweep, her eyes making small, rapid movements to keep everybody in sight. She reacted quickly to the slightest possible threat.

It was an incredible and chilling thing to see. Watching her, Shane figured that she was at least as good as he had been in his prime, if not better. He saw the look of coldness in her eyes and knew that she would not back down. She would fight until the invigilators killed her, and she would claim one of them with every shot she fired.

Across the street, Nathaniel was aware that he had lost control of the situation, and he was worried. His invigilators were hired men, loyal to the money he paid them and the promises he had made but at the end of the day their loyalty was bought, not offered, and that meant that there were limits beyond which they would not be pushed. Sooner or later, he knew one of them would disobey his orders and Chastity would die, and that was unacceptable. She was too important to what he was doing in Covenant. True, he would still have Ennis if she died, but he placed less value on that old gunslinger. Chastity was fresh. Chastity was pure.

And she was out of control.

He needed to disarm her before anybody else got hurt, but lacked the courage to go out onto the street and do it for himself. Casting about, he spied the girl's nanny, Bethan, cowering under the Grande's porch beside Whisperer. He called out to her.

'Bethan! That child's your responsibility. You get out there and you get her to put that gun down.'

Bethan's eyes went wide and she shook her head at him imploringly, but Nathaniel would not be denied. 'Don't you make me ask twice, woman! You get out there and you do as you're told.'

Whisperer closed his hand around Bethan's shoulder, adding his formidable presence to Nathaniel's demands, and the woman's will dissolved. She was crying as Whisperer pushed her out into the open, silent tears streaming down a face that became pinched and ugly whenever she cried. Nathaniel had no sympathy for her and even less concern for her safety. He called out to his invigilators again. 'Nobody fires. Is that understood?'

The invigilators kept their rifles trained on Chastity. Their fingers were on the trigger and getting tired. Soon, people would start to get twitchy.

Chastity slowly turned, keeping them all in her sights. She paid little attention to Bethan, recognising in just a single glance that the woman carried no weapon and was therefore no threat to her. As Bethan advanced tentatively out into the street, she realised that she was being ignored and grew a little bolder. She wiped the tears from her face. Bending over slightly, she offered her hands toward Chastity, inviting her to an embrace, and called out her name. Her voice was shaky, but soft.

She got no reaction and edged closer to the little girl, who

121

suddenly turned to face her.

Chastity brought her revolver up to point directly at Bethan's face. She said nothing, but the look on her face stopped Bethan in her tracks and forced a startled cry from her lips. Her courage faltered and she wavered uncertainly, poised on the edge of running for her life when Nathaniel shouted at her: 'What are you waiting for? Get her to put that gun down, woman!'

His words checked Bethan in mid-step. She burst out in sudden tears, sniffed them back and wiped her eyes. 'Chastity,' she said, her voice weak. She held out her hand imploringly to the child. 'Give me the gun, please baby.'

Chastity gave the proffered hand a suspicious look, then glanced up at the rooftops, studying the invigilators as if concerned that Bethan had been sent out as a distraction. Thinking that she was being ignored again, Bethan took a step closer.

Chastity immediately swung back to face her. Bethan was only a couple of steps away from her now, her outstretched hand just a few inches from grasping Chastity's gun. The little girl stared at her nanny with a look of pure hatred such as no child should ever possess.

On the roof of O'Malley's, one of the invigilators rose out of the half-crouch he had been holding since the first shots had been fired, stretching stiff legs. Chastity glanced his way, assessed what level of threat he represented, and dismissed him. She swung her attention back toward Bethan and the whole street waited tensely.

Bethan edged closer. 'Please, baby. Please.'

The little girl's expression remained the same. Hesitantly, Bethan stepped a little closer and that was when the gun went off.

The sound was as violent as the deed itself, shattering the silence into exploding fragments. Bethan fell over backwards, her head erupting in a spray of red. She had scarcely hit the ground when Nathaniel's voice roared out through the echoes of the shot.

'Hold your fire! Hold your fire goddamnit!'

He was not shouting at Chastity, but at his invigilators. The hired gunmen silently cursed him, angry that they could have prevented Bethan's death if he had only given them rein to. Nathaniel knew that he was losing their respect and that if he did not resolve the situation soon that they would take matters into their own hands, and the tournament and everything that rested on it would be in jeopardy.

He was not concerned by Bethan's death. She had been a good nanny but poor company so far as he was concerned, and he had been planning to dispose of her when the tournament was over anyway. His one regret was that she had been his best hope of getting Chastity to calm down. He still did not like the idea of going onto the crossroads in person to disarm her. He was an officer, a leader, and men like him did not do something themselves if there was somebody more expendable who could be told to do it instead.

He glanced about, searching for somebody who fit the bill. He could not call upon one of his invigilators to do it. He was stretching their loyalty just getting them to hold their fire. Neither could he call upon Whisperer, who was simply too valuable to put at risk. To his surprise, he found exactly the person he needed close at hand.

Madison had taken shelter as soon as things had turned bad, ducking into the nearest alleyway which, unluckily for her, was where Nathaniel had gone as well. She saw him looking at her and guessed his intentions just a few seconds too late to be able to escape him. He grabbed her fiercely by the wrist.

'You!' he said. 'Go take that gun off her.'

Madison was still hung-over and her senses were not as sharp as they usually were, or she would have known better than to argue with him. 'You have got to be kidding!' she said.

The back of his fist whipped across her jaw, knocking her silent. 'I'm not *asking* if you'd *like* to,' he said in a low voice.

The blow caught Madison by surprise, stunning her. Amazed that she had been struck, she reached up a hand to touch her face, to prove to herself that it had happened. She had the good sense not to say anything more. Nathaniel roughly dragged her from the alley and pitched her into the street.

'Get out there and do as you're told you little bitch!' he snapped.

He drew his gun and thumbed back the hammer, reinforcing his words with physical threat. Madison stared at him wide-eyed. She had absolutely no doubt that he would shoot her if she didn't do as he said.

Tears threatened at the corners of her eyes but she blinked them angrily away. She had already let Nathaniel hit her, push her and shout at her. She was damned if she would now give him the satisfaction of seeing her cry. She straightened herself up and brushed the dirt from her clothes, conscious of the fact that everybody was watching her.

Just my luck, she thought. *All this attention and I look like shit.*

She cursed herself for having drunk so much last night. Her head was sore and her stomach was unsettled and getting worse now that she was afraid. On top of all that she really needed to pee, as if things weren't bad enough already.

'One thing at a time, Maddy.' she whispered to herself.

Chastity was staring at her, intrigued by this new woman who had been pushed out into the open and made into such an inviting

ROBERT DAVIS

target. It was conspicuously tempting, and Chastity turned a slow circle, eyeing the invigilators and the other contestants and looking for danger. Madison took a hold of her nerves and forced herself to walk towards her on legs that felt heavy and strangely numb.

She got to within ten yards before Chastity swung about to face her and gave her a rattlesnake stare that stopped her dead in her tracks.

Madison had stared down the barrel of a gun before. It felt much the same this time as it had back then. A coldness seeped through her, draining her body of all feeling and leaving her numb.

Damnit Kip, why did I insist you bring me here?

She glanced back over her shoulder at where Nathaniel stood. He waved his gun at her, urging her forward and her feet scuffed in the dirt as she did as she was told. Chastity glared at her from behind the iron sights of her little revolver.

Madison was familiar with the type of gun she held. Most pocket revolvers had a five-shot cylinder, but some were manufactured to hold six or even seven rounds. She was too far away to see it clearly enough to be certain which kind Chastity held. Madison tried counting backwards to work out how many she had fired already. Fear clouded her thoughts and made it hard to concentrate.

She shuffled closer and her next step brought her level with Bethan's corpse. She told herself not to look but she could not help it. Her eyes were drawn to the hole in the back of Bethan's head and to the flies that crawled in the sticky red mess, picking their way between the matted strands of hair. Madison's stomach heaved and she swallowed down hard to resist the urge to puke.

Chastity was now only a few steps away and her aim had not wavered at all in the last twenty heartbeats.

'Nobody fire!' Nathaniel ordered.

125

Madison silently cursed him. *Try telling her that,* she thought to herself. She forced herself to breathe deeply, to calm herself and not give in to the thoughts of panic that were clamouring for her attention.

Just another couple of steps, she told herself. She was close enough that she could almost make out the details of the gun's cylinder. It was either a five- or a six-shot; she didn't think it was a seven.

Fighting her fears, she took another step closer and reached out her hand.

There was no hesitation, no suggestion of compassion or mercy or any semblance of human emotion at all.

Madison reached out to take the gun and Chastity pulled the trigger.

Madison saw it coming but had no chance of getting out of the way. She covered her face with her hands and screamed but somehow she didn't die. Seconds later, in retrospect, she realised that the sound she had thought was a gunshot had actually been the noise of the hammer falling on an empty cartridge.

She lowered her hands in surprise. Chastity stared at her as if unable to figure out why she was still alive. She pulled the trigger again and Madison flinched as the hammer fell once more onto an empty brass. Chastity became frustrated. She pulled the trigger again and again and let out an unhappy wail.

'Give me that!' Madison snatched the revolver out of the girl's hand, emboldened now that she knew she was safe. She turned and held it up for Nathaniel and the invigilators to see. 'I've got it,' she cried triumphantly.

Her words were drowned out as Chastity began to scream. The noise lanced through Madison's hangover like a bullet to the head.

Madison clapped her hands to her ears. The girl kept on screaming, filling her lungs and howling like a fiend.

Madison staggered away and fetched up suddenly in Nathaniel's arms. He took the gun away from her and pulled her hands away from her ears. 'Take her into the hotel and get her calmed down,' he told her. 'You work for me now.'

Madison was too stunned to argue with him. *Agree with him*, her mind told her. *For the time being just do as he says.* Survive now, find a way out later; it was a policy that had gotten her through many bad scrapes in the past.

Wincing against the pain in her head, she accepted Chastity's arm as Nathaniel offered it to her and dragged the child toward the Grande. She was still alive, and that was all that really mattered right now.

Nathaniel stood in the middle of the crossroads and watched her go, admiring the shape of her figure from behind. He was joined by Buchanan, who surveyed the bodies that Chastity had left littering the street.

'I think,' Nathaniel said. 'That it would be prudent if we only give Chastity one bullet in future, like Ennis.'

Buchanan did not disagree.

CHAPTER TWELVE

Jeb MacPherson had come to Wainsford for the same reason as the others. Sick of earning a living wasting small-time crooks and cattle thieves, he was looking for a last big score to set him up for his future. At twenty-eight years old, he figured it was time to stop killing and find himself a real job.

Jeb had lot of smarts, a lot more than people usually gave him credit for. His quiet, shy-seeming exterior hid a keen mind and he knew from the moment he learned that Shane Ennis and Castor Buchanan were in town that he stood no chance of claiming his reward if he acted alone. And so Jeb had started rallying together a small group of men, thinking that there was strength in numbers.

Jeb MacPherson was dead now. Three shots rang out, splitting the midday calm and sending him staggering backwards on lifeless feet.

More shots followed, a blazing frenzy of blood-letting that left his comrades dead as well, and in the centre of this maelstrom of murder Shane Ennis walked with his guns spitting lead and fire, his coat tails billowing behind him like the tattered wings of the Angel of Death.

Legally appointed as town marshal and with Castor Buchanan newly deputised, he had wasted no time in introducing a new kind of law to the bounty hunters in Wainsford. His rules were simple: 'Join me, or die.'

In just a few short hours the number of bounty hunters in town was reduced by half, leaving only those who agreed to Shane's leadership. He deputised them accordingly and paid them fifty dollars each.

One man snubbed the money and spat on the floor in disgust. 'That's horseshit! I got offered a thousand dollars to kill Hunte. Ain't no way I'm helping you for fifty.'

The other bounty hunters shuffled away from him, leaving him to face Shane alone.

'How much do you want?' Shane asked him. He spoke quietly and his voice sounded reasonable, but his hand had moved to rest on the butt of his revolver. The man glanced over his shoulder, looking for somebody to back him up.

'Well?' Shane said.

The man lost his nerve. 'Fifty dollars is fine,' he said.

Shane organised them into shifts so that there were three men covering the jailhouse at any given time. He had them set up firing positions behind barrels and crates, and had a cart wheeled out opposite the jailhouse door, where a man could crouch and fire. His men cleared out the surrounding buildings and smashed windows on the upper floors, so that every angle could be covered and there wasn't a chance in hell that anybody could get out of the jailhouse, or take food and water in without getting shot down on the way.

If Fletcher wasn't coming out then Shane would starve him into submission. And if that didn't work then in a couple of days they'd set fire to the jailhouse and burn them out. Either way, Benedict Hunte was a dead man.

As nightfall settled that evening, Shane inspected his troops. The marshal was keeping his head down and the jailhouse was silent as a church, with no lights inside to reveal the occupants to Shane's gunmen. Buchanan was keeping watch round the back, and he was sore at it. 'I don't see why you want a man here anyway,' he argued. 'Ain't no way they're coming out this way. Not unless they cut through the fucking wall.'

'Town appointed me the new marshal.' Shane said. 'And I appointed you my deputy. That means you stand guard where I tell you to stand guard.'

'Don't let this shit get to your head.' Buchanan snarled at him. 'I've shot marshals before.'

'And I've shot deputies.'

Shane returned to his hotel room. He laid himself out on the bed without even bothering to kick off his boots and stared up at the ceiling, waiting. For all the stories that had been told about him, it was rarely understood that Shane's guns were the least of his weapons. Any fool could shoot a man and sooner or later any fool who did was bound to get himself either shot or hanged. That was the way of things. But Shane was smarter than that.

He had never seen other people the way normal folk did. He didn't think of them as individuals but instead saw them each as cogs in a machine. Every person's actions affected those of the people surrounding them, whose reactions affected others, and so on.

As a child with very few friends, Shane had used to amuse himself by provoking situations and trying to predict how the consequences would ripple through the small town society in which he had grown up. By the time he had reached adolescence, he had become adept at understanding people and manipulating them. A few words in the right places could do a lot more damage than an equal number of bullets.

Shane closed his eyes. He had set events in motion earlier that day, events that would have dire consequences, but consequences that would ultimately suit his needs. Now all he had do was bide his time and let it all play out.

He woke shortly after midnight, hearing the sound of violence outside his window. It was the noise of a door being kicked down some distance away, accompanied by shouting and a woman's screaming. There were cries of protest that were answered by an animal snarl and the sound of a shot ringing out. Then silence, long and pregnant; a prelude to the horrors that were to come.

Shane did not think about what he had started. He felt neither joy nor sorrow or guilt. The crimes that Buchanan committed were of his own choosing, and Shane did not really consider that he was himself to blame. Not really. He closed his ears as the screams began in earnest, the sounds of two people being tortured by the man whose love of inflicting pain rivalled that of the Devil.

Shane rose from the bed and walked over to the window. He saw the curtains twitch in a house across the street and caught a brief glimpse of a frightened face as somebody looked out to see what the noise was about. All across town, people did the same. They looked and they listened but they did nothing to stop it. In time, an old man came running down the street. 'Marshal Fletcher! Marshal Fletcher!'

The bounty hunters stationed around the front of the jailhouse took aim as he approached. Others, woken by the noise, flocked to their positions in anticipation of the killing that was to come. Shane did nothing.

As the old man drew close to the jailhouse, Fletcher called out to him from inside. 'What the Hell's going on out there, Ed?'

'It's Ben's parents!' The old man held back, reluctant to come any closer with the bounty hunters so near. 'I'm sorry, Marshal. The bastard just kicked down the door!'

There came an almost bestial howl from within, a sound of purest human rage. Shane heard footsteps on the wooden floor inside, heard Fletcher's voice cry out: 'Don't Ben, it's a trap.'

Ben swore at him. From the sound of what got said, Shane guessed that the old lawman was trying to bar his path and keep him from opening the door. There was the sound of a fight, the hard smack of a fist against somebody's jaw and, moments later, the bolts were drawn back.

The three bounty hunters stationed opposite put fingers to the triggers and took aim.

Fletcher cried out. 'Ben. No!'

But it was too late. The door swung open and Ben ran out into the murderous night, brandishing his shotgun and a heartful of rage. He hadn't gone a step when the three rifles gave fire and illuminated the scene in a brilliant white flash. The scene burned into Shane's eyes like the image of a photograph. Ben's chest imploded as the volley struck home, stopping him dead in his tracks. He staggered, eyes wide, as if uncertain what had happened. And then a second volley blew him backwards through the open door.

A couple of men ran out and charged the doorway but it slammed shut before they could reach it and the bolts were thrown. Guns appeared at the loopholes in the wall and fired, and one man was hit, falling wounded while the others fled back to take shelter behind the barrels and the crates. They fired in return but their shots did nothing but chip splinters out of the jailhouse wall. The night's killing was over. The deed was done.

Shane slinked quietly back to his bed and Castor Buchanan played his games until late in the morning, when two gunshots brought an end to an old couple's suffering and closed another dark chapter in his list of crimes.

Shane did not know if it was something about Covenant or whether it was just his state of mind that made his memories so vivid, but he could remember that night as if it had only just been.

He did not really feel guilty for what he had done, but he was not proud of it either. It rested on his heart with a heaviness that was hard to simply shrug off and forget.

It had been the lawyer, Boyd, who had told Shane that Ben's parents lived in town and where they could be found. He had no doubt intended that Shane use them as leverage, although he had probably not anticipated that they would die in the process. Then again, it was equally as possible that Boyd simply hadn't cared.

Shane had relayed the information on to Buchanan but had made a deliberate point of telling him to leave them alone. In the brief time that he had known him, Shane had come to understand a lot about the sort of things that motivated Buchanan, and he had known that the best way to get him to do something was to specifically tell him not to.

Having planted that particular seed of rebellion in Buchanan's mind, he had then further nurtured it by giving him the most pointless assignment he could think of that night by posting him to cover the back of the jailhouse. He had anticipated that Buchanan would get bored and frustrated, and that he would abandon his post and go after Ben's parents, partly to spite Shane but mostly for his own amusement.

What had happened next was not something that Shane had

really given much thought to. He had just wanted Ben lured into the open so that he could be shot. Setting Buchanan onto his parents had simply been the easiest way of doing it.

Looking back, it was easy for Shane to see why he had done it. He had been afraid. He could have killed Fletcher the first day he arrived in town, shot Ben and Alan Grant and killed Hunte there and then instead of drawing things out the way he had. But he had been afraid to. After what had happened at the Babson ranch, he had not wanted to shoot anyone unless he was completely sure that his motives were his own and, perhaps because he had respect for him, he had decided from the start that he would not kill Fletcher, no matter what happened.

And so he had decided to wage a psychological war against the old lawman instead, to crush his spirit and wear him down. And he had started by killing Ben and Ben's family.

Shane blinked the thoughts away. On the crossroads, the invigilators were busy cleaning up the mess that Chastity's rampage had caused. Shane watched as they dragged the dead into a side street. They showed no particular regard for their own fallen brethren, treating them instead with the same casual disrespect that they showed the dead contestants. Their weapons were collected, their bodies stripped of anything valuable that could be kept or bartered.

The invigilators were hard men. They had few friends amongst each other so far as Shane could see, and viewed one another mostly as rivals, albeit rivals who were presently bound in a common cause. It was interesting because it suggested a weakness that Shane could take advantage of.

He had been thinking and he had decided that if he was going to escape from Covenant he would take Chastity with him.

He was a realistic man. He did not believe in atonement.

Nothing that he did with the rest of his life could bring back the men and women he had killed, or undo the pain and suffering that he had helped to propagate. But he could not respect himself if he fled from this town and left a six year old child to suffer a fate that he himself was afraid to meet. Whatever else he had done wrong in his life, there was still a level past which he would not allow himself to sink.

The problem was *how* would he escape?

He dared not try shooting his way out. His soul was already balancing on a razor's edge. He was halfway to Hell already and there was no way of telling how many more killings it would take to push him the rest of the way, straight into the arms of the Fastest Guns. It could be one; it could be twenty. He dared not take a chance.

But equally he did not think that he could slip past the invigilators without some kind of a fight. What he needed was an accomplice, somebody who could do his killing for him. He thought about it and, yes, there was someone who fitted his requirements. But it would all depend on who won the next match.

The crossroads shimmered beneath a watery heat haze as Vendetta and Nanache went out to face each other. The heat was sweltering and Vendetta's long brown hair clung to the back of her neck in sweaty strands. Nanache's blue army jacket was open and he played with his necklace of bones as he walked. He stroked specific joints between his finger and thumb and sang to them in a quiet voice. Shane got the impression that he was calling on their individual talents, readying himself for the battle to come.

Vendetta showed no sign of being intimidated by her opponent's alleged supernatural powers. She stared at him, uncaring and unemotional, her expression fixed in a look of grim determination. Nanache held up his hand to her and mimed cutting off one of his fingers and putting it in his pocket. He pointed at her and laughed.

The invigilators regarded them both warily. Chastity's rampage had left them twitchy and there was a palpable sense of hostility in the air.

Vendetta shook her head and rotated her shoulders, loosening them up. She adopted a three-quarters side-on stance with her left leg leading. Nanache stood square. They both glanced over at the Grande as Nathaniel rose to his feet. He held up his hands for silence.

The two contestants readied themselves.

And Nathaniel called it.

Vendetta snatched her gun from the holster, drawing and firing in rapid succession and blood splattered the dirt behind Nanache as her first shot ripped through his shoulder, snapping the tendons from his bones. He gritted his teeth against the pain, but no amount of bravery could get his ruined arm to work. He grabbed his revolver with his left hand but it cost him valuable seconds, leaving Vendetta with ample time to fire again.

She raised her gun in a two-handed grip and took aim, firing two shots that caught him in the chest and neck, and Nanache dropped to his knees. Left-handed, he fired, but the shot was the product of a delayed impulse running through his nerves. He was dead already and the shot hit the ground just six paces in front of him, kicking up a plume of dirt.

He hit the ground facedown, his last breath rattling in his throat. Vendetta regarded him coldly for a moment, her gun trained on him in case he so much as twitched, but when he did not move she turned away and holstered her revolver.

Shane watched her as she strode from the crossroads. With

skills like hers, she was exactly the sort of person he needed if he was to get out of town. All he had to do was convince her to help him, and he already had an idea about how that could be achieved.

He began to think about how he would make his move.

In the topmost room of the Grande, Madison was also thinking of escape.

Covenant had turned into something of a disappointment for her. She had come expecting to meet some of the best gunfighters in the world but so far all of the really big names had failed to show and the best she'd seen were Shane Ennis and Castor Buchanan, both of whom were way past their prime. To make matters worse, Kip was dead and she had realised too late that she had really cared for him and now, in addition to being lonely, she was trapped in a ghost town in the middle of nowhere, forced to be a baby-sitter for the youngest mass-murderer in American history.

She had never felt so low.

Her one consolation was that at least Chastity had stopped screaming now. She sat quietly on the other side of the room, perched on the edge of a wicker peacock chair like a discarded ventriloquist's dummy, legs hanging in empty space just a couple of inches off the floor.

It had taken ages for Madison to get her to calm down. Madison had never had any younger sisters growing up and she had no idea how you were supposed to deal with an upset child. She had begun by making a few ineffectual shushy noises, but when that had met with no immediate success she had fled to the opposite corner of the room and sat there with her hands over her ears, hoping that the child would settle down in her own time. Several minutes later it had become apparent that was not going to happen, and so she had plucked up the courage to go back to her and had bundled her into her arms and rocked and soothed her and, in time, she had coaxed her into being quiet. It had taken a lot out of her and Madison had finished up on the window seat, staring out through a circular window at the crossroads below, nursing her sore head and feeling sorry for herself.

The window gave her an excellent view of the gunfight between Vendetta and Nanache, and Madison was pleased to see Vendetta win. She took heart that the only other woman in town was kicking ass.

Women gunfighters were few and far between and seldom ever amounted to much. Inspired by the dime novels that she had used to read with her daddy when she was a little girl, Madison had once dreamed that she might become one, but the sad truth was that she had never turned out to be very good with a gun. Her talents lay elsewhere. She had been born with the double blessing of beauty and the wits to use it. The way she looked, the way she dressed and the way she spoke were her weapons of choice, and with them she could get a man to give her almost anything she wanted.

Nathaniel had caught her off guard earlier. If she hadn't drunk so much the night before she would have had the sense to keep out of his way, but that was largely irrelevant now. The mistake had been made and now she was suffering for it. What she had to do now was find a way to turn things about and make the situation work to her advantage before she wound up like Bethan.

And that meant establishing some kind of hold over Nathaniel.

In another time and another place, she might have willingly done so anyway. Nathaniel was not bad looking. He was older than her but that was not a problem; she liked a little experience in a man. He was powerful and he had money; two things that Madison craved. But right here, right now, it was just too soon after Kip and she would not have even contemplated it if she didn't think her survival depended on it. Nathaniel was an abusive bastard and he was dangerous. If Madison wanted to survive him and get out of Covenant intact then she needed him to be nice to her. Already, she had come up with a plan.

She prepared by smartening herself up. She twisted her hair into a couple of plaits to bring it under control and washed her face, cleaning away the marks where her tears had caused her eye make-up to run. With two hours before the next match was fought, she thought it likely that Nathaniel would want to come and check on her and Chastity and, sure enough, she heard the door bang downstairs as he entered the building. She quickly hurried over to position herself at Chastity's side, grabbing one of the child's dolls so that it looked as if she had been playing with her.

The key turned in the lock and Nathaniel entered. His expression softened when he saw Madison and Chastity together. 'I had half expected to have to send my men to look for you,' he admitted.

Madison gave him a shy smile and, ignoring his comment, said in a soft voice: 'She's quietened down now.'

'I can see that.'

Nathaniel pushed her gently to one side and knelt before the girl. He examined her face and neck and rolled up her sleeves to take a look at her arms. While he did so, Whisperer came into the room and positioned himself at the doorway, blocking Madison's escape. Nathaniel was looking for bruises, she realised, and was offended that he would think that she could be such a bitch. 'I didn't hit her,' she protested.

'No. You didn't.' Nathaniel said, finishing his examination.

'And it would be a very bad idea if you ever did.'

'I wouldn't do anything like that.' Madison said indignantly.

Nathaniel said nothing but rose to his feet again and took her by the arm. He steered her over to the one of the two beds in the room and bade her sit next to him. 'What is your name?' he asked.

Madison told him.

'Yes, I remember now. Kutcher introduced you. My condolences, by the way. But nonetheless, the fact remains that he should not have brought you here. The Fastest Guns do not appreciate spectators.'

'I understand that now, sir, and I'm sorry. I would never have come if I'd known I wouldn't be welcome.'

Nathaniel patted her on the thigh. 'It's no matter. If you hadn't come then Bethan's death would have greatly inconvenienced me. As it stands, you will make an adequate replacement. Don't you agree, Whisperer?'

'She certainly has her qualities,' the tall man replied.

'That she most certainly does.' Nathaniel said, giving Madison's chest a lustful glance. 'Although in future you will be well advised to bear them with a degree of modesty more befitting that of a lady. Kutcher may have tolerated you dressing like a whore but you're mine now, and I will have you conduct yourself properly. If you do not have anything less brazen of your own to wear then I suggest you see if anything of Bethan's will fit you. Lord knows she won't be needing it any more.'

He went on to explain what Madison's duties would be. Chastity was incapable of performing even the most basic functions without supervision. Madison would have to dress, feed and wash her. It was a lot more than Madison would have liked. *But put up with it for now*, she told herself. *The time will come later when you can ditch the little bitch and get the fuck out of here, but for now you have to toe the line.*

'What is it that's wrong with her?' she said out loud.

'She is special,' Nathaniel explained. 'Chastity cannot think for herself, not like you and I do at any rate.'

'But she's so good with a gun.'

Nathaniel smiled but didn't offer any sort of an explanation. He cupped Madison's chin in his palm. 'You will find that I can be a very kind master,' he told her. 'Attend well to Chastity and you will be rewarded. Money, jewellery; I can give you whatever you desire. But do anything to hurt Chastity, or disobey me just once, and I will give you to Buchanan. And believe me, you wouldn't want that.'

Madison knew all about Buchanan's reputation. 'I won't let you down,' she said quietly, biting her tongue to try and make the words sound sincere. In two days time, the tournament would come to an end and she was sure that the Fastest Guns would show up to watch the final bout. *We'll see how tough you are when I've got one of them to protect me*, she thought to herself.

She had lost Kip and that was bad, but it was time to revert back to her original plan and bag herself a real gunfighter.

CHAPTER THIRTEEN

The dawn rose over Wainsford, drawing back the shadows and exposing the effect of the night's crimes. Like a rape victim, the town was huddled in shock. Its population cowered, hiding behind closed doors while the men who had brought death and terror to its streets held the jailhouse in siege.

Shane stepped from his hotel and took a deep breath before he crossed the road. He had scarcely slept at all that night for he had been plagued by nightmares in which his guns had compelled him to kill over and over again; but to look at him, nobody would ever have known. He kept his inner turmoil locked away behind the implacable surface of his cold, dark eyes and he walked with the confident knowledge that, one way or another, the siege would end today.

The bounty hunters had gathered in a semi-circle around the jailhouse. They parted so that Shane could pass, then closed in again behind him. He felt the presence of their guns at his back, scratching at his paranoia, but again he was confident. Buchanan would not let any other man kill him. He wanted to prove himself against Shane too badly to let anybody else spoil the opportunity and so, for the time being, Shane could trust him like a brother.

The jailhouse stood quiet and subdued before him. The morning sun revealed the bullet marks in the door and the dark stain of Ben's blood from the night before. Shane was aware that his approach was being watched from inside and that the men in there were more likely to shoot him than listen to what he had to say but he forced himself to appear calm. To show any kind of fear right now would invite disaster.

'Are you in there Fletcher?'

The sound of a gun being cocked was his first reply.

'Back off Ennis! I ought to shoot you where you stand.'

'I'm not here to fight with you, Fletcher. I came here to make peace.'

'Why you cocksucking son-of-a-whore! You come here and say you'll talk peace with me after what you murderers did last night?'

'What happened last night was unfortunate, Fletcher. I didn't have any part in it.'

'Bullshit!'

'You have my word.' Shane called back. He did not consider that he was lying as such, since it was true that he had not actually taken part in any of the night's misdoings despite his role in engineering them. 'There are a lot of dangerous men in town. I took care of a few of them yesterday. I guess I must have missed some.'

'Why don't you stick that gun of yours in your own mouth and pull the trigger? You won't miss then!'

'You're wasting your time Fletcher. Your federal marshal's aren't coming. Federal marshals have got better things to do than get themselves killed over a piece of shit like Hunte. There's nobody here wants him alive but you. Give it up. If you come out now I swear to you that no one else will get hurt.'

Fletcher couldn't find the words to express what he thought of Shane's offer and silence was his only answer. Shane sighed. 'You're not the marshal any more, Fletcher. I am. I got a signed writ here and I've been authorised to remove you from my jailhouse with force if necessary. I'd rather it didn't come to that.'

'You can take that writ and stick it, Ennis!' Fletcher shouted back. 'That piece of paper's not worth spit, nor the men who signed it.'

Shane was beginning to lose his patience. The idea of just killing Fletcher was getting to feel more and more welcome all the time. His hand stroked the butt of his revolver.

He was distracted by a sudden shout from one of his men. The bounty hunter was pointing and Shane turned to see a band of five horsemen riding into town. They were wild-looking men. Three of them looked like half-blooded Apaches. They had long black hair that was decorated with feathers and beads. The other two were white, and one of them – the leader judging by his bearing – was built like a blacksmith's anvil.

Shane swore beneath his breath. He recognised the leader. Though he had never met him face to face, he knew of his reputation. He was an Arizona Ranger, which meant that Shane's predictions had been wrong.

The federal marshals had come to town and they had come looking for a fight.

Shane watched a dust devil spiral along the road before dissipating in a shower of grit. He did not feel the breeze that had caused it. The air was heavy and stale and hot as the fires of Hell.

'I need a drink,' he said.

'So?' Buchanan asked.

144

'So are you going to get one for me?'

'Do I look like your fucking servant?'

Shane gave him a shrug and turned away. 'It's not like you're good for anything else.' It was the sort of comment that Buchanan could not simply let pass.

'What the fuck is that supposed to mean?' he said, loud enough that the closest invigilators turned to see what was happening.

'Nothing.' Shane replied. 'Except that I notice you aren't competing in this tournament.'

He had expected this to be a sore point with Buchanan, and he was right. 'I could compete if I wanted too.'

'But you're not.'

'If you've got something to say to me then you say it.' Buchanan said, rising to his feet.

Shane rose also and turned to face him directly. They were more or less of an equal height, although Buchanan was bulkier by about twenty pounds of muscle. The invigilators started to get nervous. Rifles were cocked and, irritably, Buchanan waved them to stand down.

'Say it!' he said fiercely.

But Shane turned away, saying nothing.

'Yeah, I thought as much.' Buchanan said, his voice rancorous with disgust. 'Get out of my sight! You don't fucking deserve to compete in this tournament, you yellow-bellied bastard.'

Shane slouched away, looking defeated. A few of the invigilators jeered at him but their taunts fell on deaf ears. Shane didn't care what they thought of him. Refusing to carry a gun for the last six years, he had walked away from more fights than he could remember. It didn't mean anything to him. And besides, he had gotten precisely the response from Buchanan that he had wanted.

He crossed the street to O'Malley's without anybody trying to stop him and pushed through the butterfly-wing doors. It was dark inside but the shade offered no relief from the suffocating midday heat. Shane had not come to O'Malley's to drink, however. He walked straight through the building and out the back door, making good his escape before Buchanan thought of sending someone to keep an eye on him.

The back door led into an empty side street and Shane felt a thrill of excitement. He had been kept a prisoner of somebody or other for the past month or so and this new-found freedom felt good, even if he knew it was only temporary. It gave him a taste for more and deepened his resolve to escape from Covenant before the tournament ended.

Keeping to the backstreets and alleys, he avoided the patrolling invigilators and made his way by a circuitous route to the bathhouse, approaching it from the rear. His way was barred by a tall wooden fence but it was in poor enough condition that he was able to pull down a few planks to make a gap big enough for him to step through.

As he had suspected, the bathhouse was in use.

He had gambled on this. Yesterday when Vendetta had returned to the street to watch Nanache and Daniel Blaine fight, he had noticed that her hair had been wet. He had thought little of it at the time, but the observation had been noted and he had recalled it just a few minutes ago and recognised its significance.

Vendetta was a hard woman but she did not revel in the act of killing the way most of the other contestants did. It was distasteful to her, something that she saved for when it was necessary, and Shane suspected that she had had a bath yesterday after killing Luke Ferris, maybe to try and wash away the guilt from her soul.

That being the case, it made sense that she would do it again

146

having just killed Nanache. Shane approached the open doorway.

The tread of his footsteps must have given him away, for he heard the familiar sound of a gun being cocked as he drew near. Vendetta called out from within. 'That's far enough.'

Deliberately ignoring her, Shane walked cautiously inside. He found her sitting in one of the tubs, her legs drawn up against her chest to preserve her modesty.

Shane motioned to the gun she was holding. 'You know, if you shoot me with that thing you'll be breaking one of Nathaniel's rules.'

'Get lost.'

'No need to get mad. I only came for a bath. I wasn't expecting to find anyone else here.'

'Well, as you can see, *I'm* here.' Vendetta told him. She let the obvious gender difference hang unspoken between them but Shane chose to ignore it. Sauntering into the room, he took off his hat and waistcoat and set them down on the floor next to the tub beside her. 'It is *hot* today, isn't it?' he said, pointedly ignoring the gun that she kept trained on him.

She let out an irritable sigh. 'Get out, Ennis.'

'Why? I count three tubs. You're only taking up one of them'

'Goddammit!' she swore. 'Shouldn't you be on a leash?'

'Yeah, but I got loose.'

'So go bug somebody else.'

'Maybe I will. After I've had my bath.'

She had left some water on the hearth and Shane emptied it into his chosen tub, then went outside to draw some more. When he returned, Vendetta had evidently resigned herself to the fact that he was not going to leave. She had set her gun down on the floor on the side of her tub furthest away from him and had resumed washing herself, acting as if he wasn't there.

147

Shane mirrored her disinterest, going about the process of warming the water and filling his bath as if he was alone but, out of the corner of his eye, he kept a careful watch on her. Although it had not been his intention to, he found himself looking at her body. She was too hard for any man to call her pretty, but without her clothes on there was no denying that she was a woman, and a woman with a very fine pair of legs, Shane noted. Her wet skin glistened like honey in the golden light.

When his bath was ready, he unselfconsciously stripped off his clothes, climbed into the tub and began to wash. 'I know why you're here,' he said conversationally.

She frowned. 'Is that supposed to impress me?'

Shane did not expect her to want to listen to what he had to say, but the fact that she was naked gave her little choice in the matter. It would take her a good couple of minutes to dry herself and get dressed before she could walk out on him, and that was all the time he needed.

'You're not good enough to win this tournament,' he told her. 'You got lucky yesterday and you barely made it through today. Tomorrow you'll probably go up against Chastity, or me; and you haven't got a chance of beating either of us.'

'I can kill you,' she asserted.

He shrugged half-heartedly. 'It's been a while since I fired properly,' he admitted. 'And I'm not as good as I was so I'll give you the benefit of the doubt. But as for that little girl, I have never seen anyone who could shoot as good as her.'

Just as he had suspected she might, Vendetta got out of the tub and began drying herself. She pretended not to hear him as he continued: 'You entered this tournament to find your husband's murderer but it's not going to do you any good. You won't even see

Brett unless you win, and there's no way that's going to happen.'

'Save it, Ennis. You're not going to scare me off.'

'I'm not trying to.'

She turned her back on him and tugged on her pants.

'You know, it might not matter anyway,' he said. 'Maybe you've figured it out yourself. Nathaniel's not being completely honest with us about this tournament. I don't know what he's up to but he sure as Hell isn't working for the Fastest Guns.'

'They would have killed us all by now if he wasn't.' Vendetta said, putting on her shirt.

'That's true. Which makes me wonder what they're up to.'

Vendetta finished getting dressed. She strapped on her gun belt and pulled her hair back in a tight ponytail. 'Save it for somebody who gives a shit,' she said.

'If you don't want to believe me . . .' Shane began, but he was talking to himself; she had already gone.

He settled back in the tub and closed his eyes to think. The hook had been baited. Now all he had to do was wait to see if she bit.

The gunfight could scarcely have been called as much.

The federal marshals galloped into Wainsford in close order and fought as a team, whereas Shane's bounty hunters had no love for one another and fought as individuals. They were cut down and Shane stood in the midst of them, not moving, not even reaching for his gun. Bullets whipped past him, heading in both directions, some passing so close that they snatched at his hair. It took all of his self-control not to draw his guns, for he knew that the safest way to survive this battle was not to make a target of himself. He stood in the eye of the tornado, ignored and unscathed.

It was all over in less than forty-five seconds. Castor Buchanan and two others turned tail and fled and three of the marshals went after them. The other two shot the bounty hunters who remained and then advanced on Shane.

Their leader stared down at him from his saddle, his brow creased in an ugly frown. 'Draw your gun, mister.'

Shane met his gaze and held it. He was impressed when the man refused to look away. 'I'm not going to do that, sir.'

'Why you no good yellow bastard, I said draw your goddamn gun!'

Shane did not so much as move. 'If you'll let me prove it, I have a writ in my pocket that will identify me as the marshal of this town.'

'And I suppose those boys were your deputies?'

'That's right.'

'And you were just standing around outside of your own jailhouse, enjoying the morning air?'

It was at that point that Fletcher called out from inside. 'Don't listen to a word that man says. He's Shane Ennis.'

'I know who he is. Do you know who I am, Ennis?'

'I do.' Shane replied. The big marshal was Lyndon Appleby. He was captain of the special Desert Cadre of the Arizona Rangers and he was just as famous as Shane was notorious; a real American legend.

He had been born in Ohio in 1839 and at the age of eight he had run away from home to seek his fortune. He had drifted for a time as a vagrant and a scavenger before winding up at a horse ranch at the age of twelve, where he had learned to break wild mustangs. He had fought for the Union when war broke out and had distinguished himself at Racoon Ford but, so the story went, Appleby had grown weary of fighting his countrymen and, after the war, he had set out to the Frontier. There he had befriended the Apache and had lived with them for several years, learning their ways and sharing his knowledge with them in return. He had tried to settle a peace with them but had failed and, despairing of the wars that had broken out, he had walked away. He had become a bounty hunter, a sheriff and eventually a recluse, vanishing into the desert after the death of his wife, in which isolation he had remained until the US Cavalry had sent men to find him in 1879, to enlist him in the search for the renegade Apache chief, Victorio.

Appleby had made a permanent return to civilisation after that. He had joined the Arizona Rangers and founded the elite Desert Cadre: a group of men trained in the arts of desert tracking and survival. He was a man whose stature befitted his legend. He was tall and muscular; so strong that it was said he had once killed a man with a single punch to the head. His massive fists were too big to handle normal guns and so, in place of revolvers, he carried two sawn-off shotguns that had been specially modified to suit him. They were devastating weapons. Not as accurate or precise as a revolver, they relied on deadly brute force, spitting out a blast of 12-gauge buckshot that was instant death to anyone within fifteen yards. Appleby didn't even need to aim; the spread of buckshot was so wide as it left the muzzle that he had only to point the gun in vaguely the right direction to guarantee a kill and, because of this, he was greatly feared and respected even by professional gunfighters like Shane. Appleby was no gunslinger but he was able to stand on equal footing with all but the best.

Shane had never met him face-to-face before, although he had often wondered what would happen if he did. He could feel his gun scratching at the back of his mind, begging him to draw the bastard down, but he resisted the temptation. Appleby already had his gun drawn and he was just itching for a reason to kill Shane.

'You boys turned up in just the nick of time.' Fletcher called out.

'Telegram said you had Hunte.' Appleby replied.

'I do.'

Appleby dismounted and approached the jailhouse while his sergeant relieved Shane of his weapons and shackled his hands behind his back. 'You're making a mistake.' Shane said.

'That's right, I am.' Appleby agreed, not looking back at him. 'I'm letting you live.'

He left Shane under guard while he went inside the jailhouse. Shane waited. A crowd began to form in the street, given courage by the marshals' arrival, and several came forward to tell the sergeant what had happened over the last few days. Shane noticed several of the town councilmen in the crowd but they deliberately avoided his eyes. Already they were disavowing any involvement with him.

After a short while, the marshals who had gone after Buchanan returned. They had killed one of the men who had tried to escape with him, but Buchanan had gotten away.

'Looks like your partner's run off without you,' one of the men remarked, but Shane kept his silence.

Eventually, Appleby came back from the jailhouse and began issuing curt orders. The councilman, Boyd, stepped forward to speak with him but Appleby dismissed him briskly. He was not planning on staying in Wainsford long. There were other bounty hunters closing in and he wanted to be gone before they could catch up with him.

Shane was taken into the jailhouse. The building was dark because of the barricades that covered the windows and it smelled ripe. Four men had spent the last few days holed-up inside, eating out of cans and shitting in a bucket, but that was only the start of the smell. The worst of it emanated from the body rolled up in a blanket in one corner of the room.

Fletcher glared at Shane accusingly. 'You're gonna answer for what you've done,' he promised.

'I told you, I didn't have anything to do with that.'

'Bullshit.'

'I'd hang him if I were you.' Appleby said. 'Or put a bullet in his head.'

'No. He'll stand trial.' Fletcher said adamantly. 'I'll take him to Rosebridge.'

'You'd be better off taking him to New Mexico.' Appleby suggested. 'There's a ten-thousand dollar reward for him there and he'll hang for sure.'

They dragged Shane over to the cell. It was a metal cage set against the back wall and in it was the man that Shane had come to kill.

Benedict Hunte was a disappointingly ordinary-looking man in his mid-forties. He had thin brown hair and small eyes that darted nervously. He recoiled as Alan Grant unlocked the cell. 'Please, you can't take me back,' he cried. 'They'll kill me.'

'They'll kill you just as happily if you stay here.' Appleby said. There was not a trace of sympathy in his voice. He grabbed Hunte by the scruff of the neck and hauled him out of the cell.

'But I don't want to go!' Hunte protested.

He might as well have argued with an earthquake or a tornado. Like both of them, Lyndon Appleby was a force of nature. Nothing on earth could stop him once he set himself in motion.

Shane was thrown into the cell in Hunte's place and the door was slammed shut on him. Alan Grant took great pleasure in turning the key. 'You'll regret this,' Shane promised.

'You'll regret it more,' Grant said in return and he walked away, leaving Shane helpless to do anything but watch as Benedict Hunte was taken outside and put on a horse. Once again, he had slipped through Shane's fingers, but it was not over yet.

Shane was still alive and he still had a plan to fall back on.

CHAPTER FOURTEEN

It was almost noon – the Gunfighter's Hour – when Shane left the bathhouse. The sun was high and the water that he had spilled from the pump when drawing for his bath had already dried out, leaving the ground as parched there as anywhere else.

Covenant was a dead town and there were no birds to lend it a voice, not even a scavenger like a crow or a buzzard, and the sound of Shane's boots as they crunched on the dry earth seemed magnified as he walked towards the gap he had made in the fence. He was just nearing it when he heard footsteps approaching from down the alley that led onto West Street. There was not enough time for him to duck through the fence and so he stayed his ground, reasoning that if the invigilators had found him it was better to go quietly than risk getting shot by running away.

As it was, the footsteps did not belong to any invigilators; they belonged to Madison, Whisperer and Chastity.

'Bathhouse is popular this afternoon.' Shane said, tipping his hat to the lady. She gave him a smile in return.

Whisperer frowned at him. 'Should you be here alone?'

He was stood too close to the hole in the fence for Whisperer not to put two and two together and Shane didn't see the point in trying to play the innocent. 'Would I be here if I shouldn't?' he replied.

The tall man smiled thinly. Shane could read most men pretty well, but Whisperer was an enigma to him. Just being around him made him feel distinctly uncomfortable and he was reminded of what Nanache had told him the night before: *He is devil-kind, like you are.*

Whisperer was no gunslinger but there were plenty other demons in Hell besides the Fastest Guns, and Shane wondered what he was halfway to becoming.

'It's not often that we see you come out from Nathaniel's shadow.' Shane observed. 'Is it that he doesn't trust you? Or do you not trust him?'

Whisperer gave a secretive smile. 'Buchanan was right,' he said. 'Killing Devlin *has* changed your attitude. When I first met you Mister Ennis, you could scarcely be encouraged to say a word. Now here you are trying to bait me. Perhaps there's hope for you yet.'

'That depends on what you're hoping for.'

'No Mister Ennis, I think it depends more on what you're hoping to achieve here.'

Shane went quiet. He didn't like it when other people read his character better than he read theirs. He backed up to the hole in the fence. 'Nice talking to you,' he said curtly.

'The pleasure was all mine.' Whisperer replied.

Shane ducked through the fence and hurried away. He did not feel good about running away from Whisperer but every instinct in his gut told him to get away from him. The man scared him in a way that nobody else ever did and he was left asking himself questions that he was sure he didn't want answered.

He didn't think that Whisperer would send anybody after him but, just to be on the safe side, he circled around a bit, cutting through alleyways and old buildings and doubling back to confuse his tracks. He still had the better part of an hour left before the next fight began and he wanted to use it to get the lay of the town.

He wandered by a roundabout route to the edge of town. He didn't want to risk getting shot at by any of Nathaniel's guards, so he stopped before he reached the last building and looked out into the wasteland.

There was no cover, not as far as the eye could see. The barren landscape was totally flat with only sparse patches of a limp and withered grass to break the monotony. The ground had been baked solid and was cracked in places like broken crockery, but nowhere was there a trench or a hole deep enough to hide in. The perimeter guards had absolute mastery of the land out to as far as they could shoot, which, Shane was willing to judge, had to be a good thousand yards or more.

Simply put, there was no way he could sneak out of town. The only way to get past the perimeter guards would be to punch a hole straight through them and Shane figured he would need to kill at least three of them to make a big enough gap to ride through. That was a lot of killing and he would definitely need help.

Not heartened by this discovery, he headed back towards the heart of town and walked among the streets, getting a feel for Covenant's layout. It was simple enough. The whole town had sprung up around the central crossroads and, viewed from above, was arranged something like a rough oval with a cross etched through it. Townhouses near the centre; stockyards, warehouses and scattered buildings around the edges.

It was a dead place. A festering death trap that should have crumbled into the desert years ago. And yet everywhere Shane went he could feel the town watching him with eyes that hadn't been human in at least six years.

After twenty minutes or so, he found the feeling oppressive and turned back towards the crossroads, to where Buchanan would be waiting for him.

He was most of the way back when he passed a house that caught his attention. Its door was missing, leaving a great, dark wound in its face, from which a foul stench poured into the street. The dirt outside showed signs of heavy traffic: boot prints and a series of trails that indicated something had been dragged inside, but not out again. Shane got to thinking that he had found where the invigilators had been bringing the dead.

Curious, he covered his mouth and nose with his sleeve and ventured inside. The windows had all been boarded up, leaving only narrow gaps through which the sunlight pierced in thin, slanting beams. The smell of the place was overwhelming and Shane felt his gorge rise in disgust, making him choke.

Everywhere he looked, the room was crawling with swollen, black flies. They swarmed like shadows, deepening the gloom, and rose up in angry clouds around him the deeper he ventured. He felt them crawling through his hair and in his ears, scratching at his nose and eyes. He swatted them away, fighting to control a mounting sense of revulsion.

He found the dead piled against the back wall. By the light of the open doorway behind him, he saw that they were bloated with gases, their skin blistered and weeping pale fluids. Like everything else in the room, they were covered in the swarming flies, which made them even more unrecognisable.

Shane stared at them for some time, aware that something was not quite right about them but not sure what it was. He counted them.

He counted them again.

Back out in the street, he brushed the flies from his face and shook out his coat, retreating to a safe distance so that he could gulp at the air and try and rid himself of the stench. He felt sick and waited for the nausea to pass before reflecting on his discovery.

Eight contestants had died in the first round and so far two more had died in the second. Add to that the two invigilators that Chastity had shot, plus Bethan, and that came to thirteen dead in total.

And yet Shane had only counted twelve bodies.

Somebody was missing.

It was almost one o'clock by the time Shane returned to the courthouse. Buchanan was waiting for him, their argument seemingly forgotten. 'What have you been up to?' he asked.

'I went for a walk.' Shane replied. 'I stopped by your mortuary. Did you know you've got a body missing?'

'What?' Buchanan was genuinely surprised, which confirmed Shane's belief that the invigilators had not simply put the missing body somewhere else.

'I guess that means you didn't,' he said, deliberately antagonizing Buchanan and watching as his temper rose to the surface again. This time Buchanan held it in check. 'That bastard!' he hissed, talking under his breath. 'That fucking lying bastard.'

Shane did not press him to find out who he was talking about; he believed he had a pretty good idea already. He settled down on the edge of the boardwalk and put his back to Buchanan and looked for the two contestants who were due to fight next.

Tom Freeman and Evan Drager were evenly matched. They were both professional gunfighters and they both had more than eighty kills to their name. Drager stood by the side of the road with his head bowed in prayer. His injured leg didn't seem to have affected him badly.

Freeman sat on the steps outside O'Malley's and smoked what could very easily be his last cigar. Vendetta leaned against the wall a few yards distant from him but she looked away when Shane glanced at her and pretended that she hadn't seen him. Shane was not discouraged. He could be patient, for a while at least.

Drager finished his prayers and Freeman finished his cigar and threw the stub away. They both looked at each other, nodded, and walked onto the crossroads. All around them, the invigilators took to their stations and rifles were cocked. Nathaniel moved to stand at the edge of the porch and checked his watch.

It was time.

Both gunfighters readied themselves. If Tom Freeman was in any way intimidated by his opponent's reputation as the new messiah of the Fastest Guns, he did not show it. His right hand was poised just a couple of inches above the grip of his heavy revolver.

Drager's face looked rapturous. His eyes were distant but his body was tense. Shane recognised that look. It was the expression of a man as he surrendered his will to the gun at his hip. He envied Drager that he could be so comfortable with it.

Nathaniel made the call. 'Draw,' he shouted, and the first shot was fired almost immediately.

Evan Drager staggered to one side. He had been shot in the chest. The injury threw his own shot wild and it grazed across

Freeman's cheek instead of opening his skull. Freeman dropped instinctively to one knee, making himself a smaller target, and sank two more bullets into Drager's torso. His body jack-knifed, twitching violently as each bullet tore through flesh and bone and offal, to burst out of him again in a bloody splatter of ejected tissue, but still he refused to go down. He howled in pain and rage, spitting blood from his lips; and fanned off a lethal hail of bullets that drove Freeman to roll aside.

Freeman came up shooting. With his gun held in a two-handed grip, he grouped two shots within an inch of each other, shattering Drager's lower jaw into fragments that speared deep into his throat and head. A horrible, gurgling scream rose up as Drager wheeled to the ground, blood gushing from his mouth. He caught himself on his hands and knees and, though clearly beyond any chance of survival, he doggedly extended his gun in Freeman's direction and fired his last shot.

Startled, Freeman whipped to the side and the bullet clipped him across the ribs; a glancing blow. He retaliated with a shot that tore off the back of Drager's head and, finally, Drager slumped to the ground.

He still twitched and mumbled despite the severity of his injuries and Freeman walked over to him and kicked his gun from his hand. He reloaded his revolver and fired three more shots into Drager's head to finish him.

Silence returned to the crossroads and Tom Freeman lit a cigar.

Shane couldn't say that he was surprised. Drager had been a true initiate of the Fastest Guns but, like a lot of men, he had never quite lived up to his own reputation.

'Well, that about proves me right.' Buchanan said smugly.

Shane met his eyes. 'Being dead never stopped Priestley,' he reminded him and watched with enjoyment as the smirk abruptly vanished from Buchanan's face. Buchanan looked thoughtful then swore vehemently to himself. He called over the nearest invigilator. 'Watch him!' he ordered, and stomped off across the boardwalk.

Shane watched him hurry over to where three invigilators had gathered around Evan Drager's corpse. Apparently they were locked in some kind of argument concerning whether or not he had been any kind of a messiah. Buchanan clouted one of them around the back of the head to disillusion him and then the four of them left the street, dragging Evan's body with them. Shane waited until they were out of sight before getting to his feet.

His watchdog shot him a warning glance. 'Sit down,' he said.

Shane ignored him

The man drew his revolver. 'Sit down,' he repeated, and cocked back the hammer to prove that he meant it.

Shane gave him an insolent look. 'We both know you're not going to shoot me,' he said. 'Tell Buchanan that I've gone for a drink.' He stepped past him and crossed the street to O'Malley's, not once looking back. His watchdog made no further attempt to stop him.

Once inside, Shane walked straight to the bar and snatched a bottle of whisky off the counter. He found himself a seat against the back wall, a place where he could watch the doorway, and poured himself a drink. It was not long before he had company.

Vendetta came in casually and pretended not to see him. She walked to the counter, cracked open a bottle of beer and took a long, slow swig from it while she wrestled with her indecision. Shane decided to make it easy for her: 'I went for a walk after you left,' he said. 'Want to know what I found?'

She pretended not to hear him.

'Thirteen people have died since this tournament began. One of them has gone missing.'

That got her attention. 'Who?' she asked.

'I don't know, but it seems to me that the Fastest Guns have found someone they like already.'

He kicked out the chair opposite him and leaned back, inviting her to join him. She wandered over but did not sit, preferring to perch on the edge of the table opposite. She frowned at him. 'What is it you want, Ennis?'

'I want out of here.'

'Running away again?'

'As fast as I can. Which is what you'd do if you had any sense.'

Vendetta gave a cruel laugh. 'So that's what this is about. You want me to help you. Well forget it, Ennis. You deserve everything that's coming to you.'

She got up off the table and walked away toward the butterfly-wing doors. The sun shining through the open doorway made her silhouette shine like a halo.

'You're right.' Shane called after her. 'Maybe I do deserve what's coming to me, but you don't. I know about what happened to your husband. I know how badly you want revenge.'

'Everybody knows that story, Ennis. You don't know shit!'

'I know that if you go through with this the way you've been planning, you'll end up like I am. Is that what your husband would have wanted for you?'

Vendetta rounded on him sharply and threw her half-empty bottle of beer. Her aim was true and Shane snatched it out of the air just a split second before it hit him. 'Don't you dare presume to know what he would have wanted!' she raged. 'He was a good man.

A murderer like you would never understand him.'

Calmly, Shane wiped a few spots of beer from his face and set the bottle down on the table. 'Can you remember what it was like when you didn't feel angry at something or other?' he asked. 'That's how it gets to you at first, through the anger and the hatred. It tightens like a fist around your heart. That's what's going to happen to you if you see this tournament through to the end.'

Vendetta was a smart woman. She was not completely blind to what she was getting herself into. She turned away, not letting him see the tears in her eyes. 'It's the only way,' she said stubbornly. 'He who lives by the Gun cannot die by the Gun.'

Shane recognised the words she was quoting. He had heard them before. It was said that a member of the Fastest Guns could not by killed by a bullet unless it was fired by another member of the Fastest Guns. Some people took it as a figure of speech, but Shane knew that it had never been meant that way.

'There are other ways to kill Brett besides shooting him,' he said.

Vendetta swore. 'You'd have to be a fool to even try.'

'I'm halfway to becoming one of them. Don't you think that gives me some insight into what they are? Help me get out of this town and I'll help you kill Brett.'

'I don't need your help, Ennis. I didn't even ask for it.'

Shane leaned back in his chair with a sigh. 'You take a bath every time you kill someone like you think it can wash their blood from your soul,' he said. 'Are you really telling me that you can go out onto that crossroads tomorrow and kill Chastity in good conscience, just so you can settle your score with Brett?'

'I thought you said I couldn't beat her.'

'Just suppose for a moment that I'm wrong.'

It was clearly something that had been preying on Vendetta's mind. She looked down at the ground and was silent for a long while. 'I guess we'll find out,' she said.

'What if I said I wanted to get Chastity out of here as well?'

She gave him a hard look. 'Why would you do a thing like that?'

'Same reason you would; she doesn't deserve this.'

'I wouldn't have thought that would bother a man like you.'

'Me neither,' he agreed. 'But it does. Will you help me?'

Vendetta thought about it. Moments later, she gave him her answer.

'I think we have a problem.' Buchanan said.

The light in Nathaniel's study filtered murkily through the dirt-encrusted windows. Buchanan was feeling agitated and he rubbed the stump of his right hand as he explained about the missing body. Nathaniel's reaction when he was done made his temper boil.

'Are you sure it wasn't just placed somewhere else?'

'What are you shitting me? Where else would we fucking put it?'

'I don't like your tone, Buchanan.'

Normally the warning in Nathaniel's voice would have been enough to make Buchanan back down, but not this time. 'Fuck you!' he snapped. 'They've taken one of the dead. That means they're here, they're awake. They're not dormant. They're not sleeping. They're not in some fucking distant dimension. They're right fucking here!' He rounded savagely to face Whisperer. 'Why the fuck didn't you know that?'

Whisperer said nothing but a coolness crept into his gaze that made the hairs at the back of Buchanan's neck stand on end. Feeling threatened, his temper got worse.

Nathaniel wisely intervened before they could come to blows. 'The occult is not an exact science, Buchanan. We are dealing with the unknown here. You know as well as any off us that conditions in the field can never be accurately predicted; we need to be flexible and adapt our strategies accordingly. It is to be expected that we should occasionally encounter situations for which we were unprepared. Do you know who it is that's gone missing?'

Buchanan forced himself to calm down. Whisperer was still looking at him in that cool, oddly-knowing way and he turned away to avoid seeing it. 'It was Penn,' he said.

'Who?'

'One of your men. A sharpshooter. He came with me when I went to collect Shane from that bounty hunter. Your little girl shot him this morning.'

'And he was good enough?'

'Must have been.' Buchanan replied sulkily. 'I thought I didn't like him. Now I know why.'

Nathaniel sucked thoughtfully on his cigar. 'This is not bad news,' he decided. 'The Fastest Guns are here ahead of schedule but all they have done is steal scraps from our plate. We should perform the second incantation and close the seals.'

Whisperer disagreed. 'We should wait a while longer. If we close the seals now we risk catching only a few of them, and the others will wreak havoc to free them.'

'Fuck it!' Buchanan snapped. 'Close the goddamn seals, whatever that means. I don't trust this lying fuck.'

Nathaniel sighed. He was growing weary of Buchanan's increasing instability. 'That's enough!' he snapped. 'I trust Whisperer implicitly, Buchanan, and that is an end of it! If there is anybody here whose conduct does concern me then it is you! I understand that you have been allowing Ennis to walk around unattended.'

'So what if I have?' Buchanan replied insolently.

'So, I do not think that's wise, do you? Ennis is *devil-kind*. He may yet discover what we're doing here.'

Buchanan laughed at that, his mercurial temper changing as suddenly as it had blown up. 'I'd be very surprised if he didn't work it out eventually,' he said. 'He's sharp about things like that. He was the one who found out that Penn was missing.'

'He was what?' Nathaniel said. 'That's exactly the sort of thing I'm talking about.'

'Relax. I'm keeping an eye on Shane. He's not doing anything that can hurt us.'

'I hardly think you can be sure of that.'

Buchanan stalked over to the window and used his fingers to scrape a clear patch in the thick coating of dust. 'Let me tell you something about Shane,' he said. 'They say that the Devil can know your sins just by looking at you. Well, Shane can do that too. Stick anyone to watch him too closely and before long Shane'll be jerking their strings like a puppet. He'll be out of this town in no time. No, if you want to keep Shane on a leash then you've got to give him just enough slack to keep him from getting too creative.'

He peered out the window at O'Malley's across the street.

'Shane likes to play games,' he said. 'What he hasn't learned yet is that I can play them too.'

CHAPTER FIFTEEN

Ben's funeral was conducted on the same day that Lyndon Appleby and his marshals took Hunte away. The whole town turned out for a ceremony that included both Ben and his parents, each buried side-by-side in a dusty plot outside of town. Shane attended, his hands shackled in front of him and Fletcher and Grant solemn figures on either side. Behind them at the lych gate their horses were saddled with bags for the long journey to the state line. Fletcher was through with Wainsford and he and Grant were taking Shane with them. They were taking Appleby's advice and turning him in for the ten-thousand dollar reward.

The ceremony was a bitter, guilt-ridden thing. The preacher choked on his words and the townsfolk stood with their heads bowed. When it was over, Fletcher raised his head from prayer and wiped his eyes. Solemnly, he turned and pushed Shane toward the horses. Townsfolk who had gathered to pay their respects offered Fletcher their condolences as he passed and scowled at Shane. A few spat at him but most still feared him too much to give him any cause to remember them. It was as they drew near to the lych gate that the lawyer, Boyd, pushed his way free of the crowd and caught Fletcher by the sleeve.

'August, wait! Let's not be hasty. I know what happened was unpleasant but we had to think of the town.'

'The only thing you were thinking of was the money in your pocket.' Fletcher tugged his arm free and marched on toward the horses, pushing Shane ahead of him. 'How much did they offer you?'

'I'm sure I don't know what you mean.' Boyd insisted.

Fletcher shook his head, unable to voice his disgust. They reached the horses and Alan Grant kept Shane covered with a shotgun while he mounted.

'I know you feel that you've been betrayed.' Boyd said.

'Could that be because I *was* betrayed?' Fletcher replied testily.

Boyd pretended not to have heard him. 'We want you to stay on as marshal. We'll increase your wages to forty dollars a month.'

Fletcher mounted his horse.

'Fifty then.' Boyd said urgently. 'Think of the town, August. They'll be no one here to keep the law.'

Fletcher slowly turned to face him. 'I don't think you understand me, Boyd. I don't fucking care.' He raised his voice so that everyone could hear. 'This whole town can go to Hell,' he said, and steered his horse away.

Boyd still wouldn't accept defeat. 'Sixty then!' he called after them, but his words fell on deaf ears. Fletcher wasn't coming back.

They rode until nightfall. Fletcher was in a dark mood and said nothing the whole journey. His silence worked well for Shane, who rode with his head bowed and his brain working, a constant eye on Grant.

Up until now, Alan Grant had been a name without a face. Shane had heard him spoken of about town and had learned that he had been marshal before Fletcher. His wife had left him suddenly for a travelling salesman and, heartbroken, Grant had turned to the bottle and damn near drank himself to death. Fletcher had hauled him off the street and gotten him to sober up, but that had only been a couple of weeks ago and Grant's cravings still gnawed at him with obvious ill-effect. He sweated profusely, was clumsy and lethargic and sometimes looked on the verge of passing out. His hands shook so badly that Shane didn't think he could shoot further than ten or fifteen yards and have any guarantee of hitting what he aimed at. His friendship with Fletcher seemed about the only thing that kept him going and, in Shane's eyes, that dependence made him exploitable.

Shane drew up his plans as they rode and plotted the means by which he would win back his freedom and finish the job he was being paid to perform.

That night, as they sat around the campfire in silence, Shane turned to Fletcher and spoke. 'Hanging me won't change what happened last night.'

His words were met with a long and uncomfortable pause before Fletcher answered. 'You're right, it won't. But it's no less than you deserve.'

'What happened to Ben and his parent's was none of my doing.'

'And you really expect me to believe that?'

Shane shrugged. 'I could have killed you the day we met if that was how I wanted it.'

Fletcher had nothing to say to that. He knew that there was some measure of truth to Shane's words. Wood popped on the fire, throwing up sparks that spiralled into the air on an updraft.

'Buchanan's the man you want; not me.' Shane said.

'You could have stopped him.' Fletcher said accusingly.

'Maybe. But I didn't.' Shane spoke plainly. His own feelings on the subject were irrelevant; all that mattered was Fletcher's reaction. 'You can curse me all you want but my not stopping him doesn't change the fact that it was him that done it, not me. If you want justice, Fletcher, you've got the wrong man.'

'I'll settle things with Buchanan in due course.'

Shane let out a short, cruel laugh. 'I doubt that. You're a stubborn old mule Fletcher, but you're no match for a man like Buchanan. He'd do you like he did Ben's parents.' He paused for a moment to let the thought sink in. '*I* could kill him though,' he added softly, almost as an afterthought.

Shane and Fletcher's eyes met over the campfire and the two men stared at each other, neither saying a word. There was a reckoning in that meeting of eyes, a judgement that passed between them, and Grant did not like that it happened at all. 'Don't listen to him, August. He's just trying to save his worthless hide.'

'Buchanan and I have unfinished business to resolve.' Shane said. 'I want him dead just as much as you do.'

Grant told him to shut up, but Shane ignored him. 'If you want justice for what happened to Ben; I'm the only man who can give it to you,' he said.

'I said: shut up!' Grant drew his revolver and pointed it at Shane. The way his hands were shaking it wouldn't take much for him to accidentally pull the trigger. Shane forced himself to look unafraid and turned to Fletcher.

Fletcher sighed. 'Put the gun away, Alan.'

Grant reluctantly did as he was told, muttering to himself as he fumbled the revolver back into its holster. Fletcher got slowly to his feet and took a few steps away from the fire, his eyes distant as he stared across the plains. 'I'm almost tempted to take you up on your offer,' he told Shane. 'But I'm not that stupid. I know if I set you loose you'll only go after Hunte.'

'So what if I do?' Shane asked. 'Buchanan'll be going after him too. I find one; the other won't be far away.'

'I won't let you kill him, Ennis.'

'No, I don't suppose you will.' Shane said, his voice quiet. 'But I guess we'll cross that bridge when we come to it.'

Fletcher turned to face him but said nothing at all. Standing there like that, Shane thought he looked older than he had seemed before, older, broken and frail. As little as a few days ago, August Fletcher would never have agreed to what Shane was offering him.

But a lot had happened since then.

The butterfly-wing doors of O'Malley's swung on rusty hinges and Buchanan strode in, his boots clumping heavily on the wooden floor. He had Shane's gun belt draped over his arm and held the lacquered mahogany box that contained Shane's gun.

'Is it that time already?' Shane asked.

'Like you haven't been counting the seconds.' Buchanan replied. He tossed the gun belt onto Shane's table. 'You been drinking alone?' The way he said it made Shane think he knew that Vendetta had joined him.

'I might as well have been,' he replied, and slowly got to his feet. He fastened the gun belt around his waist. 'Did you sort out that problem with the missing body?'

'It's dealt with.' The lie was transparent. Sensing a little friction, Shane decided to press further.

'What did Nathaniel have to say about it?' he asked.

'That's none of your business.'

'It must be hard not being able to sense them for yourself any more. Are you sure than Nathaniel's telling you the whole story?'

He could see by the look on Buchanan's face that it was something that had been preying on his mind. 'That'll all change soon,' he said adamantly, and he set the mahogany box down on the table. Shane felt a shiver of excitement run through his body and immediately resented it, but he longed to open the box and hold his gun again. It awoke a yearning in him that reached deep into his soul, exerting such a power over his emotions that it filled him with self-disgust.

'What can *you* sense, Shane?' Buchanan asked. He tried to make it sound tough but even growling his words like a dog couldn't hide the raw need with which he wanted to hear the answer, like a lovelorn teenager asking to know a beautiful girl's name.

Shane cleared his thoughts and opened up his senses. He shivered as he felt a scratching at his soul. It was as if somebody had reached a spectral hand into his body and was plucking at his nerves as at the strings of a guitar. The melody they played was sweet but the song was vile.

'They're all around us,' he said. 'Watching. Waiting.'

He shook his head and broke the spell. His skin felt clammy but whether from disgust or desire Shane could not properly be sure. He tried to blank the thoughts from his mind as he reached for the box.

The gun inside had been cleaned and oiled again since yesterday and was as smooth and beautiful as a woman's naked thigh. Its smell rose up at him, sultry like musk and poisonously seductive. Shane took it into his hands and holstered it quickly, not wanting to hold onto it for any longer than he had to, not right now while his senses were still raw from the Fastest Guns' touch. He did not trust himself.

The room seemed too close. He walked to the door and stepped out onto the boardwalk, breathing deeply to ground himself. Outside, the invigilators were taking up their positions in preparation for the impending match. Their black hats and three-quarter length coats made them look like crows as they hunched on the rooftops and noisily cocked their rifles.

Buchanan walked him to his spot on the crossroads. It was hot and dusty and Shane tasted grit in the back of his throat. Buchanan gave him his bullet. 'Try not to waste it now,' he said.

The significance of his comment did not occur to Shane until after Buchanan had gone and he turned to face his opponent. In this round he had been matched against Valentino Rodrigues, the man who had fought against the Gentleman.

Given a fully-loaded gun Shane would have felt confident that he could defeat him without difficulty, but only having a single bullet changed things. It left him with no margin for error. If he fired and Rodrigues ducked out of the way again, Shane would not get a second chance to hit him.

His safest option was to sacrifice the initiative and let Rodrigues act first, then try to counteract him before he fired, but that would require perfect timing. Act too quickly and he might waste his one and only shot. Act too slowly and he might never get a chance to fire. Rodrigues knew this as clearly as Shane, and he knew that it gave him a slight advantage. He looked confident as he strutted out onto the crossroads and found his mark. He stretched his fingers like a pianist about to play a concerto and tipped his hat to Shane and smiled charmingly. Shane nodded in return. It was the last gesture by which he acknowledged the man as a fellow human being. From that moment onwards, Shane stopped seeing him as a person and viewed him solely as a threat, a danger that had to be eliminated. It drained the colours from his point of view and heightened his senses to a sharper level.

By objectifying him, Shane transformed Rodrigues into a set of probabilities. The set of his stance dictated the possible ways in which he could jump, dive or roll before firing his shot. Rodrigues was ambidextrous and wore a gun on each hip. Against the Gentleman he had drawn with his right hand and fired a .44-40 Remington but, equally, he could draw with his left and use his .38 revolver instead; a gun that was lighter and fractionally quicker to draw.

Shane looked into his eyes and tried to read his intentions, but Rodrigues had a solid poker face and he kept his thoughts locked up tight. His eyes revealed nothing.

The boardwalk creaked under Nathaniel's boots as he moved to the edge of the porch and made ready to give the call.

In only a few more seconds, the fight would begin. Shane twitched his fingers impatiently and tried to predict what Rodrigues would do. He believed he had it narrowed down to about three possibilities. It was just a matter of picking the right one.

He heard the silence around them deepen as the crowd tensed and figured that had to mean that Nathaniel had opened his mouth to speak.

There was no more time to think. No more time to doubt.

'Draw!' Nathaniel shouted, and Shane drew and fired.

The shot hit Rodrigues high in the throat and burst through his larynx. It struck against the pillar of his spine and shattered the vertebrae a couple of inches beneath the base of his skull, cutting the spinal cord. His body went limp on the spot and he coiled up on the ground like a piece of rope, having never even had a chance to move.

Shane had guessed his intentions just a split second before Nathaniel had called the shot. It seemed obvious now in hindsight. Gambling that Shane would expect him to dodge one way or another, Rodrigues had counted on him to hesitate and had gone straight for the draw. He had stood right where he was and just reached for his gun, hoping to move fast enough that he could catch Shane while he was still waiting to see which way he'd move.

It was clever and it had nearly worked. Shane felt proud of how easily he had out-witted Rodrigues and beaten him to the draw. His blood surged powerfully through his veins and he felt strong, invincible even! The sense of power that raced through him was electrifying. He wished that the gun had more bullets. Then he would show everyone in Covenant what a force he was to be reckoned with.

He forced himself to put the gun back in its holster. His hand moved slowly, reluctantly. The sensation of having the gun in his hand lingered afterwards like the memory of a parting kiss. It left him yearning for more and it frightened him; the feeling was so overpoweringly intense.

Not trusting himself, he unbuckled the gun belt and tossed it to Buchanan.

'You made that look easy.' Buchanan said.

It had been easy, Shane thought. *Too easy.* Valentino Rodrigues had been good enough to make a name for himself as a professional gunfighter, and he had been good enough to kill the Gentleman, albeit with some simple trickery, but he had never been good enough to meet the Fastest Guns' high standards.

Shane thought it about later in the quiet solitude of his cell. He was now absolutely certain that the tournament was Nathaniel's idea and that it was being held without the Fastest Guns' involvement. If that were the case though, he could not understand why they were allowing it to continue.

It did not make sense. The Fastest Guns were notoriously intolerant of allowing anybody into Covenant. Shane could only assume that Nathaniel had to be controlling them in some way or, at the very least, that he had found some way of appeasing them, and that was a thought that made him nervous. He did not know a great deal about the occult but what he did know came from having seen it face-to-face. Shane had looked into the very mouth of Hell and no man came away from an experience like that without learning something of the black arts. If Nathaniel had appeased the Fastest Guns then it was probably the opening step toward some sort of bargaining ritual, but Shane could not understand what Nathaniel expected to receive from such a deal. More importantly, how did he expect to get away with it? The Fastest Guns were not some ancient line of demons that could be held in service. They were newly-formed and so young that Hell's aristocracy had not yet bothered to even look their way. Such demons could not be bound. Only a fool would dare such a thing.

Shane felt that he was missing something, some vital piece of information that would make sense of it all but whatever it was it eluded him no matter how he tried looking at things. It bothered him that he couldn't work it out and he was still sat in determined contemplation when Buchanan came for him a few hours later.

The meeting at O'Malley's that night was little more than a formality. With only four contestants left alive, everybody knew what the pairings for the semi-final would be. Vendetta was paired against Chastity, leaving Tom Freeman to face Shane. Nathaniel avoided the Gunfighter's Hour again and the first match was set to take place at eleven and the last match to take place at one.

About the only thing that was unexpected was Chastity's

presence at the meeting, accompanied by her new nanny. Madison was dressed like a lady in an ill-fitting dress and quarter-length jacket. Her bodice had a high collar that covered most of her throat and she had piled her hair up in a way that made her look quite respectable. Shane was amazed by the transformation. It seemed as if Nathaniel had successfully tamed her.

The meeting broke up soon after the placings had been read and Buchanan returned Shane to his cell and locked him in. It was getting late and as the darkness settled the town began its eerie night-song, the creaking and groaning of every house and ruin softening gradually into melody. Perhaps lulled by the noise, Shane drifted into a light sleep and his dreams carried him back in time.

They had journeyed north the next morning, changing course to pursue Lyndon Appleby in the hope that by finding him they would find Buchanan. Grant was not happy about it. He dropped back until he and Fletcher were side-by-side, with Shane several metres in front and out of earshot. 'He'll kill us the first chance he gets,' he said.

'More than likely.' Fletcher agreed with him.

'Then why don't we just take him in? He's worth ten-thousand dollars.'

'I don't care about the money; I'm thinking about Ben.'

'Ben's dead, August. And it's that bastard there that killed him.'

'He had a part in it, I'm sure.' Fletcher said. 'But it was Buchanan who killed Ben's folks.'

'He and Shane were working together.' Grant reminded him. 'You can't trust a goddamned word he says.'

'I trust him when he says he'll kill Buchanan. And that's all I need him to do.'

'And what about Hunte?'

'He's Appleby's problem now.' Fletcher said bleakly. 'He don't need our protection any more.'

They picked up the trail at San Alejo. Appleby and his men had passed through town earlier that morning and had been followed soon after by Castor Buchanan and another man who rode with him. Buchanan was likely to be the least of Appleby's worries however. Rumour had it that there were more bounty hunters coming down from the north, at least twenty of them if the town's telegrapher was to be believed.

'They've got every watering hole, ford and mountain pass staked out between here and Sisko,' he told them enthusiastically. 'Ain't no way Appleby's getting by them without a fight.'

Shane disagreed. 'He'll slip past them like a ghost,' he said, and he drew Fletcher's attention to a map on the wall. Between San Alejo and Sisko lay a broad expanse of uncharted desert. 'That's exactly the sort of country Appleby's used to. That's where he'll go. He'll get off the trails and go deep into the wasteland. No one'll find him out there.'

He was surprised to find that there was actually a small measure of comfort in the thought of Appleby getting away from him. Hunte had brought him nothing but trouble and it was tempting to think that all his problems might go away if he simply turned his back on pursuing the man. He quickly squashed the idea. His head was so full of doubts that he was finding it hard enough to think as it was, and he needed to stay focussed if he was going to escape from Fletcher.

Fletcher gave a shrug. 'Then I guess that's where we're heading,' he said, stabbing his finger at the featureless part of the map.

They stocked up on water and provisions and headed out into the desert, ignoring every warning from the locals not to. Fletcher kept Shane's hands locked in cuffs. Shane argued to be set free, but

Fletcher couldn't be swayed.

'You know, when we find Buchanan I won't be much use to you with my hands in chains.' Shane said.

'If we find Buchanan, I'll set you loose. But not until then.'

'And if he catches us by surprise? We'll all be dead before you can set me free.'

'And what about your death makes you think I give a shit?' Fletcher replied harshly.

They rode for two days. Just as Shane had reckoned, Appleby had gone into the deepest, most inhospitable part of the desert, and the going got harder every hour. Scorching heat and the dry, arid land made every drop of water precious.

On the afternoon of the second day out, they stopped at a cool water spring and ran into trouble. A small gang of cattle herders from a ranch nearby had decided that the lure of Hunte's bounty was too strong to resist and had packed in their jobs and gone looking for him. As misfortune had it, they arrived at the spring while Fletcher and Shane were filling their water skins, and Grant did not see them coming until it was too late.

There were four of them: two young men and two seasoned hands in their mid-forties. They must have mistaken them for Appleby's men and spotted the cuffs on Shane's wrists and thought he was Hunte. They started shooting as they rode in.

Shane darted to one side and splashed through the waters of the spring to reach a pile of boulders on the opposite side. The men were armed with revolvers and didn't have much more than a basic level of skill. Their bullets chipped flakes of stone off the boulders as he dived for cover.

Grant let off a blast of his scattergun but failed to hit anybody. The noise it made gave them something to think about though, and they dismounted and moved to take cover.

Shane was cut off from his companions, and unarmed. He wrestled with his cuffs but they were too tight to slip out of and the locks were too strong to break. The cowboys closed in. They divided themselves into two teams. One group kept Grant and Fletcher pinned down while the others moved into position to catch them in a crossfire. One of the young men circled around towards where Shane was hiding. Shane got into a niche among the rocks and waited, listening to the tread of his footsteps as he came nearer. He picked up a rock and tensed himself.

He struck the moment the boy came into sight, uncoiling from the side of the boulder and smashing the rock down hard against the boy's wrist. The boy howled and dropped his revolver. Shane hooked the rock into the side of his jaw and he went down to the ground.

One of the other cowboys saw it happen and came running over. Shane quickly dropped the rock and went to retrieve the revolver but suddenly found his legs pulled out from under him. He had failed to knock the young man unconscious and the boy now wrestled into position on top of him and swung a punch at Shane's face. Shane weathered the blow against his forearm and tried to reach for the gun, but it was too far away. He rolled onto his back and fended off another couple of punches.

He knew that he didn't have much time before the other man arrived. A few more seconds at most. Ducking between the boy's punches, he threw his wrists up around the boy's head and pulled him down close to control him. The boy was stronger than him and fought violently, but Shane wrapped the chain of his cuffs around his neck and used it to choke him, cutting off the flow of blood to his brain. The boy got weaker and slipped unconscious.

Shane heard footsteps closing in. He released the boy and

scrambled for the revolver, reaching it just as the second man came into sight. Shane fired and blew off the top of his head, then turned the gun on the young man and shot him as well.

He felt less vulnerable now that he had a loaded gun in his hands, even if he was still cuffed. He checked the ammunition and reloaded, using spares from the young man's belt. On the other side of the spring, he could see that the last two cowboys were working their way towards Fletcher. There was no sign of Grant and Shane hoped he was dead.

He ducked out from behind the boulders and fired, shooting down one of the two men. Fletcher got the other.

As the last echoes of the fight died down, Fletcher turned towards Shane and saw the gun in his hand. 'Put it down.' Fletcher said sharply, and pointed his gun at him as a warning.

Up until then, Shane had not even considered killing Fletcher but now something flipped inside of him. It was like it had been back at the Babson ranch. He felt as if his mind was pushed aside and that something else seized control of his body.

He fought it. The muscles in his arms bunched with the strain as he tried to keep himself from raising his gun. He felt a surge of conflicting emotions run riot through his skull: hatred, anger, joy and ecstasy. Somehow he was able to centre himself and push it all away. He breathed deeply until he felt in control of himself once more, but it took so much effort that he did not see Grant creep up on him from behind. The butt of Grant's shotgun struck him in the side of the head and Shane sank to his knees before the ground rushed up and punched him.

CHAPTER SIXTEEN

The sound of Covenant's nightly chorus rumbled eerily through the town, its gentle rhythm surging in and out. In and out.

It was like the lapping of waves. The buildings creaked and swayed on their foundations like raptured gospel singers in a choir.

The sound crawled up West Street, past the guttering torches that burned by the side of the road and creaked its way infectiously up the steps of the porch and into the Grande hotel. The ornate chandelier in the lobby swung pendulously as the ceiling flexed slightly, and the sound rumbled on through the building.

In the great dining hall, the creaking of the ceiling prompted a shower of dust that glittered in the candlelight as it fell. Watching it settle around her, Madison felt like a bauble put in a glass dome and shaken up: a pretty thing for someone to admire. She wore her best dress – a special thing that was her own, not Bethan's – and around her throat hung a necklace of pearls that Nathaniel had loaned her for the evening and which she suspected had been given to Bethan to wear on nights like tonight as well.

Nathaniel wore his best suit and had trimmed his moustache

and smoothed back his hair. But for the naked hunger in his eyes, he looked the picture of a perfect gentleman.

Beyond the flickering circle of candlelight, the room lay in shadow and it seemed as if the two of them shared a world that was cut off from the rest of existence. The whole scene felt dreamlike, although that was possibly because Madison was a little bit drunk.

'More wine?' Nathaniel refilled her glass before she could answer, topping it generously to the brim. Chastity had been given into Whisperer's care for the evening, freeing Madison to 'indulge herself,' as Nathaniel had put it. She was well aware of what he had meant by that and was not entirely objectionable to it. Sex was a weapon that she had often used to get what she wanted from a man. She did not make the mistake of confusing it for love.

'I will have to congratulate Whisperer tomorrow on an excellent meal.' Nathaniel said. 'He really has surpassed himself considering the paucity of our supplies.'

Madison wiped her lips with a napkin. 'It reminds me of my mom's cooking,' she said.

Nathaniel let her comment pass without acknowledging it. He had made it clear from the start that he was not interested in anything she had to say; all he wanted was for her to be attentive and beautiful, to laugh at his jokes and agree with his opinions. It suited Madison just fine. Although she had resigned herself to sharing Nathaniel's bed that night, her heart was heavy with thoughts of Kip and she did not feel up to the task of maintaining a lengthy conversation. She just wanted to get the night over with as quickly as possible.

She feigned interest as he launched into another long-winded story about his travels around the world, this time telling her about Africa and the time he had spent with the *boccor* sorcerers of Dahomey. While he spoke, she absent-mindedly played with her wine glass, stroking her fingers up and down its stem in a deliberately suggestive manner. Nathaniel could hardly fail to notice it and, after a few minutes, he decided to cut his story short. 'Who do you think will win the tournament?' he asked her.

'I don't know,' she mused. 'Either Chastity or Shane, I suppose.'

'Pick one.'

From the look in his eyes, Madison guessed that he was testing her. It was clear that he wanted her to pick Chastity and it was almost certainly in her best interests to do so, but a rebellious streak in her nature had not forgotten the way he had struck her earlier and she longed for a bit of revenge. 'Oh, Shane Ennis then,' she said. She kept her expression neutral.

'You are as narrow-minded as Buchanan.' Nathaniel muttered irritably. 'Everybody assumes that Shane is the better fighter because of his reputation, but it is Chastity who will win this tournament, you'll see. I will stake my reputation on it.'

He sounded very sure of himself, and Madison wondered what secrets he knew that made him so confident. There was too much about the tournament – and about Covenant itself – that did not make sense to her. It occurred to her that if she wanted answers Nathaniel was probably the best person to ask. Her curiosity overcame her caution.

'How did Chastity get to be so good?' she asked. 'She doesn't seem to be able to do anything else.'

A cruel smile twitched the corners of his mouth. 'Your boyfriend never explained it to you?'

She shook her head.

'Interesting.' Nathaniel remarked. 'I wonder if he even understood it himself.'

His implied criticism of Kip made Madison bristle, but she

185

resisted the urge to say anything in his defence.

'Allow me to enlighten you.' Nathaniel continued. He drew his bone-handled revolver and held it up for her to see. 'Have you ever fired a gun before?' he asked.

Madison had fired plenty of guns – she liked them almost as much as she liked the men who carried them – but that wasn't what she suspected Nathaniel wanted to hear. She politely shook her head.

'There is a great deal of scientific method to firing a gun properly. Are you familiar with the principles of trigonometry? Let's say that you choose to shoot a man who is standing 20 yards away. You fire your revolver but your aim is off by a couple of degrees. Every yard that the bullet travels carries it a fraction off course. By the time it has travelled 20 yards, those few degrees of error will have caused your shot to deviate far enough to the side that you miss your man completely.

'A tiny deviation like that is all it takes to get you killed. It could be that your hand shakes a little or that you squeeze the trigger too hard and pull the weapon off target. A gunfighter learns to hold his body completely still at the moment he fires. He stands properly with his feet grounded and he grips the revolver in the most efficient manner, and squeezes the trigger with the minimum amount of force required. He even holds his breath when he fires so that the movement off his chest does not confer into his arm and lead his hand to shake.

'To the very best gunfighters, such actions are as natural as breathing. They treat their revolver as if it is a part of their body. Some of them even say that they can hear it sometimes like a voice in the back of their mind, telling them what to do.'

Madison smirked a little, but Nathaniel was being serious. 'It is not as stupid as it sounds,' he said. 'There is a belief that predates

Christianity that all things – whether they are alive like you and I, or inanimate things such as a gun – possess a spirit or a soul. It is a belief that is found in every part of the world and is still practiced in some remote places. There are holy men that can communicate with these spirits. The gunfighter, Nanache, was one of them; as is Whisperer. Chastity has a similar talent. Because she has no will of her own, a spirit may enter her body and control it as if it were its own. When you confronted her this morning, the spirit of the gun she held was controlling her, riding her like a horse as Whisperer would say.'

He returned the gun to its holster. Madison stared at him, unsure what to make of what he had told her. It sounded ridiculous and if she had heard it from someone outside of Covenant she would have dismissed it as a fantasy. But there were things about Covenant that she could not explain and she found its atmosphere unsettling. Given the circumstances, she was prepared to accept that everything Nathaniel told her could easily be the truth.

'To an extent, every man who calls himself a gunfighter invites the spirit of his gun into his body when he shoots.' Nathaniel continued. 'It is how the very best become that way. Guns are not like people; they do not have the freedom to choose what sort of life they will lead. A gun is built solely to kill and that is all it is good for. Such single-mindedness gives it incredible focus and skill.

'Whether deliberately or otherwise, men have let the spirits of the gun ride them during combat for as long as there have been guns to wield. In the beginning, they were quite simple-minded but as guns have developed, so have their spirits. The recent invention of the revolver and the cartridge bullet has made them almost as clever as we are. Buchanan speaks rather poetically of it sometimes and I am given to understand that the union between man and revolver is not unlike the embracing of lovers. There are some men who even go so far as to shoot themselves out of devotion. A gun, you see, doesn't care who it kills just so long as it kills somebody.'

He took a sip of wine to moisten his lips and Madison leaned closer towards him, eager to hear more. 'When Jacob Priestley came to Covenant in 1879, he was inspired to do so by his guns. Priestley put a curse upon this town. What he did here went far beyond a simple massacre. He killed the town. Not simply its people, you understand, but the town itself. That's why you'll not find it on any map these days. Covenant is half way between Hell and Earth.'

The building creaked ominously, making Madison shiver. She fancied that there were eyes in the darkness, watching her as Nathaniel continued to explain:

'Priestley wanted to make his union with the gun permanent. What he did to Covenant prepared the way. Killing himself was the next step. Death is not the end of existence. All those stories you were told in church about Heaven and Hell are not very far from the truth. In Hell, Priestley joined with the spirit of his guns and became a Cordite. Think of it as a kind of demon. The Cordites are the true Fastest Guns. The six men who won the first tournament joined Priestley and became Cordites too. For them it was the ultimate prize.'

Madison recalled how, in his opening speech at the start of the tournament, Nathaniel had said that recognition as one the Fastest Guns was the prize for whoever won. She had not understood what that had meant until now. It explained why there had never been any talk about prize money. The fighters had not come here for money; they had come to prove their worth in the hope of becoming a Cordite. Kip had never known that. It made her wonder how many of the others who had died in the first round had known what they were fighting for; and how many of Nathaniel's invigilators understood it either.

'How does something like this stay secret?' she asked. 'I've heard lots of stories about the Fastest Guns, and they never mentioned anything like this.'

'Would you have believed it if they had?' Nathaniel replied. 'Men hear rumours that they do not believe or that they are too small-minded to comprehend, so they change the story into something they are more comfortable with and the truth becomes distorted. In Britain they call their smokeless powder: cordite. It is not a coincidence. The name is whispered in the minds of every man who ever builds or fires a gun, but the real truth can only be discovered by those who search for it.'

'Like you?' Madison asked him.

He nodded. 'I have been a student of the occult for many years. The Cordites have something that I want and this tournament is how I am paying for it.'

Madison wanted to know but dared not ask him. He reached out and took his hand in hers. 'All of my life I have searched for the secret of eternal life,' he explained. 'It is within the Cordites' power to grant me that gift, with the added advantage that any man who is embraced by them cannot be harmed by bullets. They have a saying: he who lives by the Gun cannot die by the Gun.'

It was a saying that Madison had heard once before, years earlier, but she had never understood its significance. She felt overwhelmed by what he had told her. It was like she had lived her whole life so far in a tiny room and somebody had just opened the door, but she was not sure that she liked what lay outside.

Nathaniel patted her on the hand. 'Everything will be alright,' he told her. 'You are safe so long as you are with me.'

Madison did not believe him for a second but she was grateful for his reassurances all the same. After all that he had told her, the town felt even more sinister than it had before and she was glad that she would not be spending the night alone.

The sound of Covenant's nightly chorus rumbled eerily through the town, its gentle rhythm surging in and out. In and out.

As the noise crept inwards along West Street, it did not travel alone. A furtive shadow crept in its wake, ducking out of sight whenever the patrolling invigilators came near. It moved with infinite care and patience and made its way to the rear of the Grande. There the figure stole to the door and entered the hotel unseen.

The building creaked around her as Vendetta made her way silently along the hallway and into the lobby. She was uncomfortable skulking about like a common thief or assassin but, considering all that she had done in the name of revenge already, it was much too late for her to start having qualms now.

The lobby was dark. A faint moonlight filtered through the tall, dirt encrusted windows and made dancing shadows as it fell through the gently swinging chandelier. Vendetta moved to the foot of the stairway. The balcony above seemed to rear before her, ominously dark.

Sounds drifted down from one of the upstairs rooms: a woman's voice raised in the throes of an exaggerated passion her body did not share.

It was not the only sound that Vendetta heard. From behind her came the creak of a floorboard as a stealthy foot was lowered. Reacting on instinct, she whirled about, hand reaching for her gun.

But she was too late.

A figure stepped from the shadows opposite her. His gun was

already drawn and the grin that exposed his teeth to the murky light told her plainly that he would not hesitate to use it. Vendetta left her gun holstered and slowly raised her hands in the air in an admission of defeat.

'I'm disappointed,' the figure said. 'I'd expected you to put up more of a fight.'

She did not need to hear his voice to know who he was. Castor Buchanan was the only man in Covenant who carried a gun in his left hand. She cursed herself for not having seen him earlier. It was stupid to have come all this way only to have her revenge cut short now. She was so angry with herself that she could not find the words to speak but simply glared at him instead.

'I was wondering when you'd come looking for me,' he said. 'What did he offer you? The secrets of the Cordites, or another way to kill Brett?'

'What's it to you?'

'Just curious. I've known since this morning that Shane was trying to get you to help him, but I couldn't quite figure out what it was he'd offer that would bring you around. For a time I thought he couldn't do it, but then Shane can be a silver-tongued devil when he wants to be. He has a knack of getting inside your head. Trust me, I should know.'

Vendetta did not have the patience to deal with his taunts. 'If you're going to shoot me, do it already.'

Buchanan sighed. 'That's the problem with women. Always jumping to conclusions. I don't want to shoot you darling; not unless you make me. This here gun is purely for my own protection. You did come here to kill me after all.'

He fished the key to Shane's cell out from underneath his shirt and dangled it by its chain for her to see. 'This is what he sent you for, right?'

Vendetta neither confirmed nor denied it.

'If I wanted to kill you,' he continued. 'I'd give you this key and let you take it back to him. He'll kill you as soon as he's finished with you, or hadn't you realised that? Oh no, wait. Of course not, because you wouldn't be here otherwise, now would you?' He laughed harshly at her. 'He's playing you, bitch! He's putting your life on the line to save his own and it's lucky for you that I know what he's like, because I'm willing to look the other way for you, just this once.'

'Why?'

'Why?' he echoed nastily. 'Because it suits me to, that's why. I've got a lot resting on this tournament, darling, and I don't want Shane fucking it up. Now I *could* kill you. I could haul your ass up to Nathaniel and let him know what you and Shane have been planning.'

Vendetta clenched her fist.

'But frankly that would just be a waste of time,' he continued. 'You're fighting Chastity tomorrow and, I'm sorry darling, but that's a death sentence for you for sure.' He took off his hat and laid it against his chest as if mourning the dead. 'Pity really, nice girl like you.'

She curled her lip in anger. 'Fuck you, Buchanan.'

He grinned malevolently and walked over towards her, his gun still pointing at her. Vendetta edged backwards but she had her back to the wall and could not go far. He trapped her, putting his bad hand up on the wall next to her to cut off her escape. He leaned his face in next to hers and sniffed her hair, enjoying the discomfort he caused her.

'Nice,' he whispered. 'You know, tonight's probably your last night on Earth. It'd be a shame if you spent it alone.'

Vendetta looked him straight in the eye. 'Unless you want me to break the other two fingers on that useless stump of a hand, I suggest you get it out of my way,' she snarled.

Buchanan laughed and stepped aside. 'Time of the month, huh?' he said. He gave her a small bow and gestured towards the doorway. It took all of Vendetta's nerve to maintain her composure. She stepped away from the wall and forced herself to walk slowly.

'If I see you around Shane again I'll know you're up to something,' he told her.

'Shane Ennis can rot in Hell,' she replied. She had never much cared for Shane's promises anyway.

It was an hour later that Shane first began to suspect she wasn't coming.

From the window of his cell he had watched Vendetta creep out of the hotel and slink away into the night, but after that there had been nothing, not a sign.

Something had gone wrong.

He returned to his bunk and sat down, wrestling with his disappointment. He cautioned himself to be patient, that perhaps everything was not as bad as it seemed and that the problem was only a temporary setback. But his pessimism would hear none of it.

Haunted with bleak thoughts of failure, his mind turned in on itself and dredged up memories of the past.

He remembered the sun and how it had beaten down on the blasted white landscape, how the rocks had shimmered in the heat as if they were on fire and burned with invisible flames. He remembered the slow pace of his horse, the dry taste of dirt in the back of his mouth and the angry throbbing of his head from the cut where Grant had struck him.

It was the morning after the day when they had fought the

cowboys at the spring. Every step his horse took sent a jarring pain up his spine, igniting fireworks in his skull, and Shane was in a foul temper even without the heat and his thirst to contend with. He stared at Grant with a murderous look in his eyes and Grant stared back at him with equal venom.

Fletcher could hardly have failed to notice the tension between them but he was worn and tired and no longer seemed to care. He rode on ahead, spying out Buchanan's tracks in the dusty land and left them both to their mutual hatred of one another.

They travelled deeper and deeper into the wasteland, well beyond the civilised reaches of that place and far from the known watering holes. Grant suffered the heat worst of all and that night, as they settled down to camp, he tipped his waterskin to his lips and only a small trickle came out. Shane and Fletcher were down to less than a quarter skin each but, on Fletcher's command, they redistributed it equally. Later, as Grant lay sleeping, his face bathed in sweat, Shane approached Fletcher and told him: 'We aren't going to last long if he keeps drinking all our water.'

'If it comes to it I'll give him yours and you can go without.' Fletcher replied unsympathetically.

'We'd be better off without him.'

'Don't even think it, Ennis.'

'Send him back to San Alejo. We don't need him.'

But Fletcher was adamant. 'He stays with us.' And that was the end of the discussion.

They were able to collect some water from the morning dew but it was barely enough to wet their lips with and the following day started hot and thirsty. They walked their horses for most of it, leaving the animals to carry only the weight of their baggage so as to conserve their strength. The day grew hotter as the sun rose higher and nowhere was there any shade or any water.

Grant fell behind. At first he lagged by only ten or twenty paces but later the distance grew until Shane and Fletcher were waiting for him to catch up. As time went on, he got slower and slower and they had to wait longer. Shane again suggested that they abandon him but Fletcher would hear none of it and, when they discovered that Grant had drunk all of his water, he redistributed all they had left again, further depleting their already meagre supply.

They saw buzzards circling in the distance and went to investigate. A man lay facedown in the dirt; the victim of a short and one-sided conflict. Fletcher scared the birds away and bent to examine him. 'Shot,' he pronounced. 'At close range.'

Shane held up a cartridge that he found in the dirt. '.44 Russian,' he said. 'Buchanan did this.'

'It could have been anyone.' Grant scoffed.

'His cartridge; his style.' Shane said. 'He shot him for his water.'

Fletcher had been studying the tracks. 'He's got a couple of hours on us.'

'Then take these cuffs off me. We can be on him by nightfall.'

Fletcher said nothing, merely took the reins of his horse and set off towards the horizon. Shane swore irritably but followed him nonetheless and their journey resumed. In very little time, Grant was lagging behind again. In less than an hour, they had lost sight of him and had to wait.

'We'll never catch up with Buchanan at this rate.' Shane warned him, but Fletcher had become adept at turning a deaf ear to what he said. They waited until Grant caught up and Fletcher asked if he was okay. Grant nodded. At the time, they both assumed that he was keeping his silence out of shame because he knew that he was slowing them down. Twenty minutes later they realised it was worse than that when he collapsed and failed to get back up again.

Fletcher hurried back to where his friend lay barely conscious against some rocks. Shane followed him, but at a more casual pace. He had been patiently waiting for this to happen all day and his only regret was that it had taken so long. By the time he joined them, Fletcher was crouched at Grant's side and trying to force water down his throat. Grant retched and brought it all back up again.

Seeing him arrive, Fletcher held out his hand to Shane expectantly. 'Give me your water!'

'It's all we've got left.'

'Damnit, I don't care! He needs it.'

'Not for much longer he won't.'

Fletcher swore at him and drew his revolver. 'I'm not asking you, Ennis. Now give me your goddamn water.'

Reluctantly, Shane untied his waterskin from his saddle and threw it into Fletcher's waiting hands. He watched as the old man used it to wet his friend's lips, letting him drink it slowly so that he wouldn't bring it up again.

'I hope you like the taste of piss because that's all we'll be drinking from here on.' Shane said.

'We're going back.' Fletcher said.

Shane had expected this. 'What about Ben?' he asked solemnly.

'Ben wouldn't want any of his friends to die for him, not like this. No, this manhunt's over. We're taking Alan back.'

'Ben was no friend of mine.' Shane argued. 'I'm sure he won't care if I die out here. Take these cuffs off and let me go after Buchanan on my own. I'll make better time without you anyway.'

'I'm sure you would.' Fletcher said harshly. 'And when you find Buchanan you'll join up with him again and the two of you will go on after Hunte. I'm no fool, Ennis.'

'Sure you are. Hunte's a dead man whether I kill him or not. Even if he makes it all the way to Washington, somebody there will put a bullet in his heart. You did your bit to help him, Fletcher. Be proud of it, but have the sense to know that it's time you left it alone.'

'I said no, and that's an end of it!' Fletcher snapped. He was getting angry.

Shane gave an insolent shrug. 'Have it your way,' he said, and he stood back and watched while Fletcher tried to lift Grant onto his horse. 'You're making hard work of that,' he said after a while.

'Shut up!'

Fletcher's back was not what it had once been and he was forced to lower Grant back to the ground. While he did so, Shane surreptitiously wandered in the direction of Fletcher's horse, where his guns were stashed in a saddlebag. He had not made it a few steps when the cocking of Fletcher's gun warned him to go no further. 'Get over here where I can see you.' Fletcher warned. 'You can make yourself useful.'

He gestured towards Grant's unconscious figure. Shane groaned in protest but did as he was told. Stooping, he tried several times to lift Grant onto his back but each time he failed. 'This would be a whole lot easier if you took these cuffs off,' he said.

Fletcher considered it. The sun was beating down on them, sweating the water from their bodies and it was only a matter of time before they both ended up like Grant. Against his better judgement, he threw Shane the key to his handcuffs and let him set himself free. Shane bent to lift Grant again, finding the job much easier now but, with his hands free, he no longer had any need to do what Fletcher told him. Grant had a revolver slung from his waist and Shane drew it, turned and had Fletcher in his sights in one fluid movement.

He resisted the temptation to simply pull the trigger. 'Lose your gun, Fletcher. I could have killed you already if I wanted to so don't do anything silly. There's no need to make this worse than it is.'

Fletcher cursed him, ashamed that he been caught out so easily. He reluctantly allowed his gun to fall to the ground and kicked it away at Shane's prompting. Shane walked over to his horse and retrieved his Colts, then stripped their baggage of every gun and cartridge and added them to his own. When he was done he had an extra two revolvers, a Winchester rifle and Grant's twelve bore shotgun. It was a good-sized arsenal, but Shane would have preferred a skin full of water instead.

He turned to Fletcher: 'If you're smart and you don't waste time coming after me, you might make it to Amberville. That way,' he said, pointing. 'It's probably the closest town from here.'

'Don't play games with me,' Fletcher muttered. 'If you're going to shoot me just get it over with.'

Shane shook his head. 'You haven't been listening to me, Fletcher. I don't want to kill you; I never did.' He could not begin to explain how hard he had tried to keep Fletcher alive, or what it meant to him to have done so. Fletcher would not understand. Hell, Shane was not even sure that *he* understood it properly. Nothing was as simple as he liked it to be any more.

He walked over to where Grant lay in the dirt. With no more feeling than if he was putting an old dog out of its misery, Shane pressed the barrel of his gun to Grant's forehead and pulled the trigger.

Fletcher swore at him. 'You'll pay for all this one day, Ennis. Mark my words: your sins'll find you out.'

But Shane was not listening. He seized his horse by the reins and led her away into the wasteland. Somewhere up ahead, Castor Buchanan had water and Shane intended on finding him and making him share it.

The sound of Covenant's nightly chorus rumbled eerily through the town, its gentle rhythm surging in and out. In and out.

Save for where the torch fires burned and smoked, the town lay in absolute darkness. Dawn was still a good many hours away and not even the brush of false light touched the horizon; the sky was smooth and black as a sheet of obsidian.

The invigilators of the night watch were used to feeling uneasy in the town's strange environment. They were familiar with the half-heard sounds, the shadowy figures sometimes glimpsed in the distance, and the ever-present sense that they were being watched; but tonight they felt a new uneasiness disturb them. A presence, unseen by all, moved through the town, cloaked behind a veil of shadows. It moved, wraith-like, from the door of the Grande hotel to a place near the edge of town, where an old clapboard house creaked and groaned in time to the town's sombre melody. The hem of his long coat brushed in the dirt as he crossed the threshold, making a soft noise, like a whisper.

Once inside the house and out of sight from any passing patrol, the figure doffed his veil of shadows, shedding it like a skin. It broke into pieces as it fell away from him, each one temporarily assuming a vaguely humanoid form before it melted properly into the dark with a faint and despairing wail. Whisperer paused to straighten his collar before venturing deeper into the house.

They were waiting for him as he had expected they would be.

Three had deigned to answer his summons and they stood with their backs to the wall: tall, dark, wraith-like figures, their bodies bathed in a nimbus of grey smoke that shone with a gloaming light. Their faces they hid beneath the wide brim of their hats but

Whisperer recognised them by the guns they wore.

He began to speak: 'I am honoured that you agreed–'

'Spare us your flattery.'

The speaker's voice rumbled like distant gunfire.

'We grow tired of your rituals,' the Cordite on the left hissed.

'Why have you called on us again?' the middle one asked.

The three demons smelled bitterly of gunsmoke, dust and decay. With untold years of experience behind him, Whisperer was able to sense the demonic power that radiated from them. It was something raw and untamed. There was nothing certain in dealing with them but still, he had come this far; he could not turn back now.

'It is time we agreed on my fee,' he said.

The one in the middle raised his head slightly, allowing eyes that burned like smouldering coals to be seen beneath the shadow of his hat. He was the most powerful of the three. Jacob Priestley glared at Whisperer and his voice rumbled from the pit of his throat: 'The terms of our agreement have already been made.'

'Not so.' Whisperer argued. 'We have not properly agreed on the number of souls that I will receive for my services.'

Priestley's breath rasped harshly in his dry lungs. 'We agreed to spare you your existence. That is all you have any right to expect. We are not Faustians to be bargained with.'

'It is only that we have no use for the souls you desire that we offer them to you at all,' the Cordite on his left said.

Whisperer had observed during his previous dealings with them how they spoke as if sharing a common mind. Shane Ennis had good reason to fear becoming one of them.

The one on the right offered him a sneer, parched lips stretching back to expose yellowed teeth that were long as fangs. 'We feed you our scraps, soul-monger. Like the dog you are.'

Whisperer kept his expression neutral. A certain degree of taunting was to be expected from the one on the right. He was Michael Brett, the man that Vendetta had come to kill, and his death in the first tournament had done nothing to improve his angry disposition. Besides, the Cordites were young and inexperienced in Hell's ways. They had no idea of the value of what Whisperer was taking from them, had no idea that he was robbing them blind.

'I have brought you Ennis, and the girl, Chastity,' he said. 'I'm sure that by now you have had chance to see that she is worthy of your attention.'

Their silence was proof enough.

'I believe that twenty souls is not an unreasonable finder's fee.' Whisperer said.

Priestley breathed out, expelling a cloud of noxious-smelling grey smoke. 'Name them,' he said.

Whisperer did as he was bade, reciting the list that he had committed to memory. He did not really want them all. The only man whose soul he really wanted out of the deal was Nathaniel's.

When they had first met on the battlefield at James Point in 1861, Nathaniel had been an unremarkable officer, keen to make a name for himself. Whisperer had been stalking the countryside, scavenging among the dead and the wounded for souls to steal. He had struck a deal with Nathaniel. He had offered to turn him into a great man and had promised him money and power and all of his worldly desires. All he had asked for in return was the blood sacrifice of sixty men. To his immense satisfaction, Nathaniel had eagerly agreed.

Whisperer had tutored him patiently since then, encouraging him to delve deeper into the Satanic Arts and uncover more of its mysteries. Every demonic pact, every gift he accepted from the

Underworld, had increased the value of his soul and now Whisperer was ready to trade it in at Hell's markets and make a very good return on his investment.

The other nineteen names were just the icing on the cake, and Whisperer would just as happily dispense with them if it became necessary. The only reason he named them at all was to disguise his interest in Nathaniel. He knew that if the Cordites ever found out how much Nathaniel was worth to him they would try to keep him for themselves.

He almost smiled as he named the last name on his list. 'Castor Buchanan. That is, if you allow it.'

'Buchanan means nothing to us,' the Cordite on the left replied.

'You may take him.' Brett said.

'Thank you. I should like to take five of the ones who are already dead now, as a show of good faith.'

Priestley nodded his assent. He did not even seem interested in trying to haggle, which made Whisperer suspicious that they were plotting to double-cross him. It was not surprising given the Cordites' nature and their inexperience with Hell's laws. He could only hope that they continued to underestimate him long enough for him to get what he wanted and escape.

He kept an even expression as he thanked Priestley for his co-operation. The Cordite's eyes burned into his malevolently. 'Do not seek to cheat us, soul-monger,' he said.

'Or you will learn the limit of our patience,' the one on his left finished.

Whisperer bowed to them obsequiously, his face betraying nothing of his thoughts. One by one, the three Cordites melted back into the shadows. Whisperer left the house and returned to the

Grande in secret.

CHAPTER SEVENTEEN

By dawn, Shane had given up any hope of being sprung from his cell. He did not know what had happened; all he knew was that something had gone wrong. He had not heard any shots in the night, nor any other sound of a commotion that might have indicated Vendetta had been caught, but that silence only made things worse.

He could only conclude that she had forsaken him.

Buchanan arrived with his breakfast shortly after sunrise. He was in a bright mood and walked with a spring in his step that told Shane immediately what must have happened.

'You knew didn't you?' Shane said.

'Knew that it was time for breakfast? Of course I knew, it happens every morning.'

Shane scowled at him but said nothing more. He did not have long to wait before Buchanan's ego got the better of him and forced him to confess. 'I've been on to you from the start,' he boasted. 'You think I'd let you walk away the other day not realising you were up to something? You forget how well I know you Shane.'

'What did you do?'

'I didn't have to do anything. Your girlfriend was only too willing to turn her back on you once I'd told her what sort of gratitude she could expect. She's got a pretty low opinion of you, did you know that?'

'Must have, to have believed your word over mine.'

'Sticks and stones, Shane. Sticks and stones.'

He slid the breakfast tray under the door but Shane had already lost his appetite. The greasy smell of the food made his stomach turn.

'You'll fight Tom Freeman today and then tomorrow you'll fight Chastity. I don't know if you can beat her but I don't think that really matters. Either way, they'll take you.'

'Do you really think you can buy your way back into their favour?' Shane snapped.

'I think I know them better these days than you do.' Buchanan replied.

Shane wondered what he meant by that but Buchanan offered no further clues. He left Shane alone and the solitude closed in around him like an unwelcome embrace. He got to his feet and paced back and forth in his cell, feeling restless. His anger formed a tightness in his chest that he had no way of releasing and, in his helplessness, that anger slowly turned into despair. He ignored the breakfast tray and sat on the edge of his bunk and put his head in his hands. He had pinned his hopes on having escaped by now, but fate had slapped him down.

As the sun rose higher, it pierced through the bars of his window and fell across his face. He blinked against the harshness of the light and the memories that had been lurking behind his eyes came forth to engulf him.

* * *

The sun was his enemy, but it was also his friend.

It occupied a pale and cloudless sky, beneath which the desert shimmered as if the ground was boiling in the heat, evaporating into the scalding air. It was a hundred-and-thirty at least and Shane's throat was so dry that he almost choked on every breath he took.

He had never known a thirst so bad.

The sun was his enemy, cooking him to death in the heat of its radiation, but it was also his friend. For as long as it gave him light to see by he could follow the tracks on the ground and hope to catch up with Buchanan.

Buchanan: who had water and who would share it with him, one way or another.

The trail had led him away from the place where he had abandoned Fletcher and had taken him through a range of dry hills to a basin valley on the opposite side. Once, from his vantage on the hilltops, Shane had seen a figure in the distance, a man leading a horse, but since then he had seen nothing but tracks in the dirt and he knew that he was still behind by a couple of hours.

The sun beat down on him, sapping him of his strength. His horse was too tired to carry him and he abandoned much of the arsenal that he had taken from Fletcher. He threw away all but the most essential supplies, lightening the load to conserve his horse's stamina.

The miles disappeared underfoot. The sun was merciless and the terrain blistering. Shane wondered how Appleby and his men were holding up. A man used up four gallons of water a day in an environment such as this and Appleby had six men. They could not be carrying enough water to last them more than a couple of days each, which meant that they had to be replenishing it from somewhere but, wherever it was, Shane could not find it. He had heard that Appleby had taught his men to recycle the water from their own urine and might have tried it himself if only he was able to piss more than a single, reluctant drop.

He crossed the basin valley and climbed into rocky hills once more. The afternoon was fading rapidly and Shane knew that he had only a few more hours of light left, after which he would be unable to find Buchanan and would probably die. His thirst began to make him weary with delirium and, as his mind faded, so he felt his guns rise into his consciousness.

We can end this pain, they seemed to say. *Join with us.*

'Never,' Shane muttered. He was not fooled by the apparent simplicity of their proposal. The succour they offered was not the helping hand of a friend, but a swift and merciful bullet to the head. He did not want help like that.

You belong to us, he fancied they told him. *Do not deny that it is so.*

'I don't need you,' he said aloud. 'You need me.'

Save your lies for others; you cannot lie to yourself.

Shane snarled wordlessly, unable to answer them this time. He tried to convince himself that it was just his thirst driving him crazy, that the voices of his guns were all in his imagination. In his delirium, he misread the tracks on the ground and unknowingly struck out in the wrong direction.

Weary and dying of thirst, he wandered across the hillside until he came to a steep gully that plunged between sheer rocks down into a sheltered box canyon. The rocks had been warmed all day by the sun and radiated that heat back out into the evening air, making the canyon feel like the inside of an oven.

Natural wariness made Shane draw one of his revolvers. The canyon was filled with an eerie, expectant silence. A fine white sand covered its floor and the tracks of several horses were clearly marked. For the first time, Shane realised his error. Instead of following the tracks towards their source, he had gotten turned around and followed them back along the route they had come from. For reasons that did not immediately make sense to Shane's sun-baked brain, Appleby and his men had diverted from their course to visit this canyon.

Curious to know why, Shane left his horse behind and proceeded deeper into the canyon alone. In the shadow of the cliffside, he spied a narrow crack in the rock into which several footprints could be seen to have entered and returned. Shane got down on his hands and knees and crawled inside. It was dark and he felt his way with his hands, touching smooth, cool rocks. His fingertips came away feeling wet.

There was a source of water near the back of the cave. Shane pressed his lips to the surface of the rock and sucked at it. The taste was brackish but it slaked his thirst and he pulled off his neckerchief and used it to soak up the water, wringing it out into his hat so that he could carry it back to his horse.

The animal was drinking from it when a shot rang out in the narrow space of the canyon. Shane's hat was plucked from his grasp and it fell to the ground, spilling water from a hole that had been shot neatly straight through it.

Shane's gun was drawn and aimed before the hat landed, but he checked his fire when he recognised the man who had shot at him.

Castor Buchanan led his horse down through the gully. 'Well, well, well. Shane Ennis. We do have a nasty habit of running into each other, don't we?'

Sitting in his cell, Shane turned his hat over in his hands. He should have killed Buchanan that day. Instead, he had joined forces with him again and they had carried on the next day in search of Appleby and his men. They had caught up with them too, but that was a battle that Shane was not ready to remember just yet and he turned his thoughts to the present instead.

Despite all the passion with which he had sought to escape from Covenant, he felt strangely resigned to being there now that his hopes of leaving had been dashed. He contemplated fighting Tom Freeman not with the trepidation with which he had faced John Devlin and Valentino Rodrigues, but instead with a cool sense of detachment such as he had known in his prime.

He no longer felt afraid of becoming one of the Fastest Guns and that disturbed him faintly, but not as much as it would have a couple of days ago. His emotions felt drained. His will to resist had been broken.

Shane was all but ready to submit.

He was left in solitude until shortly before eleven when Buchanan came to collect him. He observed the untouched breakfast tray and the change in Shane's demeanour and could not resist the urge to gloat. 'Cheer up,' he said. 'You'll thank me when this is over.'

Shane said nothing. He followed Buchanan out into the sunlight and sat himself down on the edge of the boardwalk in his customary spot. To his irritation, Buchanan chose to sit next to him. 'I don't want to miss the look on your face when your girlfriend dies,' he said.

'She might win.'

Buchanan laughed at him. 'Are you still holding out a hope that she might change her mind and rescue you? Naiveté is something for the young, Shane.'

His words cut Shane's pride, all the more so because they

bore an element of the truth. Across the street, the invigilators were making ready for Chastity's arrival. There were twice as many of them as there had been yesterday and more than half of them were taking up positions where they were partially shielded behind cover. After her performance yesterday, they were taking no chances this time.

Vendetta waited patiently on the opposite side of the road from Shane. She caught him looking at her but turned her head and pretended not to have seen him. Her expression shut him out, giving him no clues as to what had passed between them. He might have been a million miles from her for all she cared; her only thoughts now were to the up-coming match.

It was clear that she was nervous. She checked and re-checked her revolver, her holster, her boots. She got up and paced a few steps before walking back to where she had started and sitting down again, only to rise a few seconds later. There was nobody in Covenant who expected her to win this fight and Shane suspected that she entertained no illusions either. He did not pity her. She had made her choices and now she would face the consequences.

All eyes turned as the door of the Grande opened and Nathaniel emerged, leading Chastity by the hand. The little girl moved woodenly, eyes vacant, tripping as she was led across the porch. Her new nanny, followed by Whisperer, came out after her and took up position at the side of the porch. Madison had fixed her hair up fancy with a few tight curls mixed among her black and blond tresses and Buchanan whistled to himself in approval.

'She's a finer bit of pussy than Bethan, that's for sure. And a real screamer,' he added, nudging Shane in the ribs. 'You can see why Nathaniel's kept her.'

She had a healthy glow about her this morning, Shane noted.

Her cheeks looked rosy and her manner was similar to how it had been when Kip had been alive. *Money and power*, Shane decided, *could end any sorrow.*

He watched as Nathaniel walked Chastity onto the crossroads and set her at her mark. Vendetta joined them, going to her position like a convict walking to the gallows. Her lips were set in a hard, thin line, her eyes fixed cold. Mary Elizabeth Becker had died already that morning and all that was left was Vendetta, sworn to her revenge. She marked out her place on the ground, kicking at the dirt with her toes.

She nodded to Nathaniel to tell him she was ready.

'Girl's got nerve.' Buchanan said. 'Three-to-one she doesn't even clear the leather.'

Shane thought they were generous odds but he kept his silence. He waited, feeling the tension as Nathaniel drew Chastity's pocket revolver and loaded it with a single bullet. He did it plainly and in the open so that his invigilators could see it happen. Then he snapped the loading gate closed and inserted the gun into Chastity's holster. She gave no sign of even noticing he was there.

Nathaniel hurried to the side of the road.

He had barely gone three steps when Vendetta reached for her gun. The shot rang out loud and clear.

It caught everyone by surprise. Nobody had expected Vendetta to cheat. She stood shakily on legs that trembled, her eyes fixed on her opponent in stunned amazement as smoke poured from the barrel of Chastity's gun.

Even Buchanan was shocked. 'Fucking hell,' he breathed.

Vendetta's hand had scarcely reached the grip of her revolver when Chastity had fired. The shot had caught her in the forehead and Vendetta blinked as a line of blood ran down into the corner of her eye. She dropped to her knees then slumped forward into the dirt.

Fearing that the invigilators would jump to the wrong conclusions, Nathaniel ran to Chastity's side and held his hands up in the air to signal that they should all stand down. He looked from Chastity to Vendetta and back again and, as his eyes came to rest on her a second time, the girl's face turned red and she began to scream.

She had realised that her gun was empty.

Her scream was a howl of frustrated rage and she erupted into a tantrum. Flinging the gun to the ground, she stamped her feet and snatched great handfuls of hair from her scalp. Nathaniel grabbed her to stop her from hurting herself and weathered her kicks and punches while he shouted for Madison to come and take her from him.

Watching from the relative calm of the sidelines, Shane made a quiet observation. 'She's gotten quicker,' he said.

'Ain't she just.' Buchanan agreed. 'Nathaniel was right. She might afford you some competition yet.'

Madison had arrived with one of the invigilators and together they carried Chastity away to the hotel. A party of invigilators came out to drag off Vendetta's body.

'I was never that quick.' Shane said heavily.

'That's not how I remember it.'

They said nothing for a moment then: 'Get me my gun,' Shane said. 'Don't load it, just give it to me.'

'Why?'

'Because I need to practice.'

CHAPTER EIGHTEEN

Benedict Hunte had become the most wanted man in America. Word of his bounty had spread far and wide, tempting bounty hunters and opportunists from every neighbouring state to come look for him. The situation had gotten out of hand and the men who had initially put the price on his head stopped offering individual bounties and joined together to offer the sum of fifty-thousand dollars to whoever brought them his head.

It was enough money that the more-organised groups banded together. They eliminated the small-time competition and made allegiances with the other large groups. They co-ordinated with one another and scoured the desert with systematic patrols, slowly gathering the net tighter until Appleby was cornered.

It was the morning of May tenth when the first shots rang out. Appleby had tried to creep past them in the early hours before dawn. His men had crept ahead in pairs and quietly assassinated the sentries that barred his path, but one man had managed to fire off a shot in warning before his throat had been slit and the sound had travelled far enough to alert the others. Within two hours, every bounty hunter in the region was closing in like sharks drawn to a feeding frenzy and, right through the thick of them, Shane and Buchanan rode like Death's servants.

As individuals they were two of the most feared gunfighters alive. As a team, they were unstoppable. Men fell on either side of them, bleeding, screaming, and thrashing their last. The crack of gunfire became so constant that it became as much a feature of the desert as the rays of the morning sun and the blistering, pitiless heat.

It was a day of bloody mayhem.

They followed Appleby by the trail of corpses he left in his wake. He fought across nine miles and killed nearly thirty men before he arrived at the canyons of Spinster's Peak. It was there that he did the unexpected and stood his ground.

Shane and Buchanan reined in and watched from a distance as the first group of bounty hunters tried to storm the canyon he and his men had sought refuge in. Its walls were steep-sided and his men were dug-in behind rocks, the horses sheltered out of sight and Hunte nowhere to be seen. The bounty hunters were cut down like an autumn harvest.

Buchanan whistled in admiration of the slaughter. 'Looks like they're jammed in there tighter than a fist up a virgin's arsehole,' he said. 'You think we can get in behind them?'

'Wait.' Shane told him.

And so they waited. Several more gangs of bounty hunters assaulted the canyon and were driven back. The bodies of the dead were left strewn among the boulders, becoming like barriers to anyone who mounted another assault. Before long, the bounty hunters drew back and began scouting for other ways of getting to their prey. Somebody must have succeeded because shots soon rang out from deeper inside the canyon, out of sight of where Shane and

Buchanan waited.

'Do you want to tell me what we're killing time out here for?' Buchanan said testily.

Shane gave him a cold smile. 'Did you never see a prairie dog lead a snake down one hole and then run out of another?'

'What the fuck are you talking about?'

Shane did not answer him but rode down towards the mouth of the canyon. There was fierce fighting going on somewhere deep inside, but it was far enough in that it did not involve them. He hobbled his horse and entered the canyon on foot. Despite some abrasive words, Buchanan followed his lead.

'We're missing all the fun,' he complained.

The canyon was a slaughter yard of dead men and dead horses. Streams of blood trickled between the rocks and the smell of it mixed with the odour of faeces, where the dead men's bowels had voided themselves. Shane stooped beside one man and relieved him of his revolver, checked it and slid it into his belt. He stole a second gun from another man.

'Come on!' Buchanan whined. 'This is bullshit. And it stinks!'

Ignoring him, Shane chose a place among the dead and lay down on his back. He positioned himself facing into the canyon, towards the distant sound of fighting. Buchanan made a noise of disgust but understood his line of thinking. He found himself a spot of his own on the opposite side of the canyon and lay down among the dead. There were so many corpses surrounding them that it was impossible to tell that they were not dead as well.

Shane waited. He blotted the smell from his mind and lapsed into a concentrated state of awareness, listening to the sounds of battle that echoed off the mountain walls. Flies, drawn to the dead, made little distinction between him and the bodies he lay amongst and crawled across his face to investigate his eyes, mouth and nose. After a while, he stopped brushing them away and lay still.

He listened to the noises that echoed from further down the canyon. There were now several firefights going on and Shane guessed that the bounty hunters were fighting each other. The alliance they had formed was dissolving now that their quarry had been found. He wondered if Appleby was even involved in the fighting any more, or if he had slipped away in the confusion and doubled-back as Shane suspected he might.

Shane waited patiently. It was not long before he heard the sound of hoof beats thundering down the canyon towards him. He readied himself, cocking the two revolvers that he held but keeping them by his sides, imitating the dead.

Appleby and his men rounded a bend further up and slowed their pace as they neared the mouth of the canyon. They were forced to dismount in order to lead their horses across the treacherously scattered mounds of dead bodies. Shane waited until they were right beside him before he sprang the trap. His guns claimed the life of the man nearest to him and felled two horses in quick order, spreading chaos among the survivors. Simultaneously, Buchanan rose up on the other side of the canyon, trapping Appleby's men in a crossfire. Horses reared and men shouted. Blood was spilled.

Shane rose to his feet and struck out, using the barrel of one of his revolvers to break a man's jaw. He shot him with the other gun as he fell, then shot him again with the first to make certain, all the while pressing forward into the heart of the fray. Hunte was his target but, before he could reach him, the man-legend that was Lyndon Appleby stepped into his path. A fist like a sledgehammer struck Shane across the side of the head and he was flung to the ground. He was dazed but responded by rolling and kicking Appleby's rifle from his hands. He scrambled instantly to his feet and drew another of his revolvers at the same time that Appleby reached for his formidable sawn-off shotgun. Less than five feet separated them and, at such close range, a blast from Appleby's gun could not miss.

Shane had but a moment to think on this before his instincts took control. He fired straight from the hip, fanning the hammer with the flat of his hand. Appleby's ribs cracked and the bullets tore through his heart and lungs and broke his shoulder blade on the way out. He dropped his gun and sank to his knees but still stubbornly reached for his second gun with his left hand. Shane emptied his remaining shots into Appleby's head, tossed the revolver aside and turned to find that Benedict Hunte had taken advantage of his protector's sacrifice to mount his horse and gallop back into the canyon. He had slipped through Shane's fingers too many times already for Shane to have him escape again. Shane seized Appleby's horse by the reins and leapt into the saddle. The horse reared, trying to buck him off, but Shane held on and raked back his spurs. He left Buchanan behind to face the rest of Appleby's men alone and galloped away in pursuit of Hunte.

The horse was spirited and fought Shane's control, but it was fast and Hunte did not have much of a head start. Shane rode up alongside him and grabbed him by the scruff of his neck and heaved him out of the saddle. He hit the ground with a heavy thump and rolled several times in the dust. Shane reined in his horse and dismounted. He reloaded his guns as he walked back to where Hunte had fallen.

Being unhorsed did not appear to have damaged Hunte badly. He had rolled over onto all fours and was crawling away like a pig. Shane kicked him in the buttocks, knocking him face-first to the ground. He screamed like a frightened woman. 'Please! Please don't hurt me.'

Shane thumbed back the hammer of his Colt. 'This won't hurt a bit,' he said coldly.

Hunte screamed again and began to cry. His lack of courage disgusted Shane but it also gave him cause to hesitate.

What kind of a threat was this man to him?

It might not have concerned him in days gone by but in the light of what had happened at the Babson ranch, it was pertinent now. Hunte was no gunslinger who would kill Shane if he did not kill him first. He was a weak and frightened man, stripped of all his defences, even his pride. He was no threat, and so that begged the further question:

What reason did Shane have to kill him?

Fifty-thousand dollars was a lot of money but it was an excuse, not a reason. Shane suspected that his real motives for wanting to kill Hunte had more to do with the Fastest Guns and their tournament. He wanted to prove himself worthy of competing in it, but that was where his thinking doubled-back on itself.

He had tasted what the Fastest Guns had to offer him and it was not as sweet as it promised it would be. The Fastest Guns tempted him with lies to bind him into slavery. They would use him for their own ends, chew him up and change him into something more suiting to their needs. He was not so enamoured with them that he could not see that it was in his best interests not to join them. What his head wanted and what his heart desired were completely at odds with each other, but Shane was a man who listened to his head. He was not by his nature a passionate man. Coldly, analytically, he weighed his options and drew the obvious conclusion.

Though he wanted to go to Covenant, he chose not to. Slowly and with a heavy heart, he lowered his gun and turned away.

Hunte raised his head and sniffed back his tears, startled to find that his executioner was leaving him. He crouched where he was for a time, fearing that it was some sort of trick, but when Shane did not look back he rose to his feet and limped to his horse. Shane let him go and he galloped away into the warren of canyons.

The sound of his hoof beats had no sooner faded in one direction than another rider came thundering up the canyon. Castor Buchanan reined in when he saw Shane walking towards him.

'Did you get him?'

'No.'

'What?'

Shane trudged past him, barely deigning to acknowledge him as they passed. 'He's all yours,' he said.

Buchanan stared at him for a moment, too stunned for words. 'What the hell has gotten into you?'

Shane did not answer. He did not even look back and Buchanan, swearing in frustration, sawed on his reins and galloped on after Hunte. Shane hoped never to see him again.

He wandered back down the canyon, stepping over the bodies of Lyndon Appleby and his men. He felt numb, dislocated from the world and from himself. He could not shake the belief that he had made a fundamentally wrong decision and that the whole of reality had been fractured somehow by his choice. It seemed to him that the sky should be falling down around him like broken shards of glass, and he could not reconcile himself to the fact that it was not.

He knew that he would regret his decision in time, but at that precise moment he could not have guessed how long it would haunt him for, or how severely its burden would break his spirit.

There was a *click* as the hammer fell on an empty chamber. Shane put the gun back in his holster and drew it again. He did not hurry and, as his finger tightened against the trigger, he knew that, had the gun been loaded, his aim would have been true. Still, he was painfully aware of how much his form had degraded in the last six years. He felt confident that he was good enough to match Tom Freeman but against Chastity he was not so sure.

He holstered the gun, readied himself and tried again. It was a sign of how far he had reverted to his old self that he was taking it all so seriously. Two days ago he would have rather died than go up against Chastity and now here he was practicing so that he might stand a better chance of beating her. A line had been crossed and he was no longer a captive being forced to compete in the tournament; he was a willing participant.

Which made it all the more important that he escape before the final round.

He thought back to the previous afternoon, when he and Vendetta had spoken in O'Malley's Saloon. 'Are you really telling me that you can go out onto that crossroads tomorrow and kill Chastity in good conscience, just so you can settle your score with Brett?'

'I guess we'll find out,' she had replied.

Her hesitance had betrayed her feelings on the matter. Vendetta had been a fighter; not a murderer. Shane had known that the thought of going up against Chastity would have placed her in a moral quandary. It had been with this in mind that he had made his pitch: 'What if I said I wanted to get Chastity out of here as well?'

Vendetta had thought about it. 'No,' she had said. 'You'll say anything to get me to do what you want me to do. I don't believe you give a shit about that little girl.'

She had turned to leave but he had called out to her. 'If I left this place tonight and took her with me, tomorrow would be the final round. It'd just be you against Freeman. Think you could deal with that?'

'Nathaniel would send his men after you.'

'Probably, but if I'm right about what he's up to, he can't afford any delays. He'll have to finish the tournament early.'

'I don't trust you, Ennis.'

'You don't have to trust me. Just pass a message on for me.'

'Who to?'

The door creaked open on rusty hinges revealing yet another room that was empty except for a few relics of abandoned furniture, all of it heavy with dust. Disappointed, Madison quietly eased the door shut and moved on to the next one.

She led Chastity by the hand, the girl shuffling along behind her. Madison had given her the rag doll that she had found and the girl carried it unthinkingly by one leg, its head dragging against the floor. Occasionally, she sniffled or moaned unintelligibly, but mostly she had settled down from her post-match temper tantrum and was content to follow wherever Madison led.

They searched among the rooms of the hotel, finding echoes of its former days wherever they went. The empty rooms were covered with dust and piled furniture. Here and there a trinket lay, discarded by somebody many years ago. But Madison was searching for something more substantial than forgotten memories.

She had woken early that morning and crawled from Nathaniel's bed feeling wretched and miserable with herself. Their lovemaking the night before felt like a betrayal of all that she had felt for Kip. Better if she could have said that she had not enjoyed it, but that was not entirely so. Nathaniel had provided her with company and the illusion of his protection had helped to comfort her. She hated herself for that.

Gathering her clothes around her, she had slipped quietly from his room and returned to the attic. Whisperer had been sat there, minding over Chastity while she slept. He had not said anything to Madison but the look in his eyes as he rose silently to leave had been cruel and mocking. *Nathaniel's whore*, they had all but said.

She had been too upset to find the strength to be angry. Somehow she had managed to hold back her tears until after he had left but, with the door closed and nobody to witness her grief she had given in to her sorrow and wept. The emptiness inside of her had yawned impossibly wide.

All that Nathaniel had told her the night before had left her challenging her grasp on reality. She felt as if she was lost and, longing for something to comfort her, she had grasped at her memories of Kip. His loss had pained her that morning more than ever and she had needed to feel his presence around her. Waking Chastity, she had left the Grande and gone back to the house that they had slept in.

She had half-feared to find all of their belongings gone. The invigilators took whatever belonged to the contestants who died and auctioned them among themselves but, possibly because Madison was known as Nathaniel's woman, they had left her stuff alone.

Her belongings lay side by side with Kip's, strewn messily about the floor of the dusty old house. Madison had walked among them, picking things up to touch them and smell Kip's scent on them. Her sadness had overwhelmed her and she had sniffed back tears.

'I'm sorry,' she had whispered.

An angry sniff behind her had alerted her to the presence of somebody else in the house. Turning around and pulling Chastity to her defensively, she had been surprised to find Vendetta standing in the doorway. The hard woman had regarded her with undisguised contempt. 'I have a message for you,' she had said. 'You were supposed to get it last night but you sounded busy.'

Colour had flooded to Madison's cheeks.

'If you want to get out of this town, Shane Ennis wants to speak with you.'

Vendetta had delivered her message without any apparent interest and had left as soon as she was done. Madison had sat down to ponder what she had said. She had been too stunned at first for the words to have any meaning but gradually it had sunk in and she had laughed out loud.

When the elation had passed, she had begun to consider things in a colder, more practical light. Vendetta had given her hope for her future but there were things that needed to be done in order to make this new opportunity work for her.

She had begun by bundling together all of her stuff, together with some of Kip's and had crammed as much of it into her carpet bag as she was able. In the process, she had discovered the old abandoned rag doll that she had hugged the night after Kip had died and she had given it to Chastity, hoping that she would like it. The girl had shown no sign of even knowing what it was but she looked more human with a doll in her hands and that made Madison feel safer in her presence.

Back at the Grande, she had washed and changed clothes and had then sat in front of a mirror and made herself up. She had covered up the puffiness that surrounded her eyes and painted the illusion of an afterglow onto her face. Even if she could not fool Nathaniel, he would know that she had made an effort and that would make him think that she was his. The more complacent he thought she was, the easier it would be for her to work behind his back.

The trick had worked. Nathaniel had been suitably flattered by her attentiveness when they had met for breakfast that morning and thought absolutely nothing of leaving her alone in the hotel with Chastity now that the day had worn on. He had business elsewhere in town. Madison was not entirely sure what he was up to but he had taken Whisperer and his bodyguards and gone to prepare the warding fires, whatever that meant.

She did not care. His absence gave her the chance to explore the hotel unobserved and she searched along the hallway, trying every door she passed until she found what she was looking for.

A door that was locked.

Crouching, she peered through the keyhole. The room inside was dimly lit. Sunlight broke through small gaps in the boarded windows, casting jagged rays through the dusty air. She could just about make out the shape of a pair of wooden panniers, each of which she was willing to bet held ten-thousand dollars.

She smiled to herself. If Nathaniel was determined to make her his whore then he could damn well pay for her.

CHAPTER NINETEEN

Buchanan came to collect Shane shortly before it was time for him to fight. Shane had practiced until the motion of drawing and shooting felt as natural as it had used to feel, but that wasn't the only way in which he felt different. The coldness in his heart had spread too. It had crawled into his arms and legs and left him feeling like a man made of steel, cast by the same processes that had forged his revolver.

It was the way he had used to feel six years ago. That didn't seem so very long ago any more.

Buchanan noticed how he was different and couldn't resist mentioning it but Shane ignored him. Better to maintain the appearance that he had resigned himself to his fate and let Buchanan think that he was beaten than to open his mouth and risk alerting him to the fact that he still had one surviving hope of escape.

He just prayed that Vendetta had passed on his message and that Madison had been receptive to it.

The sun was high overhead when he stepped out of the courthouse. It blazed in the sky like a witness to the coming bout. Tom Freeman was waiting for him on the porch.

'I always wanted to fight against you,' he said.

Shane looked down at the ground, ignoring him, but Freeman was persistent. 'I hear you've been practicing,' he said. 'That's good. I want to fight you at your best.'

'No.' Shane said quietly. 'You really don't want that.'

The dust swirled up on a sluggish breeze and drifted over the crossroads. Shane took one side and Freeman took the other. The town felt more desolate than it had the other day. There was hardly anybody left to watch them any more. All of the other contestants were dead except for Chastity, and only the invigilators remained, watching from their rooftop eyries with wary suspicion, waiting to lend their own guns to the killing if needed.

Shane drew his revolver and took the single bullet that Buchanan gave him. He loaded it like an opium addict shooting a needle into his vein. It hit him with a rush.

In that instant, he wished he had more bullets.

He wished that he could kill everyone in town.

And, in a voice that was getting quieter and quieter with every passing moment, he wished that he was somewhere else, far away from here. Somewhere where he could be free of the gun's malevolent influence and his abhorrent obsession with it.

He shook his head to clear his thoughts. The gun's mind remained like a layer of scum on the surface of a stagnant pond. Shane took a deep breath and sank beneath it. It surged from the depths of his soul like vomit, terrifying in its intensity, but as it stole over him and smothered his identity with its embrace, it soothed him like a gentle lover and coaxed away his fears. He felt a cool peace come over him, a calm self-assurity: a sense that he was now complete.

He looked into Tom Freeman's eyes and saw in his expression

that the same process was happening inside his mind as well.

Nathaniel stepped up to the edge of the porch in preparation to signal the draw. Shane became absolutely still, his muscles poised like a spring about to uncoil. He heard his heart beating. Its steady rhythm sounded like the distant beating of a drum.

All other sounds faded away, except one.

Nathaniel's voice. 'Draw!'

Tom Freeman was fast. He was halfway to firing when Shane's bullet took him through the side of the head. At a speed of almost 900 feet-per-second the 250 grain bullet smashed through his skull, deforming on impact so that, by the time it entered the soft tissue of his brain, it was tumbling end over end in a storm of shattered skull fragments, pulping everything that it struck. Freeman's momentum caused him to turn a half-revolution before he hit the ground. Dead.

Shane slowly lowered his smoking gun and shed its poisonous influence from his thoughts like a spider shedding its skin. It departed reluctantly, or maybe it was simply that he found it harder to be parted from it this time and yearned for it to stay. He shivered, in equal parts from fear and excitement.

How many more times can I do this? he wondered. *How many more times before I can't give it up?*

Buchanan strode up to him, clapping his hands together in applause. 'Now that is the Shane Ennis that I remember.'

Shane gave him a cold look and started back towards the courthouse without waiting to be led there. Buchanan held out a hand to stop him. 'Aren't you forgetting something?'

Shane still wore the gun belt about his waist, the revolver sheathed in its holster. He had not given it a second's thought. He had become comfortable wearing it again and, removing it, he understood why Chastity cried so hard when her gun was taken away from her. It was like having his skeleton ripped from his living flesh.

Buchanan saw the murderous look in his eyes and nervously backed away from him. He summoned over two of the invigilators and they escorted Shane back to his cell. Nathaniel came to visit him once he was locked up and congratulated Shane on his victory.

'Buchanan always assured me that you would make it this far,' he said. 'I confess that I did not believe him but here you have proven me wrong. Well done, that is not something that happens often.'

'Save it for someone who cares.' Shane muttered sulkily.

The smug look vanished from Nathaniel's face. 'You'll face Chastity tomorrow,' he said.

'Tell me something I don't already know.'

'At twelve noon.' Nathaniel told him.

The Gunfighter's Hour. Shane had guessed it would be then. The tournament was finally coming to an end and its secrets would soon be revealed.

'Tomorrow,' he echoed dumbly. 'Twelve noon.'

If he had not escaped by then, he never would.

The storm had been building for some time, massing its energy until the air seemed heavy with it, tensed to the point of bursting. When it finally chose to erupt, it did so with apocalyptic violence, as if it was the storm that would end the world. Winds of more than a hundred miles an hour stripped the desert like a scythe, choking the landscape in a cloud of razor sharp sand and airborne debris.

Shane would have kept on running had it not been for that storm. He would have kept on running and maybe, in the end, Castor Buchanan would have stopped chasing him. Maybe. It was academic now because the storm had put Shane's back against the wall and trapped him, and now Castor Buchanan had caught up with him.

The walls of the boarding house shook under the onslaught of the ravenous wind. Every eye in the place was watching him, waiting to see what he would do. Buchanan stood outside, bellowing over the roar of the wind, calling him out.

'You'd best go out there, son,' one of the old timers said. 'I don't think he's going to go away.'

Shane wasn't listening. He was afraid, but it wasn't Buchanan that scared him. He should have known from the beginning that he could not simply walk away from the Fastest Guns. He was too far gone for that. Two weeks had passed since Spinster's Peak and he had still not laid down his guns. Instead, he had found more and more reason to use them. He had killed without provocation. The influence that they held over him was growing and he could scarcely think any more without their thoughts intruding on him. He had barely slept in days.

He knew that if he fought Buchanan and won that everything he was would be consumed by his guns. The man he was would cease to exist, and he did not like to think of what they would make him become. And yet his heart cried out for it, tearing his soul in two.

Buchanan's voice roared from outside. 'Hunte's dead, Shane! Let's finish this.'

There was no escape. Buchanan could not go to Covenant until he had proven himself, and neither could Shane. Bowing to the inevitable, Shane wrapped a scarf around his face. He turned his collar up high, drew the brim of his hat down low to shield his face and went to the door. He had to put his shoulder to it in order to push it open against the force of the wind.

Outside, he was met immediately by a stinging blast of sand. The small town was lucky in that it was only catching the edge of the storm; its full fury raged in the heart of the desert, where it could sometimes be glimpsed through a gap in the sandstorm as a towering pillar of black dust that reached from land to sky. Its noise was tremendous. In addition to the howling of the wind there were the sounds of the town straining against its foundations: the creaking of poorly constructed homes; the whip-crack of tarpaulin roofs half torn away in the wind; and the singing of wires in the scaffold above the main pit.

Shane bowed his head and forced his reluctant feet to bear him onto the road. Buchanan was waiting for him. He turned and walked slowly down the high street, and Shane followed him to the edge of town.

They stood with ten paces between them, their hands poised above their revolvers, the wind casting sheets of black sand between them.

Shane felt as though he had already been beaten. He was certain that he could kill Buchanan; he felt no doubt about that at all. It was his destiny to become one of the Fastest Guns and it filled him with a righteous fire that stirred his spirit.

But Shane did not trust his feelings. He believed in his thoughts. The war between his heart and his mind had ended, and it seemed that his mind had lost.

A dust cloud blew between them and Shane reached instinctively for his gun, knowing that Buchanan would do the same. He drew and fired, expecting to be damned. But in the last moment he found the strength to resist.

The bullet that was meant for Buchanan's heart tore through his fingers instead.

Shane woke from his memories, hearing footsteps outside his cell.

He rose slowly, not daring to get his hopes up in case they were for nothing, and crossed to the window.

Madison and Chastity stood in the alley outside. Madison looked nervous and glanced repeatedly towards the street, afraid that somebody would see her. Shane's sudden appearance at the window startled her and she recoiled with a gasp, only to be brought up short when Chastity refused to follow her. The little girl stared up at Shane with what looked like wonder, her eyes focussed and oddly intense.

'Shit!' Madison exclaimed. 'You scared me.'

'You got my message?'

'Yes.' She looked down at Chastity, who still stared fixedly at Shane. 'What's the matter, honey?' Madison asked her.

'She recognises her own kind when she sees one.' Shane muttered.

Madison glanced sharply at him. He was surprised to see that she understood his meaning. He guessed that Nathaniel had been educating her. How accurate Nathaniel's information had been, and how much of it had been shared with her, Shane was curious to know. The more ignorant she was, the easier it would be for him to manipulate her.

'I want to get out of this town tonight,' he told her. 'How about you?'

'I've got no reason to want to stay,' she agreed. 'What's your plan?'

'First I need you to get me out of this cell. Buchanan keeps a key around his neck and acts like it's the only one there is. That's bullshit. Nathaniel's the sort who'd want to have one as well. Think you could get it for me?'

'If I can't, I'll take Buchanan's.'

'Go after Nathaniel's.' Shane told her firmly. He did not rate

231

her chances of tackling Buchanan. 'Bring it to me here after it gets dark tonight,' he said. 'And bring food and water for the three of us.'

'Three of us?'

'Chastity as well,' he said.

'Okay.' She was secretly relieved that he wanted to take Chastity. Despite the circumstances under which they had met, Madison had grown quite protective of the little girl. Like her, she was trapped in Nathaniel's service and that had forged a bond of sorts between them, at least so far as Madison was concerned. She did not want to leave her behind to what Nathaniel had in store for her. 'I have a condition,' she added.

'What?'

'Nathaniel's money; the bounty he put out for your capture. I know where he's keeping it. I want half of it. You can have the other half if you want.'

Shane frowned at her. 'Getting out of here is going to be hard enough as it is,' he started.

'It isn't guarded,' she said quickly. 'Nathaniel keeps it in a locked room on the ground floor of the Grande. I've got a pretty good idea where he keeps the key.'

Shane was not interested in going after the money. They would have problems enough to contend with without adding to their burdens, but he needed Madison's help if he was to get out of his cell and so he nodded his head. 'Okay,' he said. 'But get me out of my cell first. We'll get the money together.'

'Sure.' Madison cast a hurried glance back towards the end of the alley. 'I'd better get going. I told Nathaniel I was taking Chastity for a walk but he'll get suspicious if I'm gone too long. I'll be back later.'

'Be careful,' Shane warned, and watched as she hurried away.

He was not happy placing his trust in her; she did not seem like the sort of person who could be relied upon, but he presently had no other choice. She was the only ally he had.

As soon as she had served her purpose, however, he decided that he would kill her.

CHAPTER TWENTY

That afternoon passed slowly for Madison. The hours dragged by torturously. She tried to go about her activities as if everything was normal, but every time she saw Whisperer and Nathaniel look at her she felt certain that they would observe something in her manner that would betray her plans.

Whisperer especially seemed aware that she was more nervous than usual. Several times, she got the impression that he was spying on her. He appeared no matter where she went and she often caught him looking at her with a strange look in his eye and a half-smile on his lips, as if he knew something secret. He unnerved her, and she dared not do anything to prepare for Shane's escape while he was around.

At supper, she picked listlessly at her food and retired early, claiming that she was fatigued by the sun and the heat. The lie gave her a good pretext to go to the well and draw some water, supposedly to cool her down but in reality to fill the canteens that would see her, Shane and Chastity safely across the desert. She hoped that her alleged sickness would also discourage Nathaniel from demanding her presence in his bed that night.

She put Chastity to bed early and lay in the darkness, listening to the eerie melody of the town. Nathaniel and Whisperer stayed up late making preparations for the final round of the tournament and Madison fancied that it was past midnight when they finally retired. She waited a while longer to give them time to fall asleep, then threw back the bedcovers and hurriedly got dressed. She put on a pair of black pants and a black shirt that had once belonged to Kip, and tied her hair back in a pony tail.

Grabbing her carpet bag, she filled it with the things that she did not want to leave behind and stuffed in some of Chastity's clothes as well. She could not take everything but that didn't matter; she figured that she could buy plenty of new clothes with her share of Nathaniel's twenty-thousand dollars when she made it back to civilisation, and the thought lifted her spirits a little.

She tucked her only weapon into her right boot. It was a straight razor that a previous boyfriend had given her years ago, fearing for her safety. She had seldom found need to use it and had never killed anybody before, but if Nathaniel woke while she was lifting his keys from him, she felt certain that a quick slice across the throat would deal with him.

The hotel creaked about her, sounding as if it approved of her murderous thoughts. She shivered and made sure that Chastity was sleeping soundly. Then, with her heart beating furiously in her chest, she opened the bedroom door and crept soundlessly into the hallway.

She timed her descent down the stairs to coincide with building's rhythmic creaks and groans, letting them mask the sound of her footsteps. The grey light of the moon pierced through cracks in the boarded-up windows and provided the only illumination. The shadows were deep and seemed to shift in strange ways, as if the source of the faint light kept moving. Madison could not shake off the sensation that she was being watched.

She crept up to Nathaniel's door and put her ear to it. There was no indication that he was still awake and, cautiously, she turned the handle and opened the door a crack. Peering through, she could see that Nathaniel lay on the bed with his back to her. He looked to be asleep but Madison was not convinced. She lingered in the doorway, too afraid to go any further.

Seconds ticked by while she wrestled with her anxiety. If somehow he had learned about her plans to escape, he might only be pretending to be asleep, waiting for her to come inside and walk into his trap. She tried to dismiss the thought as simple paranoia, but it was not easy. The fear remained and it took all of her courage to finally enter the room.

She padded softly to the side of the bed, where Nathaniel's waistcoat hung on the back of a wooden chair. She had seen him put the key to her room in his waistcoat pocket the day before when she had first been pressed into caring for Chastity, and hoped that he kept the rest of his keys there as well. She was right. She found three keys: one of which was probably the key to Shane's cell, another the key to the locked room where the money was kept, and the last no doubt fit the room where she and Chastity slept. She was glad that she had made an effort to win his trust and that he had not felt it necessary to lock her in overnight.

She pocketed all three keys and turned to leave. At that moment, Nathaniel rolled over and turned his face towards her.

Her heart froze. His eyes were still closed, she realised with relief, but for a moment she had thought he was looking at her. Adrenaline coursed through her veins, making her feel light-headed and weak. She took a deep breath to steady herself, then crept urgently back to the doorway. She closed the door softly behind her and breathed a sigh of relief. The first step of her ordeal was over.

Next came the tricky part.

She woke Chastity and dressed her. The girl was docile and did not make a sound but, to be on the safe side, Madison put the rag doll in her hands. She seemed to have grown fond of it in as much as she was capable of liking anything, and she clutched it to her chest.

Madison hefted her carpet bag over her shoulder and took Chastity by the hand. There were butterflies in her stomach as she left the room and made her way downstairs again in the dark. She raided the drinks cabinet in Nathaniel's study and stole a bottle of cognac, which she slipped into her bag. In the kitchens, she grabbed some bacon and flour, enough to last a few days, and slipped out the hotel through the back door.

The night air felt hot and sultry, bitter with the coppery scent of gunsmoke. She dragged Chastity down and hid in the shadows while a couple of invigilators walked by. The town's song growled at the furthest edge of town, the sound turning as she listened to roll back towards her like an approaching tide.

It creaked past her as she dragged Chastity across West Street and over to the side of the courthouse. She knew that Shane was probably expecting her to bring the keys to his window, but that was not her plan. She knew what sort of a man he was and suspected that he would probably abandon her as soon as he had no more need of her. If she was going to get his help, she needed to prove her worth to him.

Avoiding the invigilators, she crept around to the front of the courthouse and let herself in. It was dark, but a lantern burned in

237

a distant room. As Madison made her way towards it, she freed her hair and arranged it so that it fell attractively about her shoulders. Her looks couldn't actually kill, but they could easily stun a man for a while.

There was only a single invigilator standing guard in the room. Madison had gotten to know several of them since her arrival in Covenant. She had flirted with the better looking ones even while Kip had been alive, favouring them with a smile and a lingering glance. She knew that this one's name was Jeff, and she had seen him admiring her when he didn't think she was looking.

He looked surprised to see her. 'You shouldn't be here,' he said.

Madison put a finger to her lips and shushed him. 'The girl wouldn't go to sleep so I thought I'd take her for a walk,' she told him.

'The Colonel's orders are for nobody to come in here. That includes you, miss. I've got to ask you to leave.'

'My feet are sore. Do you mind if I sit down for a moment? Come on, what harm is it going to do?' She did her best to look helpless and appealing.

'The Colonel's orders—' Jeff began, but she interrupted him before he could finish.

'The Colonel wants Chastity fit to beat Ennis in the fight tomorrow. Please, I've got find a way to get her to go to sleep or he'll be really angry in the morning. Just let me sit down for a couple of minutes. I won't cause any trouble.'

She picked her words carefully, knowing that Jeff wouldn't want to do anything that might put him on the wrong side of Nathaniel. Reluctantly, he stepped aside and let Madison take his chair. She perched Chastity on her lap.

'Are you any good with that thing?' she asked, gesturing towards the Sharps rifle that he had propped against the wall.

Like any man in the company of a pretty woman, Jeff was only too happy to boast about himself. 'It depends,' he said. 'If you call twelve shots grouped in a five-inch bull at three-hundred yards good then, yeah, I am.' He thought for a moment and decided that she might not understand what a measure of his skill that was. 'That *is* good by the way,' he added.

She smiled. 'I'm going to have a drink,' she announced, digging the bottle of cognac out of her bag. 'Would you like one?'

'I can't, miss. The Colonel's orders.'

She set the bottle down on the table. 'You're good at following orders, aren't you,' she teased.

'The Colonel would have my hide if he caught me.'

'Well, you're a good boy. Oh!' Madison bent forward sharply as if hurt. 'Oh, my leg! I've got cramp. Take the girl, quick!'

She pushed Chastity into Jeff's arms before he could object and stood up, making a show of stretching the muscles in her leg. Jeff held Chastity awkwardly with both hands. He bent over to put her down and, as he did so, Madison stepped behind him and grabbed the bottle of cognac. She brought it down hard across the back of his head and he sank to his knees. He was dazed but not unconscious, and she hit him again before he could recover his senses. This time, she put her weight into the blow and he collapsed against the floor. Hastily, she pulled off his belt and used it to tie his wrists behind his back, then gagged him with a neckerchief and bound his ankles. He was coming round by the time she was finished.

She took his knife and revolver from him and opened the door that led to the cells. 'Wait here, hon,' she told Chastity.

Shane had been alerted by the noise and was waiting at the

door to his cell. 'What was all that about?' he growled.

She put her hands on her hips. 'You had a better way of dealing with the guard?' she challenged him.

He thrust a hand through the bars of the cell. 'Give me the key.'

Madison gave it to him. 'I've also brought food and water,' she said, as he opened the door. 'Oh, and you'll want this.' She offered him Jeff's revolver.

Shane sprang back in horror. 'Take it away!' he snapped.

'What's the matter?'

He pointed into one of the open cells. 'Throw it in there. Now!' He did not trust himself to be near a gun tonight, not when he was so close to escaping. The temptation was too strong.

Madison tossed the gun away. 'Jeez, I'm sorry,' she said, a hurt look on her face. She walked back into the next room and picked up her carpet bag. Jeff had woken up and was struggling against his bonds. 'Did he have a knife?' Shane asked.

'Do you want it?' Madison asked.

He held out of his hand. She gave it to him and was startled when he knelt down and slid the blade harshly across Jeff's neck. There was a bright splash of blood and Jeff made a horrible, gurgling cry. His body jack-knifed and he flapped about like a fish thrown on dry land, his movements becoming slower as the blood drained out of him, stealing his life away.

'What did you do that for?' Madison hissed.

'It wouldn't have taken him long to work himself loose. Now, he's no longer a problem.' He wiped the knife off against Jeff's shirt and sheathed it. 'I'll take the girl,' he said. He lifted Chastity into his arms and carried her to the door.

'Are we taking his rifle?' Madison asked.

'No.'

'But we'll need it.'

'I said, no.'

Madison pouted angrily. 'How are we going to escape from this town if we don't have a gun?' she asked.

'Very quietly,' was his answer.

They made their way out onto the street. The crossroads was lit by smouldering torch fires that illuminated the town with a reddish hue. Invigilators could be seen patrolling in the distance. Shane made for the nearest alley and ducked in out of sight. Madison followed and crouched beside him, pressing her body against his as she pointed over his shoulder towards the Grande. 'Nathaniel keeps the money in a locked room on the ground floor,' she said. 'It's the fifth one on the right from the lobby.'

She dug the keys from her pocket and gave them to him. 'One of these should open the door.'

Shane could see that she had her mind set on taking the money. He decided not to risk starting an argument with her now and said nothing of his intention to leave it all behind. 'Horses first,' he told her.

Keeping to the shadows, they made their way towards the stables. The town creaked and groaned around them, maintaining its usual rhythm. The sound crawled out towards the edge of town and then turned about and came rumbling back in again.

In and out. In and out.

In.

The noise abruptly stopped. Shane looked over his shoulder in alarm. All along West Street, the invigilators were turning to face the crossroads, confused by the silence.

And then the clock above the town hall began to chime: dull, leaden peals that echoed ominously throughout Covenant, striking the count of noon.

'What the hell is going on?' Madison asked shakily.

'The Cordites,' Shane whispered. 'I don't think they want me to leave.'

TWENTY ONE

The silence that came after that dread tolling of the bell seemed to resonate with its memory. In dark places across the town an eerie grey smoke began to rise. It poured from holes in the ground and from the cracks between floorboards, its smell a bitter mixture of sulphur and nitric acid.

And men emerged from that smoke.

They strode out of it with solemn purpose in their gait: stern, wraith-like figures in clothing that was ragged with holes. Their skin was dry as parchment, pale and yellowed and stretched tight upon their bones. Beneath the shadowed brim of their hats, all that could be seen of their faces were their lipless mouths, grimacing with long, sharp teeth.

Howard Anderson was one of the first invigilators to see them. His patrol had taken him off West Street to the yard behind the bath house and he was startled to see one of the figures striding from the alleyway towards him. Not recognising him, he shouted out a challenge and called for two of his comrades to back him up. The figure did not slow his pace. As he drew closer, his hand reached for the gun at his waist and Anderson did not hesitate to shoot him. At such close range, Anderson could not miss. The shot hit him in the chest, at a place where it should have torn through his heart, but the man did not go down. He drew his revolver and fired, dropping Anderson and his two colleagues in three deadly-accurate shots.

The Cordite stepped over their bodies without a second glance and moved onto West Street. The killing had begun.

The sudden noise of gunfire carried clear across town and alerted the sentries who guarded the perimeter. Frank Hammill was one such man. He twisted on his rooftop perch and looked back across town, where he was surprised to see what looked like mist crawling through the streets. It was the colour of soft lead and seemed to glow softly with an ethereal light.

Curious, Frank brought the scope of his rifle to his eye. It was a powerful German-made Vollmer sight, as expensive and precision-crafted as the rifle it was mounted on. The gun had previously belonged to another invigilator: the man called Penn, who had died in Chastity's rampage two days earlier. Frank had traded his own rifle and the last of his tobacco to possess it. It was a .45-120 Sharps Creedmoor with a heavy thirty-two inch target barrel and gain-twist rifling. It was a truly exquisite instrument.

The scope had an incredible twenty times magnification and the faint light of the mist made it possible to see in good detail. Frank scanned the road until he spotted two men that he recognised. They were shooting at another man who was walking down the street towards them. Frank had never seen the stranger in town before. He was thin and wiry and carried a single revolver, which he drew lazily, as if unconcerned by the shots that were being fired at him. Looking more closely, Frank fancied that he could see the man's clothes twitching, as if the bullets were striking him, but he showed no sign of being hurt. He fired his revolver from the hip and Frank tore his eye away from the scope, unable to believe what he was seeing.

The man's hand moved impossibly fast, fanning the hammer in a blur. Flame spat from the barrel and a volley of shots erupted like a burst from a Gatling gun. Impossibly, he seemed to fire ten times more than just the six shots that the cylinder should have contained, and the two invigilators were ripped down where they stood, falling in a red rain of blood and shredded flesh.

The colour drained from Frank's face. He was no stranger to violence but he had never witnessed murder on such a scale before. It horrified him, and yet it exerted a sickening urge in him to see more. He put his eye back to the scope and watched as the man stalked past the bodies of the men he had just killed and move on in search of more.

The rooftop creaked behind him but, like everyone in Covenant, Frank was used to the noise of the town settling at night and he thought nothing of it, despite the fact that the buildings had all been eerily quiet since the clock tower had struck twelve. He kept his eye glued to his scope, feeling insulated from the bloodshed by his distance from it. A foul smell washed over him and, suddenly, his scope went black.

Jerking his head back, he was astonished to see a man towering over him. He gripped the barrel of the rifle in one hand, blocking the view through the scope. 'What the–'

Frank's words died in his throat as he saw the gaping hole in the man's forehead: a wound that no man could have taken and survived. It didn't disfigure him so badly that Frank could not recognise him. 'Penn?' he asked incredulously.

Penn's eyes were as deep and as cold as gun barrels. 'You're holding my rifle,' he said.

Frank's mouth became too dry to speak. He scrambled to his feet in a burst of energy and tried to wrench the gun from Penn's grasp and shoot him with it, but Penn's grip was stronger. He twisted the rifle from Frank's hands and turned it on him. The gun went off and Frank felt a chilling numbness engulf his chest. He stepped backwards and lost his footing. Silently, he toppled backwards from the roof and landed heavily on the sun-baked earth below, his neck snapping on impact.

'I don't understand.' Madison said.

Shane was not running but he was walking quickly and with such long strides that she was finding it difficult to keep up. 'I thought Nathaniel said he could control them.'

'I don't think Nathaniel ever really understood what he was doing.' Shane told her. His words were drowned by the sound of gunfire close-by. Shane pressed himself flat against the wall as a small group of invigilators ran past him. They had only just woken and one man had not even had time to tug on his boots before joining the fray.

They did not see him and Shane waited until they had gone before hurrying out across the road. He held Chastity tightly in his arms. The atmosphere of the town had changed since the clock had struck. Whereas before it had seemed like a dead place, now the streets felt horribly alive, coursing with an energy that sang deep within Shane's soul. It touched him on a primal level, exciting him with promises that tempted him to go to the Cordites and join them. It was only that he understood the price they demanded of him that he found the strength to resist them.

Chastity had no such insights. She squirmed and wriggled

against his grasp and cried out from time to time in a voice that was choked with need. Shane held on to her tightly, determined not to let her go. If he had doubted before that he should take her with him, those doubts were gone now. He was certain that what he was doing was right. It was not about redemption. It was not about atonement. It was just something that needed to be done. For all of his many failings, Shane refused to be the sort of man who would abandon a girl like her to become a Cordite.

He refused to be that much of a coward.

Resisting the urge to run, he strode purposefully along the edge of the street. Another invigilator ran out in front of him but did not see him. He was too intent on escaping from whoever was chasing him. There was the sound of a shot and Shane ducked as the side of one of the nearby houses exploded as if hit by a cannonball.

The invigilator was blown from his feet. Splinters of burning wood rained down around him and he screamed as he tried to stand. One of the splinters had become embedded in his thigh. He clutched at it, his hands becoming slick with blood as he yanked it out.

A Cordite strode through the smoke and flames of the devastated building. He was a tall man with broad shoulders and a straight back. In his hand he gripped a breach-loading pistol, from which he tugged a spent cartridge and inserted a fresh one.

The invigilator scrambled to his feet and started running again, favouring his wounded leg and gasping with pain and fear.

The Cordite took aim and fired. He did not miss and the invigilator's body exploded like a pumpkin hit by a shotgun blast.

Madison covered her face with her hands and looked away, whimpering. The Cordite opened the breach of his pistol and plucked out the empty cartridge, then inserted a new one and walked on by, seemingly attracted to a band of invigilators who had gathered further down the street. He did not seem to be aware that Shane and Madison were nearby.

'That was Mark Crowood,' she whispered, once he was out of earshot.

Shane nodded in agreement. Crowood was one of the six men who had won the first tournament. He had always been known to favour the heavy .50 calibre Remington 1871 Rolling Block pistol over the more popular six-shooters, reasoning that it was better to fire one shot and make it count than shoot six and waste them all.

The .50 calibre pistol was well-known for its devastating stopping power but since Crowood had bonded with it and become a Cordite it had clearly become an even more devastating weapon. Shane had seen horse-drawn artillery that hit with less force.

He noticed that Madison's face had gone white with shock and her eyes were distant. He thought about killing her. From this point onwards she would only slow him down. Then again, she might yet be useful to him. She carried the food and water and he would need somebody to mind Chastity while he saddled his horse. He grabbed her by the wrist and dragged her after him.

The stable door was open when Shane got there and several of the horses were missing. No doubt some of the invigilators had tried to get out of town; the ostler being one of them. There was nobody guarding the horses, for which Shane was thankful.

The building stank of sweat and fear. Horses had senses that humans lacked and knew as well as Shane what sort of nightmare was loose in town. A couple of them looked ready to kick down the gates, and their panic was spreading among the others.

Shane closed the door behind him and lit a lantern. While he did so, he heard a retching noise as Madison doubled over and was sick onto the floor.

'Feeling better now?' he asked her.

She wiped her lips and nodded. 'I never . . . .' She could not finish her sentence.

Shane gave her the courtesy of not looking at her while she cleaned herself up. He had been a few years younger than her and fighting in the Civil War when he had first witnessed killing on such a massive scale. He set Chastity down on the floor and gave her into Madison's care. 'Keep a close eye on her,' he warned.

Madison grabbed her tightly by the wrist. The girl stared straight past her, looking about the room with wide eyes as if tracking things only she could see.

'You could be one of them couldn't you?' Madison said. 'Like Crowood, I mean.'

'That's right.' Shane replied.

'So why don't you?'

He looked at her sternly. 'You'd want to be one of those things?'

'Rather one of them than one of the invigilators right now,' she replied, and in a weak voice added: 'I don't want to die here.'

Shane turned his back on her. 'There are worse things than dying,' he told her.

Buchanan had been dreaming when the striking of the clock tower woke him. He surfaced from red memories of rape and bloodshed not knowing if the sound was real or just an echo of his dreams and he lay still for a time, uncertain of himself, until the first gunshots made him sit upright and reach for his revolver.

He crossed to the window in his jeans, his heart hammering with excitement, and looked out onto the bedlam that had seized the town. Alarm had been called and he saw invigilators running to the summons through streets that were choked with luminous grey smoke.

He knew at once what was happening.

He tipped his head back and whooped with joy, his voice echoing through the building, dropping slowly into a manic laughter.

They had arrived!

Buchanan was rapturous. His long wait was finally at an end. The Cordites had arrived and he would meet them! At last, after all this time, all his long years of faithful patience would be rewarded. He was so moved that he wept.

He shouted his encouragement as the gunfire cracked in the streets below. The invigilators were dying and he revelled in it. There was scarcely a man of them who had the slightest idea what the Fastest Guns really were and Buchanan had despised them for as long as he had known them. He had suffered their boasting, their claims of how they were worthy. Well, now they would learn the truth.

He paused, a worm of fear gnawing at its gut. As the ecstasy of his joy evaporated, it occurred to him that this was not the great arrival that Nathaniel had envisioned. The trap had not been sprung. The Cordites had not been bound by Whisperer's magic; they were free.

And Buchanan suddenly knew fear, because the truth – the awful truth that it hurt so badly to admit to himself – was that *he* was no more worthy of the Fastest Guns than the invigilators he despised. Maybe once they would have embraced him, taken him to their breast and shared with him their power. But not now. He stared at his stunted hand in loathing. He was nothing!

He stepped away from the window, sobbing to himself.

Crestfallen, his joy and his fear hardened inside his gut, tightening into a knot of white-hot anger that exploded from him in a rage. He scattered the room's furniture, smashing it against the walls, spitting a violent stream of cuss-words without sense or meaning.

It was not fair!

He had waited. He had been patient. He had been faithful. And yet it was all for nothing.

'Nothing!' he roared. He slammed his good fist into the wall, breaking through the thin plasterboard and bloodying his knuckles. The pain meant nothing to him. All he could think of were the people who had brought this failure on him: Nathaniel, Whisperer, Shane.

'Shane.' He hissed the name to himself.

Yes, it made sense now. Who else could have lured the Cordites out of hiding? It was because of Shane that the Cordites had turned their back on him last time; now he was doing it again! Buchanan's rage hardened into something tight and compressed. It formed a black hole inside his chest that dragged in all his wayward thoughts with the crushing weight of its emotional gravity, focussing his intentions. The red mist of his anger dissipated and he could see clearly again.

Buchanan knew he was going to die. There was no escaping the Cordites, no defeating them. But if he was going to die then he would make certain that he took Shane with him. He would have the satisfaction of completing his revenge.

Beyond of the stable's walls, Madison could hear the continuing sound of gunfire as the Cordites stalked the streets, killing everyone they found. Inside, the horses were getting more and more nervous and Madison was becoming anxious. She suspected that they could sense when the demons were getting closer.

'Do all the Cordites carry guns like Crowood's?' she asked Shane nervously.

Shane was in the stall, saddling his horse. 'No,' he replied. 'It depends.'

'Depends on what?'

'Depends on the fighter, and the gun. The qualities they possessed in life get exaggerated. Crowood carried a powerful gun, so now it shoots like a cannon. A man who was quick on the draw would probably move even faster. Someone who could shoot long-range might be able to shoot you from over a mile away.'

'How do you know all this?'

'I just know,' he answered vaguely.

He finished and climbed out over the top of the stall. 'Which one's yours?' he asked.

Madison's horse was nothing special. She selected a better-looking one instead. 'Him.'

'He is a she,' Shane corrected her, but he did not argue. He chose a saddle and bridle and climbed into the stall. The horse snorted at him. 'Easy,' he told her, and put out a hand to touch her, to reassure her that he meant her no harm.

From somewhere outside, a loud burst of rapid gunfire rang out like a jagged crack of thunder. The horse stamped away from him.

'Get over here and help me,' he said.

Madison came over and set her carpet bag down on the floor. She waited while Shane attached the bridle, then held the reins for him while he put on the saddle. The horse shook its head nervously.

'Hold her steady!'

'I'm trying.'

Madison was holding onto the reins when she heard the door

open behind her. Cold fingers of alarm seized hold of her heart and she glanced over her shoulder to see a man walk slowly in. Thinking that he was one of the Cordites, Madison let go of the reins with a cry and snatched hold of Chastity's hand. The newcomer fired at her as she dragged the girl into the nearest empty stall, but the shot missed and took a splinter out of the gatepost as she ran through.

The shot startled the horse and Shane narrowly leapt out from under its legs. He took shelter, pressing himself flat against the wooden wall, and drew his legs up against his chest to keep them from getting trampled on. He peered between the bars of the stall and saw the man come stalking towards him. He cursed silently under his breath when he recognised that it was Castor Buchanan.

'I thought I'd find you in here, Shane. It's a long way across the desert to go it on foot.'

The layout of the stalls blocked his line of sight, preventing him from taking a shot, but he could tell where Shane was and strolled leisurely down the aisle towards him.

'Were you going to leave without saying goodbye?' Buchanan asked maliciously.

Shane moved to avoid Madison's horse stepping on him.

'I can hear you!' Buchanan called in a sing-song voice. 'Come out and play with me, Shane. You too, girly!' he called out to Madison. 'Don't think I've forgotten about you.'

Shane contemplated trying to rush him but didn't favour the odds. There were too many obstacles barring his path and Buchanan was a good enough shot with his left hand to make short work of Shane the moment he got out in the open.

The horse in the stall next to him snorted nervously as Buchanan drew closer. Shane looked through the wooden bars that separated them and regarded the animal with a critical eye. It was a healthy stallion, but frightened by what was happening in the town. By the look of things, it had already kicked the gate several times and the hinges had broken.

Shane had an idea. He drew his knife and slashed out, raking the blade across the horse's rump. The animal reared in panic and bolted for the gate. It broke through with a single kick and the beast ran out into the aisle. Buchanan leapt out of its path and narrowly avoided getting trampled beneath its hooves. He swore loudly and the horse, wild with terror, reared up onto its hind-legs and kicked at him. He retreated, firing into its belly at close range. Shane leapt the gate during the confusion and ran across the aisle to where Madison was cowering. He snatched Chastity out of her arms and bolted for the back of the stable, where there was another door.

Buchanan saw him and opened fire but the rearing stallion got in the way. Two shots sank into its neck and the horse pitched sideways and fell to the ground. By then, Shane had already reached the door and was out into the night. A bullet gouged splinters from the doorframe as Madison ran after him.

'Run Shane!' Buchanan yelled after him. 'Go on, run! It won't do you any good.'

The stallion lay before him, blocking the aisle, still kicking and thrashing in its death throes. Buchanan broke open his revolver and reloaded six cartridges into the cylinder. He shot the horse until it stopped moving and then stepped over the body.

'You won't escape me this time, Shane,' he promised.

CHAPTER TWENTY TWO

In the Grande, Nathaniel had just been told the extent of the problem. He stared at the invigilator who had brought him the news, his hands tightening into fists. 'What do you mean she isn't there?'

'She's gone, sir. The woman must have taken her.'

'What?'

A bead of sweat formed on the invigilator's brow as Nathaniel's look became fiercer. 'They must have crept out earlier in the night, sir. It looks as if she's packed her things.'

'Then find her, damnit! And bring back Chastity. I don't want her harmed.'

'Yes, sir!' The man snapped a clumsy salute and hurried away.

Nathaniel turned to Whisperer as soon as he had left. 'I am surrounded by incompetents,' he muttered. 'I have guards patrolling every inch of this town and two girls are allowed to slip away?'

Whisperer said nothing. He was a silent presence in Nathaniel's wake as the occultist stormed down the hall. Nathaniel searched in his pockets as he went. 'Damn it!' he hissed.

'She took the key?' Whisperer asked.

'She took them all.'

He stopped outside the locked room where the money was stored. The door was still locked and Nathaniel rattled the handle in frustration. He could not understand how things had gone so wrong after all his careful preparation. He stormed back towards his study and, on the way, met the man he had sent to check on Shane's cell.

'He's gone, sir. And the guard's been killed.'

Nathaniel swore vehemently. With Shane and Chastity both gone, he had no leverage with which to bargain with the Fastest Guns. 'Where's Buchanan?'

'I don't know.'

'Well find him!'

The man glared at Nathaniel insolently but he voiced no argument. He turned on his heels and walked away.

'Buchanan has gone to kill Shane.' Whisperer observed.

'Then we'd better find him first.' Nathaniel hastened to his study and began rifling through his books. There had to be something that he could use to buy some time.

Whisperer lingered in the doorway. 'Your men are no match for the Cordites. They will abandon you.'

'You think I don't know that?' He walked to the window and peered out. 'Damnit, have the wards been lit?'

'It's too late. The wards will not offer any protection. Not now.'

'Well there must be something we can do.'

'Against the Cordites, nothing.' Whisperer said flatly.

Nathaniel resumed flipping through his books, refusing to accept that there was not some course of action that could snatch victory from this mess. He looked at page after useless page of magical formulae and circles of conjuration, seeing nothing that looked like it would work. 'This shouldn't be happening,' he raged. 'You said that they weren't ready to manifest yet. You told me that they wouldn't come until Chastity and Ennis fought.'

'I said many things.'

'That's right, you did. And I'm beginning to think that I would have better off listening to Buchanan.'

'That would have been wise.'

The tone of his voice suddenly made Nathaniel feel very uncomfortable. He turned to face him. 'What do mean by that?' he challenged.

Whisperer ran a finger along the top of the sideboard and inspected the dust as if it mattered more to him that Nathaniel's predicament. 'Do you remember the first lesson I taught you?' he asked.

Nathaniel thought back to the day he had first struck a deal with Whisperer, back at James Point.

'I warned you,' Whisperer reminded him. 'That you can never trust what a demon tells you. I told you that from the beginning, so that you would understand our agreement. You should have taken heed of what I said.'

Nathaniel stared at him, dumbfounded. He felt icy fingers crawling down his back. 'I bound you to me!' he said fiercely, but Whisperer only laughed.

'A binding is a contract, Nathaniel, and a contract that is poorly written is not worth the blood you sign it in. I warned you about that as well,' he added.

'So this is your doing?' Nathaniel said, angrily waving a hand at the window to signify the massacre that was taking place in his town.

Whisperer shook his head. 'No. Ennis escaped from his cell

of his own accord. I suspect he persuaded the girl, Madison, to assist him. The Fastest Guns value him too highly to allow him to escape, so they have taken it upon themselves to stop him.'

'That's all?' Nathaniel had never understood why the Fastest Guns – and Buchanan – attached such importance to Shane when he had always thought it was obvious that Chastity was the better fighter.

'Ennis has a strong will.' Whisperer explained. 'He has the power to resist the gun's allure. If he Descends and becomes a Cordite, he may become the first man to ever do so whilst still alive. All of the others killed themselves in the process. Or each other. A living Cordite would have greater freedom to come and go in this world. He would have more power than any of the others possess. He might even replace Priestley as their leader.'

'And Priestley accepts this?'

'Priestley does as his gun commands.'

'And Chastity?'

Whisperer shrugged. 'She will only ever be a puppet to them.'

'But she would have won the tournament!'

'That has yet to be proven.' Whisperer reminded him.

Nathaniel slumped, his will gone out of him. 'So what happens now?' he asked.

Whisperer regarded him emptily. 'You came here to bargain with the Cordites,' he said. 'You can still try, if that is what you wish.'

'But they are not bound.'

'They are as bound as you could ever make them. You may not have the power to force their co-operation, but you may still strike a deal with them if you have the wit. And the courage,' he added slyly, goading Nathaniel slightly. He gestured towards the door. 'Shall we?'

Nathaniel did not see that he had any other choice.

* * *

They were waiting for him outside the Grande. All seven of them had gathered in a semi-circle facing the porch. The secret inner core of the Fastest Guns: the six triumphant contestants from the first tournament and the unholy messiah himself, Jacob Priestley.

Nathaniel's courage faltered at the sight of them. Despite that they had been human until only a few years ago, their Descendence had left its mark upon them and they radiated power like the smoke they seemed to sweat.

The bodies of his invigilators lay scattered upon the streets for as far as he could see, the grey mist curling around them, exposing torsos that were shot full holes, heads that had been split open. It was like a battlefield. In the distance, Nathaniel could hear the voices of survivors calling out to one another, re-grouping, trying to find shelter or escape from town.

The Cordites had allowed a temporary ceasefire in which to face him.

Nathaniel could not see their eyes for they wore their hats tipped low, concealing the upper half of their faces in shadow, but he could feel the chill of their gaze. He looked back to Whisperer for support but the ancient sorcerer offered him none. He was on his own.

He took a hesitant step forward and called out to them:

'I, Nathaniel, created in the image of God, constrain you by the sacred names of God: Tetragrammaton, Adonai, Agla, and Jesus Christ; that the might of Hell be now conquered by the power of–'

'Do not threaten us in His name.' Priestley rasped.

'It is you who has come to our world. We have not come to yours,' a second Cordite said.

Nathaniel felt his confidence waver. He summoned another passage from the lines he had memorised: 'By all the things beneath the heavens, I offer you your wayward brother, Shane Ennis, and the girl, Chastity, who is worthy of your kind. I offer this tournament to you in your greatness, and the souls of those who have died. By this offering I invoke you powerfully in the name of those that strike fear and terror in you, that you shall grant me the power that is yours to grant. Grant me the power of eternal life.'

They stared up at him resentfully. Nathaniel could feel the waves of their hatred assailing him like a psychic battering ram.

'There are none who strike fear and terror in us,' one said. 'We will take Ennis for ourselves. He is not yours to offer.'

Another spoke: 'We will take the girl. You have nothing to offer us.'

Not to be outdone, Nathaniel stepped to the edge of the porch and called out in a powerful voice: 'By all your princes, kings, lords and superiors–'

Priestley cut him off. 'Their word is not heard here,' he said. 'We have no masters.'

Nathaniel was taken aback. He finally understood what Whisperer had meant when, during the early stages of their preparation, he had warned that the Cordites were a young cacophony of demons, newly formed. At the time, Nathaniel had assumed that he had meant they were weak and easily-exploited; that had been his inference. But that was not the case at all. The fact that the Cordites were young simply meant that Hell's legions had not yet figured out what to do with them. They were a minor power, as yet unclaimed; and so there was no one a sorcerer could call upon to constrain them to his will.

Nathaniel's heart sank. With despair, he finally grasped just what a mistake he had made.

The Cordites began to move, the three on either side of Priestley retreating, forming a corridor down which Priestley faced Nathaniel in a stand-off. 'If you want to join us,' he said. 'You will have to prove yourself.' He beckoned Nathaniel down onto the crossroads.

Nathaniel balked at the idea. 'But I can't beat you.' he said. 'My bullets can't hurt you!'

Priestley's lipless mouth stretched in a grin. 'That,' he said in a voice that dripped with sadistic intent. 'Is not my concern.'

He took his mark on the crossroads and waited for Nathaniel to join him. Nathaniel twisted his neck around and glanced imploringly at Whisperer, who merely shook his head. There was no backing out now.

Nathaniel swallowed nervously. His throat felt painfully dry. He walked down the steps with heavy feet and stepped out to take his place. As he passed between the first two Cordites, one of them hissed at him between its teeth, the sound like steam rising from a hot gun barrel. Nathaniel flinched away from it and the Cordite leered. In all other regards, they were eerily silent. They let him take his place opposite Priestley and Nathaniel kicked the dirt at his feet, levelling it. He shook his hands to try and hide the fact that they were trembling.

He had never been very good with a gun. He could hit a target but he was no gunfighter. He could not draw fast and he could not shoot well. He stood no chance of winning.

Perhaps they just want to test your mettle, he thought hopefully. *See if you have the guts to stand-up to them.*

But again he was deluding himself, and he knew it this time. The Cordites did not respect courage; they only respected skill.

Nathaniel's courage deserted him. He turned and ran but had only taken three steps before Priestley's shot thundered out over the crossroads. It hit him in the knee and Nathaniel fell to the ground, screaming. He rolled over and went to clutch at his wounded leg but one of the other Cordites shot him in the elbow. He howled in agony and rolled onto his back.

The Cordites closed in to surround him. There were seven of them. They each fired a single shot and killed him one piece at a time.

With smoke curling from the barrel of his gun, Jacob Priestley looked up from the Nathaniel's bullet-riddled corpse and turned to face the Grande. Whisperer stepped slowly down off the porch.

One by one, the Cordites parted before him, giving him leave to do as he pleased with Nathaniel's body. 'Take him.' Priestley said. 'And the others that we have agreed.'

'Take them and leave,' said another.

Whisperer bowed his head to them in thanks. He crouched at Nathaniel's side and reached out with one hand to brush the air above his chest. In his mind's ear, he heard Nathaniel's scream of outrage.

Behind him, Priestley watched with darkly burning eyes. He said nothing and made no signal but the other Cordites sensed his mood and they closed in to surround Whisperer on all sides. This was the moment of betrayal that Whisperer had anticipated. He tightened his grip on Nathaniel's soul and tore it from his cooling flesh.

'We had a deal,' he reminded Priestley.

'Did you get it in writing?' the Cordite replied sardonically.

Whisperer reacted at once. Splitting the barrier between worlds with his bare hands, he pulled forth a dozen struggling figures, who were bound to him by ethereal chains. Their bodies were like smoke and he weaved them about himself like a shield.

The Cordites' guns thundered and the shield was stripped apart, the wraithlike bodies that composed it flying into tatters. But their sacrifice spared Whisperer any lasting harm and he reached again into the space between worlds and yanked out more of the naked, emaciated creatures and set them upon the Cordites like rabid dogs. They charged in ghostly silence and leapt upon the Cordites and tried to strangle them with their chains. Gunfire blazed and the ghostly figures were cut down in seconds, but during that time Whisperer was able to break clear of the melee and escape.

Lowering his smoking gun, Jacob Priestley extended his senses out through the town, feeling for Whisperer's presence the way a spider feels for vibrations in its web. He could not find him; the soul-monger was somehow able to conceal himself, hiding his aura amongst the surviving invigilators.

'Kill them all.' Priestley demanded. 'Find him.'

CHAPTER TWENTY THREE

Shane ran. Every few steps, he made an abrupt right-angle turn, ran a few more steps, then turned again, trying to keep Buchanan from getting a clear shot at him.

Shots rang out frequently, some of them passing close enough that Madison yelped in panic. A quick glance over his shoulder told Shane that Buchanan was gaining on them.

Shane was out of breath. He held Chastity tightly against his chest but he wasn't used to sprinting with her extra weight and he knew that he could not keep it up for much longer. Blasting out of the alleyway, he emerged onto West Street and ran straight into the path of a group of invigilators. They were startled to see him but quickly recognised that he was not armed and therefore not a threat to them. Shane and Madison ran between them and sprinted on towards the far side of the street. Behind them, Buchanan let out a wordless bellow and fired off a volley of shots. One of the invigilators was caught in the line of fire and fell as a bullet punched through the side of his head. Startled, the others turned and brought their guns to bear upon Buchanan. They fired and he ducked back into the alley for cover. Their shots blew splinters out of the corner of the wall.

Laughing maliciously to himself, Buchanan emerged again and fired from the hip. Both men carried breach-loading rifles that took time to reload. He shot one but his gun clicked empty before he could shoot the second.

Angry, he closed the distance between them in a loping run and smashed the barrel of his revolver into the invigilator's teeth. The man dropped to his knees and Buchanan floored him with a devastating kick, then stamped on his neck until he felt the man's spine break beneath his heel. He spat on the corpse while he broke open his revolver and ejected the spent cartridges.

Shane and Madison had reached the general store on the far side of the street meanwhile, and Buchanan saw them disappear inside.

'Gotten tired of running, have you Shane?' Buchanan crooned to himself, reloading fresh bullets into his revolver. 'Think you can fight me, do you? Well, that's good.'

He snapped his revolver shut and advanced towards the store. 'Let's finish this properly.'

Shane stood at one of the boarded-up windows, looking out through a gap in the boards as Buchanan crossed the street towards him.

Madison was on the far side of the room. There was a door behind the counter that led into an alley out back. She had hold of Chastity's hand and urgently gestured for Shane to follow her. 'Come on!' she hissed, but Shane stayed where he was.

They would never escape from Covenant if they kept on running. Sooner or later, Buchanan would get a clear shot or, even worse, they would run into the Cordites. The only way they would

265

ever get out of the town alive was if they started to take control of their circumstances, and that meant they had to deal with Buchanan.

Shane glanced over his shoulder at Madison. 'Hide!' he told her.

She ducked behind the counter and dragged Chastity down next to her. Shane edged to the side of the door and waited in the shadows. He did not experience the familiar calmness that usually came over him when he fought. Instead he felt a nervous chill.

He was not accustomed to fighting without a gun.

He listened to Buchanan's footsteps as he mounted the boardwalk and approached the door. Buchanan was no fool. He could guess that Shane would be waiting for him. He hesitated at the threshold.

'Are you in there, Shane?'

He struck the doorframe with the palm of his mutilated hand, making a loud, sudden noise. He was trying to psyche Shane out and frighten him into making a move, but Shane kept his cool and waited in the dark, his hand on the hilt of his knife.

Buchanan hit the doorframe again, harder and more aggressively than before. He had never been a patient man and Shane did not think he would wait out there for long. He gave the doorframe another strike, but when that failed to illicit a reaction, he strode inside.

Shane sprang on him the moment he entered the door, chopping his knife down in a strike aimed at the back of Buchanan's hand. It cut the skin and Buchanan dropped his revolver and swore. Shane reversed the direction of his cut and thrust the point of his knife at Buchanan's belly, but his adversary had recovered from the surprise of his attack and managed to turn the blow with the back of his arm. He hit Shane with his elbow and knocked him staggering across the room. The knife slipped from Shane's fingers and slid away across the floor.

Buchanan roared in anger and charged him like a bull. He hit Shane low and scooped his legs off the ground. The wind was punched out of Shane's lungs as Buchanan drove him backwards against a rack of shelving on the wall. Shelves broke and an assortment of dusty jars and empty bottles rained down onto them. Buchanan dumped Shane roughly on the floor and stamped on his belly.

Shane somehow managed to get to his feet, fending off the blows with his arms. He ducked and weaved and managed to avoid Buchanan's strikes long enough to get his measure. Buchanan was a fierce and aggressive fighter, but his movements were clumsy. He made up for the disadvantage of his mutilated right hand by striking with his elbows more often than his fists.

Shane timed his moment and ducked under a wild haymaker. He seized hold of a broken shelf and swung it into the side of Buchanan's head. The man let out a howl and staggered sideways, but he had taken enough beatings in the past that pain had little effect on him. He shook his head to clear it and waded back into the fight. Shane tried to hit him with the shelf again but this time Buchanan was expecting it. He lunged inside of Shane's reach and hooked one arm around his head. Then, with scarcely any exertion on his part, he slammed Shane's head against the wall.

Shane managed to break free of his grip and danced backwards across the room. He ducked and weaved past Buchanan's strikes and retaliated with a fierce punch that struck Buchanan square on the jaw. It stunned him for a moment and Shane pressed his advantage. He snapped two fast hooks into Buchanan's kidneys and then swept a vicious uppercut into his solar plexus.

Buchanan staggered up against the side of the counter and

gave a hacking cough. He recovered quickly and caught Shane by surprise. Countering a punch, he hauled Shane in close and slammed him up against the counter. Buchanan was enraged now, and his face turned blood red. His eyes bulged and spittle flecked his lips. He cursed as he hit Shane with his elbows, driving each blow with numbing force. Shane felt his legs buckle beneath him.

Buchanan got hold of him by the collar of his shirt and threw him against the wall. Shane smacked into it, too weak and too dazed to absorb the impact. He grabbed hold of a shelf and used it to steady himself, but Buchanan was upon him again in an instant. He drove his knee into Shane's stomach and threw him across the room into the counter again. Shane hit it and slithered to the floor. He rolled over and tried to stand but his strength deserted him. He crumpled onto the floor, breathing heavily, his whole body in pain.

'Did you think you could beat me, Shane?' Buchanan asked.

It took a moment for Shane to find his voice. 'I did the last time,' he croaked.

'You had a gun last time, fucker!'

He swung a kick into Shane's ribs.

'Look at you! You're nothing without a gun!'

'What about you?' Shane replied with a groan. 'You're nothing even with a gun.' And he laughed, even though it hurt his ribs.

Buchanan bellowed savagely and kicked him. 'Let's see you laugh in a minute, after I've ripped out your fucking tongue.'

He was so intent on kicking Shane that he did not see Madison creep out from behind the counter, a wooden stool in her hands. She stole up carefully behind him and raised it above her head to strike. He whirled about abruptly.

'I thought I smelled cunt,' he snarled, and snatched the chair out of her hands.

He punched her in the face and sent her to the floor, where she sprawled unconscious. Buchanan hurled the stool across the room and it broke against the wall.

Shane tried to get to his feet but only made it as far as his knees before Buchanan kicked him back down. 'I've waited a long time for this.' Buchanan sneered, drawing a knife from his belt. It was long and the blade had a wickedly serrated edge.

'I'm gonna carve you up slow, Shane. Starting with your fingers.'

Shane tried to scramble away as Buchanan advanced on him but he was too weak and could not move fast enough. Buchanan slammed his knee onto Shane's chest and sank his weight on top of it, pinning him down. His face was cut and bleeding from the few blows that Shane had landed, but he did not seem to be badly affected by them. He grinned, blood dribbling from his gums.

He brandished his knife to the light, letting Shane take a good long look at it. Buchanan had never liked to kill his enemies too quickly. He much preferred to draw out their suffering, and with Shane he had a big grudge to settle.

The gunshot was sudden and abrupt. It caught them both by surprise. Buchanan blinked and looked down at his chest, where a red stain had appeared and was rapidly getting bigger. He swore quietly and looked over his shoulder to see who had shot him, but his strength gave out and he collapsed onto the floor.

Shane saw Chastity standing close to the doorway. She held Buchanan's Smith and Wesson revolver awkwardly in her tiny hands and there was smoke curling from its barrel. Her face was like china. Her eyes were ablaze.

Shane found a hidden reserve of strength somewhere deep

inside of himself and rolled to his feet just a split second before she fired at him. The heavy revolver bucked in her grasp and blew a hole in the floorboards where he had lain. It was a much bigger gun than she could handle and the recoil lifted her hands up into the air. She brought them level again and fumbled to draw back the hammer. In that time, Shane lurched for cover. He vaulted clumsily over the shop's counter just as she fired and felt the bullet rip past the side of his head, narrowly missing him. It struck a bottle on the shelves in front of him and blasted it into shards.

He dropped down behind the counter, breathing heavily, and clutched painfully at his bruised ribs. The sudden movement had hurt him badly.

Beyond the counter, he heard Chastity cock the hammer.

The sound gripped him with a icy chill. The wooden front of the counter was perhaps an inch thick at best and offered no protection from the .44 calibre slugs that Buchanan's revolver fired. He scrambled forward on his hands and knees, ducking flat to the ground as Chastity fired blindly at him. The first bullet smashed through the counter behind him and embedded itself in the wall beyond. The second was aimed in front of him and showered him in the face with splinters.

He came to an abrupt halt, gasping for breath. On the other side of the counter, he heard her draw back the hammer and knew that the next shot was coming straight at him. He grabbed hold of the counter and vaulted over it just as she fired. The bullet smashed through the wood, passing beneath him as he jumped.

He cleared the counter and landed running, pushing his body to the limit of his endurance. He rushed Chastity head-on and tackled her, propelling her down to the ground. The gun toppled from her hands as she tried to cock it again and she screamed with frustration.

She kicked and scratched him and spat and wailed.

Shane smothered her in his grasp and pinned her to the floor, holding her immobile while she raged. She was fierce, but she was also tired and she quickly wore herself out. As she quietened down, Shane eased back and sat down with his back against the wall. He felt exhausted. Wincing at the pain in his ribs, he pulled Chastity into his lap and sat there, nursing her while he got his strength back.

CHAPTER TWENTY FOUR

From the upstairs window, Travis could see all the way across Covenant to the far side of town. South and West Street divided it into quarters and the old clock tower reared up at the crossroads, looking like an enormous headstone in the night.

The streets were bathed in a luminous grey smoke that seemed oblivious to the shifting patterns of the wind and seemed to flow instead in whatever direction the strange new gunmen went. Here and there, Travis saw the smoke light up with muzzle flash and heard the rumbling thunder of gunfire, and knew that the strangers had tracked down another isolated group of invigilators.

He saw all of these things, but he could not see the one thing that he was looking for: the man who was trying to kill him.

Parker and Eddings were both dead. They were the two sharpshooters who manned the nests on either side of his position. Parker had abandoned his post shortly after the fighting had broken out. He had gotten scared and decided to make a run for it. Travis had been thinking about shooting him himself when Parker's head had suddenly split open and the sharp crack of a rifle shot had pierced the night.

Eddings had died next. It had happened quietly. Travis had heard the shot and some time later he had noticed Eddings' arm hanging off the side of the roof where his body had fallen.

Now Travis knew he was next.

He had expected this. Travis handled a rifle so well that it was often said that he had been born with one in his hands. He was proficient enough that he had just recently begun to hear it whispering at the back of his mind. He knew what was loose in the town, killing the other invigilators, and he suspected that one of them – a Cordite rifleman – was coming for him.

There had been rumours that one of the dead sharpshooters, Penn, had been taken by the Fastest Guns and invited to join their number. His body had gone missing from the charnel house and Travis had a feeling that it was Penn who was stalking him now.

He hoped it was. Travis had respected Penn, had been envious of his talent and the expensive rifle that he carried. He had often wondered if he could beat him in a fight.

He searched the dark rooftops for him, peering watchfully through his rifle's optical sight. He was crouched far enough back from the window that he felt confident that he could not be seen.

Sniping was a waiting game. Whoever moved first, died; and Travis was confident that Penn – or whoever it was – would have to come out into the open in order to take a shot at him. And when that happened, Travis would get him.

He scanned the line of buildings in front of him, keen eyes dwelling especially on those places where a man would be able to get a good shot at him. He saw nothing but shadows.

And then a figure appeared abruptly, stepping from an open doorway about a hundred yards away.

Calmly but quickly, Travis brought his aim to bear and made a quick adjustment to take the distance, air temperature and wind speed into consideration.

Through his scope, he saw the man bring his rifle smoothly to his shoulder and take aim. He zeroed in precisely on Travis' position.

'Shit!' Travis cursed.

The glass lens of his optical sight shattered into fragments and the back of his head exploded. He fell down with a heavy thump, bleeding through the hole where his right eye had been.

Madison regained consciousness with a groan. She sat up and clutched at the side of her head, which she must have banged on the floor when she fell. Her head ached and she felt nauseous.

She saw Buchanan's body lying only a short distance away and her breath caught sharply in her throat. For a moment, she had thought that it was Shane. Groaning, she looked around and saw Shane sitting against the wall, holding Chastity in his lap. The girl looked tired. Shane looked exhausted. His face was bruised and bloody and she could tell that he was in pain.

'What did I miss?' she asked croakily.

'Chastity killed him.' Shane replied, matter-of-factly. 'And then she tried to kill me.'

'Oh my god! Are you all right?'

'I've been worse,' he replied with a groan, and rose awkwardly to his feet, leaning against the wall for support. 'Can you take her?' he asked.

Madison nodded and took the girl away from him, leading her gently by the hand. Chastity was half-asleep and she did not try to resist her. Shane retrieved his knife from where he had dropped it and was just about to move towards the door when a figure suddenly appeared within it.

Madison started in alarm and stepped behind Shane for protection. There was no time to run for cover. Shane gripped the handle of his knife and grimly resigned himself to another fight.

The figure moved forward into a dim shaft of moonlight and they saw that it was Whisperer. He was slightly out of breath and walked favouring his right leg. He gestured for Shane to lower his knife.

'You've nothing to fear from me,' he said. 'For what it would cost me to have you, you and Chastity are not worth the risk.' He saw Buchanan lying on the floor. 'Your doing?' he asked Shane.

'The girl's.'

He accepted Shane's explanation without question; Whisperer understood Chastity's nature perfectly. 'Yes, of course,' he said.

He moved to Buchanan's side and knelt down. Shane stepped back and watched while he made a few strange passes in the air above Buchanan's torso with his hand. The darkness seemed to thicken under his palm. It moved like the tail of a tornado, becoming more and more solid as Whisperer stirred the air.

'What's he doing?' Madison asked, peering over Shane's shoulder.

Shane said nothing. He thought he knew but wanted to have his suspicions confirmed before he said anything.

Buchanan's body began to twitch. His arms and legs jerked fitfully and then his whole body began to shake like a fish dragged from the water, his toes kicking at the floor. The spiral of darkness that Whisperer gathered under his hand grew more substantial until Shane thought he could see a face within it. A face that resembled Buchanan's. His eyes were wide, like a man trapped in a nightmare, and his mouth stretched open in a silent wail.

Abruptly, Whisperer clenched his fist and Buchanan's body became still. There was a sound, distant and confused, like the howling of a far off wind, and then Whisperer rose. He lowered his fist and turned to leave.

'Nanache was wrong about you.' Shane told him.

'Oh, in what way?' Whisperer asked innocently.

'He said you were *devil-kind* but you're not, are you? You're the real deal.'

The tall man smiled knowingly. 'Now that would be telling,' he answered. 'And these walls have ears.'

Shane understood now why Whisperer scared him so badly. A full-blooded demon was bad news, and one who openly crossed the Cordites on their own ground was sure to be powerful. He took hold of Chastity's hand and steered her and Madison towards the back door. He had not gone far when Whisperer called out to him.

'This is only the beginning, Mister Ennis. You do know that, don't you? The Cordites are young. They have not yet learned the extent of what they have become, but that will change. They will grow stronger and they will not forget about you.'

'They won't forget you either.' Shane reminded him.

Whisperer gave a shrug. 'Maybe not, but by the time they catch up with me they will have had plenty of time to learn my worth. No matter who you are, it always pays to have a good merchant on your side.'

He fell silent, hearing the sound of footsteps on the boardwalk outside. Grabbing Madison by the arm, Shane steered her behind counter and they hurried for the back door. Whisperer did not try to stop him. As Shane glanced back, he saw that the tall man no longer stood alone. He was surrounded by half a dozen shadowy figures, each of whom was tethered to him by chains of ethereal steel. Their bodies looked smoky and insubstantial, naked and painfully thin.

One of them turned to face Shane and opened his mouth in a silent cry of anguish. It was Castor Buchanan.

At that moment, the footsteps outside drew level with the shop doorway and a Cordite strode into the room. Whisperer unleashed his wraiths and the Cordite's gun blazed. Shane did not wait to see the outcome of the fight. He fled out the back door and hurried away.

Alex and Jim Bening were brothers, both in their late-twenties, both professional killers, and both hired by Nathaniel to serve as invigilators. It had been Jim's idea. He was the oldest by three years and the most headstrong. He had only to hear of the Fastest Guns to know that he wanted to be one of them. His younger brother Alex had been more cautious but a job was a job, especially since they were hard up for money.

The two of them were now running for their lives, together with a third man, Glenn Short.

When the shooting had started, the three men had gone to bolster a counter-offensive. They had found themselves battling just one man, but that one man alone had wiped out all of their companions. He would have killed them too, but they had had the sense to run away. They had tried to reach the stables but the route was blocked by another gunman, who had fired his revolver with preternatural speed. Fanning his hand against the hammer, he had blazed off a hail of lead that drove them into the mouth of an alley in search of cover. His shots chipped splinters off the wall.

'What the fuck is going on here, man?' Glenn spat. He risked sticking his head round the corner and saw that another group of invigilators had blundered onto the street. They looked like they were running from somebody else, but their path took them straight into the fast-shooter's line-of-sight. He unleashed a volley of shots and the men fell down.

'No way.' Glenn said. 'No way is that fucking possible. No one can shoot that fast.'

Alex grabbed him by the shirt. 'Forget it!' he snapped. 'Let's just get out of here.'

'But the horses—'

'Fuck the horses! I'd rather take my chances with the desert than fight those bastards.'

His brother agreed and they fled down the alley, winding their way from there towards the edge of town. They steered well clear of the fighting as much as possible, doubling-back when necessary and keeping out of sight.

They were almost at the edge of town when a shot rang out. Alex felt as if he had been punched in the back. The pain was so intense that his overwhelmed senses simply went numb and he fell with a cry. His brother turned back to help him but Glenn pulled him into the shelter of a nearby alley. 'Sharpshooter,' he hissed.

There was no sign of their assailant. He was on a rooftop more than three-hundred yards away, watching through a Vollmer sight as Alex rolled about on the ground, moaning and clutching at his stomach.

Glenn's hand tightened on Jim's shoulder. 'You can't help him,' he said.

Jim shook him off. He was not going to leave his little brother behind. He ran out to get him and the side of his head erupted in a gush of blood. Moments later, the sound of the rifle shot echoed over the rooftops.

Jim sank down to the ground, deaf to his brother's anguished cries. Alex knew that the sharpshooter had used him as bait to draw Jim out into the open. He understood that he was partly to blame for his brother's death. He cursed with impotent rage. Clawing through the dirt, he reached out his hand imploringly towards Glenn, but Glenn was not going to risk his life for a man he barely knew. He turned and ran.

He did not look back and so never saw the silhouette that rose up from a distant rooftop, standing tall and taking aim, his finger brushing the trigger with the gentlest amount of pressure. Glenn was shot through the back of the spine, just an inch above his shoulders. He did not even feel the shot that killed him.

On the distant rooftop, the sharpshooter adjusted his aim and finished off Alex with a well-placed shot to the head, then melted back into the shadows.

Shane and Madison ran out the back of the store and into a wide open yard. Behind them, the blazing of gunfire stopped as abruptly as it had begun. Madison looked at Shane inquisitively, but he shook his head. He could not imagine that the Cordite had been killed. It was more likely that Whisperer had escaped by some arcane means and that the Cordite had moved on in pursuit of him.

Better him than us, he thought. The Cordites' interest in Whisperer might just be the break he needed in which to make good his escape.

Glancing about, he took stock of his surroundings. They were close to the edge of town. A few run-down buildings teetering on rotten foundations were all that now stood between them and the open desert. Safety was but a short distance away.

Madison set out hurriedly but Shane held back near the edge of the yard and studied the way ahead with suspicious eyes.

He did not trust it. Covenant was like a spider's web, its leaning ruins sensitive and almost alive. There was nothing within its boundaries that the Cordites could not sense and there was absolutely no way that they did not know how close he was to escaping from them.

He felt a curious prickling sensation over his skin and decided that, somewhere, somebody was watching him down the barrel of a gun.

He caught up with Madison and drew her into cover against the leaning wall of a clapboard house.

'We need to split up,' he said.

She looked at him sharply. 'No,' she said.

'Listen. You heard what Whisperer said. Chastity and I are too valuable to the Cordites. They're not going to let us just walk out of here.'

'Then why'd we come this far together? What was the point?'

He grabbed her by the shoulders and looked her in the eye so that she would listen closely to him. 'You remember in the alley outside my cell, the way Chastity looked at me? I said she could recognise her own kind. The Cordites can sense us both in the same way, especially when we're together like this. If we both try to leave at the same time they'll come and stop us. I'm going to go back and get the horses. You take Chastity and go on without me. I'll catch up with you.'

She pouted sulkily. 'Okay then,' she said. 'But don't be too long.'

She did not say anything about Nathaniel's money. Shane guessed that either she had forgotten about it or, like him, she had decided that it was not worth dying for. 'I left my bag in the stables,' she added. 'There's food and water in it.'

'I'll bring it.' Shane promised. They would need it if they were to survive the journey across the desert.

Madison nodded glumly and set off, leading Chastity by the hand. Shane stood and watched her go for a moment, quietly reckoning the distance she had to travel. He had lied to her. He was going back to the stables to fetch the horses, but first he was going hunting.

And he was going to use Madison as bait.

So far as he knew, nobody had ever killed a Cordite before. They killed each other often enough, but as the saying went: *he who lives by the Gun, cannot die by the Gun.* No Cordite could be slain by a gun fired by anyone other than another Cordite.

But that didn't mean that they couldn't be killed. Shane had told Vendetta it was possible and his theory was sound. It had just never been done before.

He broke into one of the crooked buildings nearby and found his way upstairs to a window that gave him a view out towards the edge of town. He spotted Madison picking her way through an old stockyard. She was making slow progress. Chastity was too tired to move quickly and Madison was not strong enough to carry her. They moved clumsily and even though Madison did her best to stay behind cover, Shane knew that they would be an easy target for whichever Cordite was hunting for them.

He suspected that it was the rifleman, Penn. The greater accuracy of his rifle over long range made him the ideal choice to guard the town's perimeter and to pick off anybody that tried to escape his brethren. Shane hoped that it was Penn anyway. Having only been a Cordite for about a day, Penn was probably still the weakest and therefore the easiest to kill. If it was somebody like

Priestley then Shane was in big trouble.

He looked at all the places where he thought the Cordite might be hiding. He figured that Penn would favour a long shot and that he would probably be on a rooftop, balcony or upper storey window somewhere with a clean line-of-sight. Shane failed to spot him but, refusing to give up, he left the building that he was in and moved across the street to another one and continued his search from his new vantage point.

Madison was two-thirds of the way to the edge of town now and Shane focussed his search by drawing imaginary lines from her position out towards suitable shooting points. His rigorous approach paid off. A few streets away, he spotted a shadowy figure creeping across a rooftop at the edge of town. The shadow carried a rifle.

Got you! Shane thought to himself.

He stole quietly from the house and circled around to approach the Cordite's position from behind. Gunfire crackled from other parts of town and he reasoned that there must still be a few invigilators left alive.

He moved hurriedly but with caution. He did not think that the Cordite would shoot Chastity; only Madison, and she was not so important to Shane that he was overly concerned by the prospect of her dying. He crept up to the house and entered through a downstairs window. It was dark inside but enough grey light penetrated the windows that he was able to find his way to a staircase and climb to the upper storey.

He found himself in a room with a sloping ceiling, whose rafters were bent and crooked and slowly succumbing to rot. The roof had come down on one corner and the floor was littered with debris: warped planks and broken beams, rotted furniture and some empty bottles. The floorboards were dry and they creaked loudly under Shane's weight.

The noise carried and Shane immediately threw himself to one side, hearing movement above. A shot rang out and a hole was blasted through the roof. The bullet punched down, passing through the empty space where Shane had been standing and put a hole in the floorboards.

The roof flexed, shedding a cascade of dust as the Cordite stalked across it, ejecting a spent cartridge from its rifle and inserting a fresh one into the breach. Shane threw himself into a dive as a second shot punched down. It passed so close to him that he felt its heat in the air.

He landed with a roll and snatched up an old, discarded book that lay amongst the debris on the floor. He tossed it a few steps ahead of himself, in a direction that he might logically have travelled coming out of his roll. The book landed with a heavy thump and a third shot came down through the roof a split second later and ripped the book in half.

Shane stayed motionless where he was, not making a sound. He listened to the Cordite as it paced across the roof above him, the wooden rafters creaking and bending under its weight. It did not believe that he was dead. Its senses were not as finely attuned to the town as its brethren and it could not sense exactly where he was, only that his heart was still beating.

Crouching, Shane reached out for a broken chair leg that lay nearby. His movements caused the floorboards to creak softly and the Cordite stopped moving and turned to listen. Shane froze. He dared not even breathe in case he moved whilst doing so and allowed it to locate his whereabouts.

His muscles burned from the strain of staying in one position for so long. Above him, the rafters creaked, raining dust into the room. The demon was moving again. It had gotten tired of playing cat-and-mouse and was heading towards the place where the roof had fallen so it could climb down and confront him.

Shane moved like a mountain lion. Leaping forwards, he struck the chair leg into the rafters at a place where they looked to be particularly rotten. The wood split where he struck it and there was a crash as the ceiling caved-in. Shane rolled out of the way as it came down around him. The Cordite fell and landed heavily nearby, dropping its rifle. Shane was on it in an instant. His knife flashed in the dim light and plunged down into the demon's chest.

Shane felt the blade turn as it struck bone and he wrenched it out and stabbed again. The Cordite tried to dislodge him but he batted its defences aside. He had no way of knowing if it would die like a normal man. Its wounds did not seem to bleed and so he kept on stabbing it, burying the blade up to the hilt in its chest, belly and neck. He attacked it with focussed aggression and did not stop hitting it until it stopped moving.

Shane guessed that he must have hit it more than forty times. His attack had left its torso badly mauled. He eyed it suspiciously but there was no sign that it would get back up again. As he had suspected, those who lived by the gun could apparently still die by the blade.

CHAPTER TWENTY FIVE

Shane retrieved his knife and limped over to the window. He moved stiffly, wincing at the pain from his bruised ribs. The Cordite had landed a couple of good punches while he had fought with it and the adrenaline was wearing off, allowing the pain to come creeping in.

He looked out and saw that Madison and Chastity had reached the edge of town and were starting out into the desert. It was time he fetched the horses and joined them.

The sound of killing still rumbled across town as Shane made his way stealthily back along West Street towards the crossroads. Despite the fact that it was the middle of the night the air was unpleasantly warm. It seemed to clutch at Shane like an unfamiliar hand and left his skin damp with sweat.

The ground was thick with a knee-high layer of gunsmoke that glowed blood red where it surrounded the burning torches. The smoke parted as Shane waded through it, revealing the bodies of dead invigilators. Their guns lay beside them and Shane sensed them calling out to him, inviting him to take them into his hands. It was hard for him to resist them, and he squeezed his hands tight into fists and held them rigidly by his sides, determined not to give in to their siren-like calling.

There was no point in denying that his heart yearned for him to stay. The Cordites offered him more than the world outside of Covenant could ever give him. He would never find anybody else with whom he belonged so rightly. No mortal love could ever hope to eclipse what he felt for them and by denying them he knew that he was consigning himself to a life as a hollow man, deprived of joy and purpose.

But it was the price they demanded of him that settled his decision, as ever. To go the rest of his life alone, denying his heart's desire, but to be free to make his own decisions and live a life of his own choosing was infinitely better than to become a slave.

It might only be a temporary salvation. He was *devil kind*. His soul belonged to the Cordites and they would claim it on the day he died, if he could resist them for that long. But for now, even a temporary reprieve was better than the alternative.

He found the stables and made his way in through the back door. The smell of blood from the dead stallion, coupled with the Cordites' hellish rampage in the streets outside had gotten the horses even more anxious than they had been earlier, and several of them reared and screamed when they saw him. His own horse and Madison's were calmer but would not stay that way for long with the panic the others were creating.

Shane opened up the main doors and carefully released the horses one by one, freeing them to bolt out into the streets. The stables felt eerily quiet after they had gone. Shane stroked his horse until she calmed down a little, then released her and did the same with Madison's horse. He found Madison's carpet bag and tied it onto his saddle.

Gunfire pounded from somewhere not very far away and Madison's horse stamped its feet nervously, its eyes rolling. Shane tied its reins to the pommel of his saddle and led both horses into the night. He felt something dig into his thigh as he mounted up and checked in his pockets and discovered the two keys that Madison had given him earlier. They were the ones that she had taken from Nathaniel. One was the key to the room in which Nathaniel's money was stored.

Up until now, the money had not been important to him, but he was not far from the Grande and holding the key got him thinking. The last six years had taught him how difficult it was for a man to live without a gun. People didn't look too favourably on pacifists in a land where any display of weakness invited trouble, and Shane could scarcely remember a town where his unwillingness to start a fight hadn't landed him in trouble. With twenty-thousand dollars he could buy himself a place in society, set himself up with some property and a new identity. He could find Chastity a family who would raise and take care of her.

The more he thought about it, the more he became convinced that he needed the money just as badly as he needed the food and water in Madison's bag. It would certainly make his future a hell of a lot easier to bear.

He tethered his horse to a hitching post and went back into the stables to grab a pair of saddlebags off a peg on the wall. He realised that he was probably making the very last mistake of his life, but he turned around and led the horses across the street towards the Grande.

The clock tower of the town hall reared against the skyline, its pale, round face gleaming like an enormous baleful eye. Beneath it, the crossroads were knee-deep in smoke that writhed and boiled with currents of its own formation. The familiar, dark buildings were ominously still and silent.

The fighting had all spilled out onto the edge of town and Shane crossed the street unmolested and went around the back of the Grande. He tethered the horses to a tree in the yard and entered the crooked building through the kitchen door, the two saddlebags slung across his shoulder.

The hotel had already acquired a dead feel to its musty halls, the memories of its occupation turned to ghosts now that the Cordites had reasserted their dominance. Shane followed the directions that Madison had given him and found the locked door. He tried the keys in the lock until he found the right one and the door swung open upon a small, dark room.

The two panniers lay on the centre of the floor. They were locked with stout padlocks but Shane broke one open by prising the blade of his knife under the hinges and applying leverage, tearing the screws from the wood. The box was filled with money, which he hurriedly began to transfer into his saddlebags.

He had emptied one box and was working on getting the other to open when he became aware that a lengthy silence had fallen across town. He paused in his work and cocked his head to listen.

The shooting had stopped.

Shane felt a cold chill of fear gush through him. The silence could only mean one thing: that the last of the invigilators had been killed and that Whisperer was either dead or had escaped. Shane was the only man left alive in Covenant and now the Cordites would be coming for him.

He abandoned the second box. His saddle bags were swollen with roughly ten-thousand dollars and that was enough. He slung them over his shoulder and started for the door only to find that his way was blocked.

A tall, dark figure stood in the doorway, wreathed in pale grey smoke. 'Reduced to the level of a common thief,' it said. 'This is beneath you, Shane.'

Shane stood his ground against the demon that had once been Jacob Priestley. His hand fingered the hilt of his knife wonderingly but, the moment he tensed to step forward, Priestley drew his gun.

The weapon was aimed and ready to fire before Shane had a chance to move, but Priestley did not shoot. He grinned, exposing teeth that were long and sharp and stained like a dog's. 'We knew that you would come to us in time,' he said.

'I'm not here to join you.' Shane replied.

The demon chuckled. It was a vile sound, like a man choking up blood. 'You are one of us, Shane. Why seek to deny it?'

'Because it's not what I want!'

'Your mouth says no, but your heart pleads yes.'

Priestley turned the gun around in his hand so that it was no longer pointed at Shane, but was instead presented to him as a gift.

Shane yearned to take it. He craved it with an emotion that was rooted deep inside his soul. He had to fight to resist it.

'You *will* join us.' Priestley said. 'Even if you leave here today, you will one day come back to us. You cannot escape; this is where you belong.'

Shane clenched his fists to stop himself from taking the gun. It felt as if his mind had split in half and that his will was pouring out through the resulting chasm. He thought about the last six years of his life: the weakness, the constant burden of fear, the fights that he had been forced to run from because he had not possessed the power to defend himself. And against that he considered the years that had gone before it, the years in which he had been a legend, the years in which the name of Shane Ennis had been synonymous with Death.

There was no contest when he asked himself which of those times he would choose to live in if given the choice but, when he looked to his future, he saw that there was a third option. He had ten-thousand dollars and the rest of the world thought he was dead. He had an opportunity to start afresh.

He brought his eyes up level with Priestley's and looked at him straight. The two of them stared into each other's souls.

And Shane stabbed him.

Priestley bellowed with a sound like mortar fire as the blade sank into his arm. His hand spasmed and he dropped his gun and Shane barged into him, driving him up against the doorframe before punching him in the face.

Shane did not waste his time prolonging the fight but charged on by, pushing his way briskly into the hall. He turned towards the kitchen but another Cordite stood at the end of the hall. It reached for a gun and Shane pushed sideways through an unlocked door. Bullets chewed up the doorframe in his wake, flinging jagged splinters of wood across the room.

He heard footsteps in the hallway. The Cordites were closing in for the kill and he rushed to a boarded-up window and kicked through the boards. He cleared himself enough space to climb through and tossed the saddlebags out before scrambling after them. The Cordite entered the room behind him and fired a blaze of shots, but by then Shane was safely through the window.

He ducked his head and rapidly skirted the outside of the hotel. Figures rose up out of the gunsmoke on the crossroads and began to advance on him. He ducked around the side of the building as a shot was fired.

The horses were where he had left them. Shane thanked his good fortune that the Cordites had not killed them. He unwound his reins from the crooked tree and vaulted into the saddle.

At that moment, the kitchen door swung open and a Cordite stepped out into the yard. Shane was caught in its sights, helpless to do anything but stare at it.

It was not too late to change his mind, he thought. He could still join them.

He wavered in his indecision for a fraction of a second before the fear that he might actually submit galvanised him into action. He savagely yanked on the reins, sawed his horse's head around, and laid his heels into her flanks.

The Cordite took aim as he galloped away but a gnarled hand closed upon his wrist. The Cordite turned and stared questioningly into the face of Jacob Priestley.

'No.' Priestley said, his eyes fixed on their fleeing brother. 'He is not leaving us. He is only delaying the inevitable.'

The other Cordites gathered in the street to watch as Shane escaped. One by one, they faded away into the smoke until only Priestley remained. He shimmered, becoming insubstantial as a ghost.

'We can be patient,' he whispered. And Covenant breathed a sigh as if in anticipation.

The noise trembled through the ruinous buildings, a soft whisper of creaking wood and disturbed dust that spread outwards from the centre of town and chased at Shane's heels as he galloped for safety.

He rode like a madman, kicking back his heels and hunching

down in the saddle. His frightened horse was only too glad to be fleeing the town and galloped with all the speed she had, her hooves kicking up a thick cloud of dust in their wake.

Shane did not expect to make it. He felt certain that they would shoot his horse out from under him, but the Cordites did nothing and he rode out into the desert without any sign of pursuit behind him. Even then he did not believe that he was safe. He rode hard and did not curb his horse until the town was far behind him, a dark and brooding thing on the horizon.

He caught up with Madison in the early hours of the dawn. 'You made it,' she said happily.

Shane tossed her carpet bag to her, then threw her one of the saddlebags. She caught it and her eyes widened when she looked inside and saw the money.

'Your cut,' he said. 'Like we agreed.'

She ran over and threw her arms around him. Her lips were on his before he had chance to realise what she was doing. She kissed him and he drew her close, feeling her firm young body pressed against his. She was a poor substitute for what he had turned his back on in Covenant but she would suffice, he thought grimly.

He disengaged himself from her and lifted Chastity into his arms. The girl rested her head sleepily against his shoulder and sobbed quietly. There were tears on her cheeks.

'I don't think she wants to go.' Madison said. 'Will they come after her?'

Shane honestly did not know. 'Maybe,' he said. 'One day.'

'What about you?'

Shane did not answer. He could still hear Priestley's words in his ear: 'You are one of us.' That was why they had let him escape; he knew it. They were sure that they would have him in the end.

But Shane had bought himself some more time, and maybe that was all he needed. Given another thirty or forty more years, maybe he could find a way to break the chains that bound him to them. He could not undo the crimes of his past, but perhaps half a lifetime spent well could even the score a little, and maybe in the end he would cheat the Cordites of their due. Maybe.

He climbed into the saddle and seated Chastity in front of him. 'What's your surname?' he asked Madison.

'It's Dorney,' she said. 'Why?'

According to the newspaper that Buchanan had shown him, the rest of the world believed Shane Ennis to be dead.

Shane Dorney, on the other hand, maybe had a future.

Lightning Source UK Ltd.
Milton Keynes UK

171546UK00001B/130/P